ALL OF ME

THE SAFEGUARDED HEART SERIES
BOOK TWO

MELANIE A. SMITH

WICKED DREAMS PUBLISHING

Published by
WICKED DREAMS PUBLISHING
info@wickeddreamspublishing.com
Boise, ID USA

Edited by Jennifer Gardner

Cover design by Wicked Dreams Publishing

Formatting by Wicked Dreams Publishing

eBook (K) ISBN: 978-1-7323900-2-7
eBook ISBN: 978-1-7328154-7-6
Paperback ISBN: 978-1-7323900-3-4
Hardback ISBN: 978-1-952121-03-6

CONTENTS

PROLOGUE

Alessandro

I'm jolted awake by the plane beginning what surely must be its slow descent. I run my hands through my messy hair and over my beard, smoothing the chaos as well as I can. I've always been able to sleep on airplanes, though my rest this time was unfortunately short and more disturbed than usual.

I rub my chin contemplatively, knowing it will be a long time until I sleep peacefully again.

To avoid succumbing to the anxiety that is tearing my insides to shreds, I begin ordering my belongings for landing, starting with removing and coiling the headphones that were piping classical music into my ears as I slept.

Partially to soothe the turmoil, partially to avoid the overly interested, middle-aged woman seated next to me.

Sure enough, as if my removing the headphones was the invitation she had been waiting for, she offers me a simpering smile and puts her hand on my bicep, running her fingers along its hard length to the edge of my short-sleeved black polo shirt. I resist the urge to recoil, my jaw tensing with the effort of smoothing my features into relaxed indifference.

"They announced that we'll be landing in half an hour," she says softly, suggestively, her dull blue eyes staring longingly into my own dark eyes. "Last chance to use the lavatories." She raises her painted-on eyebrows delicately and flips her poorly dyed ashy-blond hair over her shoulder coyly. Then she rises slowly, excusing herself past the elderly woman in the aisle seat. Pausing dramatically, she gives me a meaningful look before heading down the aisle. As if we'd had some interaction, some conversation that made her think I'd want to fuck her in a cramped, disgusting airplane bathroom. Or anywhere, for that matter.

The elderly woman huffs and rolls her eyes at the woman as she departs.

"On behalf of womankind," she croaks to me, "I'd like to apologize for that dingbat."

The humor is an unexpected shot of light in the dark,

and a deep rumble of appreciative laughter rolls through me despite myself.

"Thank you," I reply sincerely. "But there's no need."

She smirks unreservedly in response, leaning her head toward me conspiratorially and says, "It's okay to not be a gentleman sometimes. Women like her," she jerks her head toward the back of the plane, "only see that as encouragement."

For that exact reason I've purposely avoided turning on the charm until now, though I've also been too broken and tired, too distracted. But this white-haired, feisty old woman has cut through my foul mood. And for that I give her a wink, and a genuine crooked smile.

"I'll keep that in mind," I assure her amiably.

And, as usual, the charm works its magic, and even this weathered, wise lady blushes and waves me away coquettishly, pretending to turn back to her knitting.

"Save it for someone your age," she admonishes me.

Her words bring a whisper on the wind to my ears — *Serafina* — and the smile drops abruptly from my lips. My chest tightens and breathing becomes difficult. I turn and stare out the window, but as the plane descends through the clouds, there is nothing to distract me. I close my eyes and try to breathe through it.

When I reopen them, I find the old lady considering me carefully, her shrewd gaze seeming to pierce straight through me.

"Sometimes we don't know just how much we love someone until we lose them," she says quietly. She returns to her knitting, her needles clacking softly.

I note the sense of sorrow within her words, and the delicate, gold band on her ring finger. I examine her for a moment. Her features are fine and soft, gently curved amongst her wrinkled skin. Her hands, however, are strong and calloused. This is a woman who has worked hard and known life, and love, and laughter. I suddenly wish I'd been seated next to her this whole flight.

"Is it worth it?" I ask her, abruptly breaking the silence.

She looks up in surprise, dropping a stitch. "Love?" she replies.

I nod. Her answering smile lights up her whole face.

But before she can respond, a flight attendant announces our final descent and requests everyone to return to their seats and buckle up. The old woman focuses on stowing her knitting, so I take the last moments of opportunity that the added space of the empty seat beside me provides to stretch my long legs. Window seats are not meant for someone who is six feet tall, and I can feel the tension in my neck and cramped limbs.

Moments later the seats creak and a heavy bottom drops into the chair next to me. Its occupant pointedly ignores me, and I suppress a smile as I prepare to land. To start the search that will hopefully yield answers. Answers that will, in turn, hopefully give me the power I need to shatter the obstacles keeping me from what I want. From the woman I love. Before I've lost her forever.

I stare blankly out the window as the ground swells to meet us, itching to get out of the plane and begin hunting.

Finally, the wheels meet the earth in a mighty jolt and the reassuring pressure of the brakes engaging pushes me forward in my seat. Another ping sounds throughout the cabin, followed by the calm, smooth female flight attendant's voice.

"Ladies and gentlemen, welcome to San Francisco International Airport. Local time is eleven twenty-seven a.m. and the temperature is a foggy sixty-two degrees."

ONE

"San Francisco? Are you sure?"

Bryce drops a file on the coffee table in answer, removes his just-from-church tan blazer and collapses into the chair across from the couch I'm seated on. The stiff, white dress shirt and brown slacks he wears underneath are rumpled, and he looks exhausted. His long, muscled legs splay out comically as he sinks his six-foot-four frame into the relatively small chair.

"I'm sure," he responds grimly, running a hand through his chestnut hair, his blue eyes dark and hard.

Ignoring his moodiness, I snatch up the file and eagerly peruse its contents. It's quick, as there's not much there.

"And you're sure he didn't catch a connecting flight out of the country?" I press.

Bryce levels a look at me, the closest to annoyed I've ever seen him get. "I'm sure, Sera," he huffs. "He was only ID'd boarding a flight to San Francisco. No scans through customs or to any other destinations."

I shake my head, confused. "It's only been six days. Maybe it's a stopover?" I flop back onto the couch.

Bryce eyes me, his gaze trailing over the last yellow remnants of the bruising that only a week ago sprawled the complete center of my face. The evidence of the attack by a mentally unbalanced woman shouldering a massive grudge against me that almost ended my life — the end of a long saga of sabotage and betrayal. I sweep my long, wavy brown hair in close around me self-consciously.

"I'll keep an eye on it," he replies, hesitating. "But my monitoring him is not exactly on the up-and-up. I've got to be careful about what I dig into and how often."

My eyes flick up to his in surprise. "I'm sorry, Bryce, I didn't realize I was putting you in that position," I respond.

A half-truth, really, as I know my request for help finding Alessandro made Bryce deeply uncomfortable. I thought they'd forged some sort of peace in rescuing me from my attacker and the aftermath, but Bryce's cautious protests have made it clear that he's as angry with Alessandro as ever, and that he's only helping because I asked. Well, insisted, really.

He leans forward in his chair, his sky-blue eyes now

reserved and contemplative. He chews his lip, clearly carefully choosing his next words.

"You know I'd do anything for you, Sera," he breathes. "But this guy. He relentlessly pursed you until you fell for him while lying about being married. And then right after what you just went through, he hurt you again. And now it seems there are lies around that too." Bryce shakes his head sadly, running another hand through his hair, aggravated.

"I can tell he didn't want to," I insist. "And whatever his reason for not telling me he was married in the first place, it's moot now. He's not married anymore. What I can't understand is why he insisted he had to go back to Italy, but now he's in San Francisco?" I shake my head. "I don't get it. But there *is* an explanation. I just don't know what it is. And I *need* to know what it is, Bryce." I mash my lips together, willing him to understand.

"I guess I'd want to know why too," he admits, sighing deeply. "But I'd like to go to San Francisco with you."

My answer vehemently escapes my lips before I can stop it. "NO."

Alessandro made it clear before he left that he had no intention of providing me with answers, possibly even that he *couldn't*. If Bryce were there it would drastically reduce my odds of getting through to Alessandro.

Bryce smirks at me, shaking his head. "You know I could follow you. Whether you want me to or not."

I glare at him. Of course I know. It's why I hired him as a security consultant in the first place, when my attacker and her girlfriend were working together to sabotage my company, raining down chaos on my client list through various attacks, and eventually attacking me physically when their attempts to damage my business didn't work. And it was Bryce who cracked the case and saved me from being beaten and almost shot by that maniac. But while I know I should be grateful, his obvious threat still annoys me, and I can't stop my nostrils from flaring in outrage.

But I do manage to bite back my angry response. Because I know how deeply Bryce cares for me. And not just because he's clearly in love with me, as evidenced by his attempt to date me while Alessandro and I were broken up. But because through everything we've become close. And if the tables were turned, I'd probably be protective of him too.

"But you won't," I finally reply. I try not to let my sorrow seep into my tone or my expression. I hate that this is driving a wedge between Bryce and me.

"You're right, I won't," he agrees, "not if you really don't want me to. I just wish I had a better understanding of why you're doing this."

I ruminate on that for a moment. I decide to skip the obvious "because I love him" as he's heard it before, and I know it's a sensitive subject for him.

"Because even if it doesn't work out, I'd rather regret doing something than doing nothing," I finally offer.

He considers me thoughtfully for a moment. "Well, I can't argue with that," he admits, giving me a half-hearted smile. A ghost of the bright-as-sunshine smile that usually radiates from him so easily. The smile I haven't seen since before that awful night. But once again I shut down the thought before it can go far. I know someday I'll have to process everything that happened. But not today. "When are you leaving?"

I breathe in deeply through my nose and out through my mouth. "Tomorrow," I answer.

"What about ERS? Sutton?" Bryce presses.

ERS. Evans Realty Services. The company I've slaved to build for nearly five years. The company that will be no more as Charles Sutton, my last client, agreed to absorb it into his own, larger company. In exchange for me. Well, when I'm done figuring things out with Alessandro anyway.

I can't help wondering if Charles Sutton only wants to mentor me, to shape me for his own purposes, because my grandfather did the same for him. Or if, as he says, he truly sees potential in me. Either way, it was an opportunity that came along at exactly the right time. And I'm ready to give up the burden of being in charge. At twenty-nine years old I'm already burnt out. And I'm ready to go after what really matters.

"Everything is already in motion," I reply softly. In less than a week, I've managed to arrange for the absorption of my company into Sutton Developments. It's far from over, but there's nothing that can't wait a few days. I meet his gaze. "I didn't see anything in that file on where he's staying."

A muscle twitches in Bryce's jaw. "He hasn't checked in to a hotel or made any other purchases. He must be using cash. Which may make finding him difficult."

"Where would you start?"

Bryce looks like he doesn't want to answer that question for a moment, but finally he says, "If he doesn't want to be found, if he gets wind that you're looking for him, from what you've told me, he will probably leave. I'll run a banking and credit history report, see if there are any places in the area he used to frequent. That's where you'll start."

A heavy pause ensues before he speaks again. "If that doesn't work, there's also a short list in the file of his known associates who are still in the area. He's likely staying with one or more of them. See if anyone on the list rings a bell with you. Before you approach any of them, observe first. Once *casually* during the middle of the day to get a lay of the land. Then again in the evening — find something inconspicuous to do with yourself and watch from a distance for a couple hours." He spits his instructions out tersely, and I know he's incredibly uncomfortable, for many reasons.

"And what if I need to approach someone?" I ask tensely. I hadn't even thought of needing to undertake such subterfuge, and the dawning realization of the challenge before me is sending ripples of apprehension through me.

"The safest people to approach are the ones who work at the places he's frequented," he explains. "Bring a picture. Ask if they've seen him. The less you say, the better. If you need to tell them why, have a simple, clean story ready."

"And if I have to approach someone he knows?" I press.

"Would you be comfortable pretending to be from immigration again?" he asks, cracking a smile.

In my desperation for his help, I'd ended up confessing many of the details of my relationship with Alessandro, including its downfall. He was extremely impressed with my detective work of the day I tricked Alessandro's wife into confirming that he was, in fact, married and much more. He even jokingly offered me a job. Clearly, it's something he's going to remember for a while.

"I can do something *like* that," I agree. "But he may know about that."

"Then probably not worth the risk," Bryce concedes.

I rub the back of my neck and pick up the file again,

searching for the list of names. And I pause with it in my hand, a thought occurring to me.

"Do you think he'd tell me where he was if I just asked him?" I ask. "It sounds silly, but maybe it's worth a shot?"

"First," Bryce replies slowly, "you'd have to be able to get ahold of him. And his cell number and email address no longer work."

I blanch at the information. "How do you know that?" I ask stupidly.

Bryce looks around blankly for a minute, then when his eyes land on me again he jumps a little in his seat theatrically. "Oh, hi! I didn't see you there," he says leaning forward, offering me a hand. "I'm Bryce Hoyt, and I work for a *security* company. It's nice to meet you." I smack his hand away, feigning a glare. "That was the first thing I tried, Sera. This ain't my first rodeo."

He winks at me, and I stick my tongue out at him in response. He laughs honestly, and the sound unravels the tight coil in my chest just a bit. I can't help but smile back.

I mull suggesting I ask Marco Rossi, Giovanni Bianchi, Maria Greco, or Francesca Del Vecchio, Alessandro's former team here in Seattle, but immediately dismiss the thought knowing even if they were open to helping me find him that they'd also likely tell him. Especially since Marco and Alessandro are like brothers. He'd never give me information Alessandro didn't want me to have, much less go behind his back to do it. The hard way it is.

I stand, wandering to the window wall and gazing out at downtown Seattle. I feel rather than hear Bryce approach.

"Where'd you go, Sera?" Bryce asks quietly from beside me.

I snap my head up to catch his concerned gaze more than half a foot above my own eye level. I smile at the reminder of how much bigger than me he is with his towering, broad, muscled frame. Because at five-foot-nine and curvy I'm not used to feeling so small. And somehow it makes me feel safe.

He reaches out and tugs absentmindedly at a lock of my hair. I can feel the heat in my face at the affection in his gesture.

"Sorry," I reply sheepishly. "I'm already mentally preparing, I guess."

"Good. You're going to need to do a lot more of that."

THE NEXT DAY, AS MY TAXI DRIVES OUT OF SOUTH SAN Francisco and into the city proper, my first thought is that it looks an awful lot like Seattle — there are gorgeous vistas in every direction and some stunning architecture. But it's also dirtier, more run-down, and more crowded. With the tech industry continuing to migrate north, though, I realize I may be looking into a crystal ball of Seattle's future. Both cities by a bay, both havens for not just tech giants but other professionals and urbanites. And while San Francisco is a shade more temperate, the beauty and outdoorsy lifestyle of the Puget Sound is drawing more and more people into the area. Not to mention the vastly more affordable housing. Which is, of course, exactly how I came to meet Alessandro Giordano, as his real estate investing company expanded into territory rife with opportunities for savvy investors.

I know Buone Case, the company he owned, still has offices here in San Francisco. But in my gut, I know he didn't come back here to work, so trying to find him there isn't at the top of my list. And the thought of lists reminds me to pull up the email from Bryce on my phone with the three locations that Alessandro used to frequent. All are within walking distance of the hotel I'll be staying at near the Museum of Modern Art, though San Francisco, like Seattle, seems to be very walkable, if not just as hilly.

As we arrive at the hotel, I realize just how close to the museum I'll be — literally a stone's throw. I glance longingly at the simple façade. While it's exactly the kind of place I could spend hours upon hours losing myself, not this trip. I step out of the cab into the early afternoon sunlight, and, luggage in tow, head into the hotel so I can quickly check in and get moving.

∽

Remaining in the lavish hotel room is ridiculously tempting. Apart from a spacious and lush living room and bedroom, my suite comes with its own personal butler and gorgeous city views on two sides of the generously sized common area. I suppose I should have expected as much, as it is a five-star hotel. But I don't travel often, so I figured what the hell. And while I'm glad I splurged, I have to resist the urge to ask my butler for help combing the city.

Smiling thinly to myself, I lean back into the plush, grey couch to plan my route for the afternoon. Plotting the three stops in my map app shows a near-linear path, not much more than a mile from the hotel. I grab my purse and slide on my sneakers, heading back out into the cool sunshine of the day.

Walking through the city, it feels like Seattle too. The mile to the bookstore isn't even very sloped, and the tall buildings and bustling traffic are a familiar and comforting backdrop for my stroll. There's even a faint whiff of salty sea air from the bay.

As I go, I try to practice what I'll say in my head, but I've never been terribly good at planning that sort of thing ahead of time, so I give up quickly. It'll just have to come in the moment, like it always does.

Before I know it, I can see the bookstore ahead on the opposite side of the street, the salmon and black building squatter than those around it. As I look left before crossing the road, I'm stopped short by the sight of the Transamerica Pyramid thrusting into the sky behind me, its iconic architecture drawing the eye of many on the street. Some, like myself, have stopped to gaze upon it in awe.

Briefly the tallest building west of Chicago, it still commands the eye and the imagination with its unique shape and sheen. I remember suddenly that it was another Italian — Amadeo Giannini — who actually founded the Transamerica Corporation. And just like that I'm slammed back to reality.

I take out my phone, pulling up the snapshot I took of the photo Peyton, Alessandro's now ex-wife, gave me the day I tricked her into confirming they were married. I zoom it in on just Alessandro and step down into the bookshop.

The shop has a funky vibe, with shelves upon shelves of tightly packed books, posters of all kinds, and signs directing its patrons to yet more books. It's neither stuffy like a library nor tidy and cold like a chain store. Rather, it's cozy and full of life, and I instantly understand why Alessandro came here often.

Unfortunately, it's also clearly a very popular stop for both locals and tourists, as the kind gentleman behind the counter is skeptical he'll recall the "friend" I'm searching for even before I've shown him the picture. And as he suspected, he doesn't.

I thank him, though I'm more than a little disappointed. But I'm also too enthralled by the store to not take a quick stroll through their fiction section, lovingly fingering some of the unique finds as I meander. When I leave, I thank him yet again and head to my next stop, a café only a few blocks away.

I have to stifle a laugh as I'm greeted by the bold colors of the Italian flag and the word "ESPRESSO" emblazoned under the shop's name like a beckoning call to the coffee-obsessed true Italian.

Entering the small shop, the aroma of coffee and pastries wraps me in a warm cocoon of happiness. The woman behind the counter greets me with a smile.

"Welcome! What can I get for you today?" she asks warmly. She looks to be a few years younger than me and has a kind face framed by a sharp, golden-brown bob.

I smile back as my eyes rove over the pastries displayed. "An espresso, please," I reply. "And," I point to a gorgeous, heart-shaped jam thumbprint cookie, "one of those too, please."

"My favorite," she replies, plating a cookie. She rings me up before making the espresso. "Anything else today?"

"Actually, there is. I'm looking for a friend," I hand her a large bill for the tab and measure her reaction carefully. Since she still seems to be eagerly listening, I continue. "He moved away about eight months ago and we lost touch, but I think he's back now. He used to come in here all the time, though, so I thought maybe you'd seen him?"

"It's certainly possible. We have a lot of regulars, and I know most of them — I've been here almost three years," she replies, and excitement unfolds in my gut. "What does he look like?"

I bring up the picture on my phone and show it to her. Her face lights up with recognition.

"Alessandro," she says in an exaggerated imitation of his accent as she heads to the espresso machine. "Doppio espresso, every day as soon as we opened."

I make an effort to laugh casually, trying not to let my excitement show. "That's him. Have you seen him lately?"

"Not in months," she responds.

And I deflate like a popped balloon. She hands me my espresso.

"Thanks anyway," I reply, dropping my considerable change in the tip jar with a smile.

"No problem," she says, her eyes widening slightly as she watches the bills settle. "Do you want to leave your name and number in case he stops by?"

"Oh gosh, no, that's okay. I'm sure I'll catch up with him sooner or later." She shrugs, and I take a seat at a nearby table.

I examine the espresso, noting the perfect crema on top. I sip it, and the rich flavor wraps around my tongue. I follow it with a bite of cookie, and I'm instantly hooked.

"Damn, that's good," I remark to myself. I can see the barista give a faint smile behind the counter. A little embarrassed, I finish my espresso and cookie quickly, giving her a smile on my way out.

"Come back soon," she calls after me, and I nod faintly as I leave.

Emerging into the fading afternoon light, it occurs to me that Alessandro may yet stop there, and I silently hope I'm able to find him before super-memory-chick back there blows my cover.

I start trekking the short walk to the last stop on the list — unsurprisingly, an Italian restaurant. Supposedly *the* best Italian restaurant in San Francisco. I arrive to a more muted display of the colors of the Italian flag at the entrance of another small, cozy establishment. Unfortunately, it's currently closed. I glance at my watch. The restaurant won't open for another hour. And after the cookie and espresso, I'm not particularly hungry.

Realizing I should have thought this through a bit better, I decide to return to the hotel and come back later for dinner. On the bright side, I get a long look at the Transamerica building once more as I make my way back.

Once in my room, I opt for a soothing shower. The hot water unknots my tense muscles, and the fluffy robe afterward feels like heaven. I sink onto the bed to rest my eyes for a minute before getting dressed once more.

I WAKE IN THE DARK AND CURSE MYSELF FOR NOT SETTING an alarm. A glance at the clock on the nightstand tells me its two a.m. I strip off my robe and crawl between the sheets, making a mental note to make a reservation once I'm up. The bed is so luxuriously soft, and I'm still so tired from my travels, that I'm asleep again almost instantly.

WHEN I WAKE FOR THE DAY, MY FIRST ACT IS TO MAKE the reservation at the restaurant for eight p.m. that night. That done, I pull on a pair of jeans and a white T-shirt and sit down to review the list of Alessandro's known contacts in the area.

The list is only five names long, and none of them sound familiar. I decide to rent a car for the day as the addresses are scattered around the city, and my lack of results yesterday has me itching for progress.

By ten a.m. I find myself in a blue coupe headed for the Presidio. Even at this late hour, traffic is slow going. I roll my windows down and try to enjoy the warm breeze as I crawl toward my destination.

As I roll by the marina, I see signs for a Fourth of July party at Pier 39. I glance at my phone's display, surprised to see that it's Tuesday, July third. The Fourth of July is *tomorrow*.

I scrunch my brow, wondering where the time went. But I guess I've had other things on my mind these last weeks. I tap the steering wheel impatiently, knowing I better make the best of things today, as I'm unsure whether trying to run covert surveillance on a holiday is a good idea.

When traffic finally breaks up, it's smooth sailing to the address my phone is guiding me to. Until I see the guard gate at the entrance to the community. It's unmanned, only offering a mounted keypad with a speaker box. I look around apprehensively, wondering if I should hover nearby and wait for someone to open the gate, or even try to bluff my way in. But the impressive houses beyond give me pause, as I have no idea what kind of security the community might have. I decide against chancing it, opting to move on to the second stop on my list.

I head south to the Richmond neighborhood, toward Golden Gate Park, noting wryly that at least my hunt will take me on a decently comprehensive driving tour of the city.

As I approach the next address, with thankfully zero barriers, the rather average looking neighborhood has me itching, not for the first time today, to pull up my real estate agent apps to check prices in the area. I resist, trying to focus on the task at hand.

In classic San Francisco style, the buildings are packed against one another, each climbing close to their likely regulated height. I pass by the address on the list slowly, and the building's tan exterior and drawn shades give no hint as to what's inside.

Unfortunately, there is no way to "casually" observe much more than that, as there's not really anywhere to park, nor any pretense under which to approach the house. Not that I think it would do much good if I don't intend to knock anyway. I take a lap around the block and approach from the opposite direction, but a second look doesn't yield any new information. I decide to come back this evening, I'll have to park at a nearby business and walk by to get a closer look.

I spend the rest of the morning and into the afternoon visiting the other three addresses, stopping only briefly for a quick lunch. The third address was nearly identical to the second, tan house, but purple and in a slightly more run-down neighborhood. The one after that had so much junk piled in the yard that I didn't even bother with a second look; I simply crossed it off the list and continued on, unable to see Alessandro, with his immaculate attention to detail and appearance, staying in a place like that. The final address has a for sale sign out front, and a quick look at the listing clearly shows that the house is empty.

With two viable options for evening surveillance, I return to the hotel to regroup. Once back, I step into the shower, again letting the hot water work the tension from my back and limbs. It's short-lived relief, but I take what I can get.

As afternoon shifts into evening, I decide to return to the second, tan house to observe until my reservation. I opt for a comfortable, stretchy black shirtdress over black leggings, bringing a maroon cardigan along, since I know temperatures will drop when the sun sets. I slip on a pair of black flats to complete the look, allowing both a decent appearance for the seemingly casual restaurant but enough comfort to stroll inconspicuously by the house a few times.

Due to traffic, it's nearly six p.m. when I find a play-ground to park near, a few blocks from the house. I note, ironically, that it's called Rossi Playground. I think of Marco and wonder how he's handling running Buone Case since taking it over so Alessandro could do whatever it is he's doing.

Willing myself to focus, I step out into the cooling evening air and start my stroll.

∾

On my third lap past the house, I've run out of convenient excuses to stop within sight distance. I have no shoelaces to tie, and I can only pretend I dropped my keys so many times. None of the passes offer up anything of further use. While I can see that there are now lights on inside, no cars are in the driveway, and I haven't been able to catch anyone going in or out, or even peeping out of the drapes. There isn't even a nosy neighbor to feign conversation with about looking to buy a house in the area. Nonetheless, I persist until it's time to return to the car to make it in time for my reservation. By the time I do I'm starving and discouraged, with sore feet.

I'm especially grumpy when I'm not able to find a parking spot close to the restaurant and am forced to walk another good distance. I slip on the maroon cardigan against the slight chill of the evening and make my way slowly past the few blocks of shops. As I approach, I take a deep breath and try to let go of my frustrations. I'm going to need to be charming and approachable to get answers without raising suspicion.

Fixing a neutral expression on my face, I enter. The hostess stand is just inside the door, and a plump, friendly looking middle-aged Italian woman greets me.

"*Benvenuto!*"

"*Grazie*," I reply, slipping into my best impression of a warm smile despite my exhaustion. "I have a reservation for one under Evans."

As she examines a list on her podium I note that the small restaurant is absolutely packed, with every seat at the bar occupied as well, and I wonder where exactly she's going to seat me.

"Serafina?" she asks in her lovely, lilting accent.

"Yes," I agree. "Sera."

"Sera," she replies, smiling. "I'm terribly sorry, but with the upcoming holiday we've unfortunately over-booked for the evening. Would you mind sharing with another single? There's a gentleman you could join who just ordered. He's a friend of the family, and I can promise he's very well behaved." She smiles encouragingly. "Or you're welcome to wait a few minutes for a table to open up. It shouldn't be long."

I bristle slightly but considering I'm hoping to get information from her, refusing doesn't seem like the best option. And her warm smile and mannerisms tell me that she really would understand if I'd rather not. But it also occurs to me that if this person she wants to seat me with knows the owners, he may be able to help too. And agreeing would certainly put me at an advantage regardless.

"I'm happy to share a table," I respond, returning her smile.

"*Grazie mille*," she responds sincerely, clasping her hands together. "It is much appreciated, and we'll get you something good for your troubles." She lifts a menu from a pocket on the side of her stand and gestures for me to follow her.

She leads me through the dimly lit restaurant, heading for the very back corner. The back few tables are tucked behind a waiter's station, so I can't see my table companion through the packed tables between us.

"*Ciao*," she greets him. "*Ti dispiace condividere?*"

"*Nessun problema*," a deep, melodic voice replies. And I freeze before she even steps aside, gesturing to the chair across from him, as I don't need to see the shock of artfully tousled, dark brown hair nor the warm, liquid brown eyes that meet mine to know that I've just found Alessandro.

TWO

Alessandro

As Sofia steps aside to reveal the young lady she's asked me to share my table with, I'm confused for a moment wondering if, having just been thinking of Serafina, my vision is playing tricks on me. But as I realize it's not, that Serafina is really standing before me, looking alarmed but as beautiful as ever, my heart skips a beat before it starts pounding madly.

Thankfully the shock renders my face blank, though I'm sure it registers in my eyes. I work to keep my expression fixed as Sofia glances nervously at Serafina's stunned look.

"Is it okay?" Sofia asks her uncertainly.

Serafina doesn't take her eyes off me as she answers.

"Yes, thank you." She slides into the chair, dazed, and Sofia hands her a menu before glancing at me questioningly.

Gathering my wits, I shrug lightly and, mollified, Sofia returns to the front of the restaurant.

It takes me a moment of examining my unexpected dinner companion, of absorbing that she's really here, before I can speak. "How …?" But my words fail me before the question can even fully form.

Her face is pale and drawn, and I can tell she's still recovering from the shock of seeing me as well. Interesting. "It's my turn not to give up," she replies with a meek, apologetic smile.

I want to laugh, and cry, and kiss her, and admonish her for using my words against me, but I don't know who might be listening. And if I've learned anything this past week, it's that the danger I'm in, the suspicion of which drove me from Serafina's side in the first place, is very real. And if those pursuing me learn what she means to me, I dare not even think of the consequences.

"What I meant to say is, how, exactly, did you know I'd be here?" I ask, scanning the restaurant nervously. I'd tapped in to my cash reserves when I followed the trail here and took pains to stay out of the system as much as possible, thinking I'd be practically untraceable.

"Bryce. He told me you were in San Francisco. But I didn't know you'd be here tonight," she replies. "I mean, he told me you used to come here often." Her expression is all apologies and longing. "How else was I supposed to find you? Apparently, I can't call or email you anymore."

I frown, running a finger under my chin. The giant sent her here. That's a twist, though with his expertise it explains how she found me. Though I was fairly certain when we spoke last, while Serafina lay unconscious in the hospital, that his threat to "make sure bad things happened to me if I hurt her again" meant he didn't want her coming anywhere near me. And yet, he helped her do exactly that.

"You weren't supposed to find me at all," I respond bluntly.

"You're not glad to see me?" she asks, catching my eye. A gentle tease, and I can tell she's searching for a warmer welcome. But she has no clue the danger at hand, and I can't find a smile or cute response to give her. My only thought is to convince her to forget me, to protect her, and to get her back on a plane to Seattle as soon as possible.

I simply stare at her for a moment before shrugging noncommittally. "It's nice to see you again," I reply casually. "If you're hungry, I recommend the house special."

She arches her eyebrows at my indifferent response, but the waiter arrives, blocking any immediate reply. As suggested, she goes ahead and orders the house special. I add a bottle of wine for good measure. Something to take the edge off. When he leaves, she sweeps her long hair over one shoulder and places her shapely arms on the table, leaning forward on them.

"I need to know why," she says baldly. Her beautiful, light brown eyes are flecked with green, and I have to resist the urge to reach out and touch her.

I lean back in my chair, crossing my legs under the table and smoothing my dark gray linen trousers as I consider my response carefully. Thankfully the waiter is already back with the wine, giving me a bit longer to gather my thoughts. He uncorks the bottle, pouring a small amount in my glass. I swirl it carefully, inhaling deeply as I watch Serafina shift uncomfortably in her chair. I take a sip, barely tasting it, and nod to the waiter. He pours our glasses slowly, then leaves the bottle behind and departs once more.

I take a long drink, then set my glass back down. I mirror Serafina's posture and lean forward so our faces are close enough to speak quietly and avoid being overhead, but still a respectable enough distance away to not raise the interest of a casual observer.

"I can't offer you any more information than you already have," I reply lowly. "Especially not here. Let's just enjoy our dinner, shall we?" I lean back in my seat once more, making a point to keep my expression neutral.

"Then where?" she demands quietly but firmly. "When? When are you going to trust me enough to tell me what's going on? To let me make the decision for myself?"

"I think we can agree," I reply guardedly, "that there are some things best not shared, *especially* with people you trust."

She looks at me, clearly confused. "What is that supposed to mean?"

I smile cryptically. "How's the giant? Still in love with you?"

Her nostrils flare and she clenches her jaw. Good. My comments are hitting their mark.

"At least he's honest with me," she retorts.

I raise an eyebrow. And I hate myself before I even say my next words. "Then maybe you should go back to him," I suggest casually, draining my wine glass.

Her mouth opens and closes several times. "You don't mean that."

Her voice is low and breathy. It sends a shiver down my spine. I pour myself another glass to mask my reaction.

"Oh, but I do." I level a sharp look at her. "I thought I made it clear where things stood." *Forgive the pain I must cause you, mio tesoro, and just go*, I plead silently, *before something much worse happens to you.*

"You're not going to get rid of me that easily," she counters, her eyes narrowing.

"I don't see that you have much of a choice," I reply calmly.

"Don't I?"

This time I can't hide my smile. I wonder sometimes if she remembers everything I've ever said to her, the clever girl. Her answering smile is hopeful but sad. But before anything further can be said, our food arrives.

"*Buon appetito*," our waiter says softly.

We each mumble our thanks as he leaves. We eat in uncomfortable silence for a bit before she sets her fork down and pushes her plate back.

"Something wrong with your food?" I ask archly. She's barely eaten anything.

"I'm not as hungry as I thought," she says quietly, taking a deep drink of wine.

"Then maybe you should slow down on the alcohol," I remark drily, glancing pointedly at her now-empty glass.

"Maybe you should mind your own business," she retorts hotly.

I can feel anger rising in me at her words, but I master it before it can get far. "I'm just trying to look out for you," I explain. *And not just about the alcohol, damnit.*

"I can take care of myself," she pouts. She shakes her head lightly. "This isn't what I came here to talk about, Alessandro. I thought …"

I set my fork down and lean over my plate, hands clasped in front of me. "You thought what? After I told you why I was leaving that it was a good idea for you to follow? That I'd want to involve you? You thought wrong."

I stare intensely at her, trying to tell her with my eyes what I can't with my lips. *The threat was more real than I thought. They've been watching me. If they don't already know about you, I can't risk them finding out.* But I know if I tell her these things it won't deter her, stubborn as she is. And the last time she underestimated a threat it nearly got her killed. I can't let that happen to her again.

From the anger in her eyes, in her demeanor, I can see that she doesn't understand what I'm trying to say. And she's furious.

"This isn't you."

As usual, she sees straight through me. I smile grimly. "Maybe you just weren't listening closely enough before," I suggest, spreading my hands in front of me.

She rises from her chair, quietly fuming. She shakes her head and turns to leave.

"Where are you going?" I ask as indifferently as I can.

"Back to my hotel," she seethes. She drops a card on the table, with the name of a nearby luxury hotel. "If you come to your senses you know where to find me. But I'm leaving before I say something I don't mean. Or worse, something I *do* mean."

I watch her silently as she walks out. And I'm angry. Not at her, but at myself, for having to be that way with her. Returning my eyes to the card, I flip it over. She's written her room number on the back. I quietly shred the card and tuck the remnants into my pocket. And then I pick up my fork and return to eating my dinner in solitude.

As the restaurant clears, I continue drinking until Sofia and her husband, Luca, are done for the evening and sit down at the table next to mine.

"Who was the girl?" Luca asks, rubbing his round belly.

"Leave him alone, Luca," Sofia chastises him. "And I told you not to eat so many cannoli."

Luca grins widely at her.

"It's okay," I reply. "She was just a friend. I told her about this restaurant, but she didn't expect to run into me here." I suppress a heavy sigh. I dislike lying, despite what others seem to think.

"Good! Tell all your friends," Luca laughs. The chef pokes his head out of the kitchen and signals Luca. "I'll be back." He rises slowly, shuffling away.

"I know it's not my business, Alessandro, but I saw her when she left," Sofia says softly. Her kind, brown eyes, so much like my own mama's, meet mine. "*Sei più gentile di così.*"

I shoot her an angry look. *I* know *I'm kinder than that. That was the point.*

"You're right," I agree, finishing yet another glass of wine. "It's not your business."

Sofia raises her hands in a gesture of surrender. "If that's how you want her to remember you."

Her words are like a punch in the gut. "That's low, Sofia."

She stands to follow Luca into the kitchen and fixes me with a stern look. "*È vero.*"

Yes, it's true. But it's still a cheap shot.

She turns and starts walking away but can't resist a parting parry. "I hope I don't see you back at the house later."

I shake my head. Sofia has always been a busybody. But when she's right, she's right. Before I can stop myself, I'm out in the cool night air.

∽

It's only a little after ten p.m. when I knock on her door, so I know she must still be awake. But she doesn't answer, and I'm suddenly afraid she's already gone. I knock again, louder, and wait a good while. And still no response.

I do the only other thing I can think of — I call the front desk. But they say she's still here and connect me to her phone. Sure enough, I can hear it ringing inside. And ringing. And ringing. Now I'm really starting to panic, wondering if she ran into trouble on the way home. But finally, she answers.

"Hello?" She sounds annoyed.

"Open your goddamn door," I order her.

A moment later, the door cracks open and she peeks out at me. I push the door open, step inside, and close it behind me. Her hair is up in a messy bun and she is dripping wet with a large, fluffy white towel wrapped around her. I breathe a sigh of relief. She's here. She's safe. She was just taking a shower.

"What the hell?" she asks angrily.

"I've been knocking for fifteen minutes," I tell her. "I thought something had happened to you."

She glares at me and turns away. "What do you care?" she scoffs, heading toward the bedroom.

She's still mad. And she has every right to be. But her dismissal roils the anger I'd suppressed earlier in the evening, and like the flip of a switch, I'm mad too. I stride quickly for her, spinning her around by her wrist.

"You damn well know that I care," I respond hotly.

She yanks her arm out of my grasp, clutching the towel to her naked body. And I'm suddenly very aware of how much of her is showing, and it's been long enough since I was with her that I'm suddenly finding it very hard to keep my wits about me.

"Are we Dr. Jekyll now? What, no more Mr. Hyde?"

I huff a short laugh, unable to stop staring at the hand clutching the edges of the towel together over her chest. "I'd say I'm usually a bit of both, honestly."

"*Honestly*," she scoffs. "Glad we're being *honest* now." She waves a hand around as she speaks, and in her fervor her towel slips from her grip slightly, exposing the top of her round, heavy breasts.

A bolt of lust shoots through me and I squeeze my eyes shut tightly. "Can you please put some clothes on?" I ask. I open my eyes to see that she is smiling, realizing suddenly that she has the upper hand.

"No, I don't think I will," she replies serenely.

"Serafina," I beg.

She takes one step toward me, letting the towel slip just a bit more. I swallow hard, and my cock twitches.

"Tell me why you had to leave," she prompts.

I shake my head dimly, my eyes on her chest. She takes another step toward me, within touching distance. She drops the towel so she's holding it in by a corner in front of her, clinging to a small scrap of the fabric that keeps her from exposing herself to me completely. Though one perfect, rosy nipple is just visible around the edge of the towel.

"Tell me," she repeats.

My breathing is heavy, and my palms are itching to grab her. "It's not safe," I say dumbly.

She cocks her head to the side. "For who?"

I open my mouth to protest and she removes the clip holding her hair up and shakes out her long, damp tresses.

"Tell me." Her sexy whisper sends a shiver down my back once again.

I'm hypnotized, and the tight rein I keep on what I

want her to know has evaporated. "For either of us," I breathe. "I wouldn't have left if I had any other choice."

She steps forward, her body pressing against mine, only the towel between us. My hand has a mind of its own as it lightly wraps around her glorious, naked backside.

"There's always another choice." Her sweet, cinnamon-honey scent fills my senses and my head swims.

"No," I protest. "There's not. Not until I stop whoever is after us."

The words tumbling out surprise me, as I have no recollection of forming them. All I can think of is her hand on the towel. And her nipple, ripe for sucking. My lips part and I know I'm breathing heavily.

She raises an eyebrow. "Who threatened you? Let me help you, Alessandro," she purrs.

I shake my head, trying to clear the fog of my desire for her. "No," I whisper.

She smiles seductively up at me, with a look of triumphant lust and fire. "I think I can change your mind," she murmurs. And she drops the towel, sliding her arms around my neck.

And I have no more words, no more conscious stream of thought, only the burning need to feel her, taste her. I lean into her, my lips searching for hers. When our faces meet, I'm wrapped in her scent, my hands sliding over her soft, delicious body. My hands slip under her backside, lifting her to me. Her legs wrap around me, and I carry her through the bedroom door, laying her out on the humongous, cloudlike bed inside.

I pull my mouth from hers and slide my hands down her chest, over her hips, lightly grazing the dampness between her legs. I control myself long enough to get an eyeful of her large, firm breasts, those perfect nipples peaked with anticipation, her soft stomach and the stunning curves of her thighs an invitation for the heat roiling inside me. She pulls a leg up, exposing herself to me, her gaze fiery and taunting.

And like a summons, I drop to my knees, my mouth finding the glistening, wet mound between her thighs. My tongue probes for the small bundle at its zenith, and when she gasps loudly I know I've found the spot. I work it with increasing ardor, adding a finger, then two, then pumping them in time with my circling tongue. She writhes under me, her gasps egging me on, her fingers entwined in the bedding, her salty-peachy taste filling my mouth. One of her hands reaches for me, and I grasp it with my free hand. Her grip is as tight as she is under my provocation, and I don't think I can wait much longer to take her.

But I press through, controlling the churning heat inside, determined to see her through to climax. I switch my assault, squeezing the small bundle of nerves between my thumb and forefinger, plunging my tongue into her. She cries out and tightens around me, and I know she's on the edge. I let go of her hand and search for her nipple. I'm just able to reach it, rolling it between my fingers as I work her below. It's enough to push her over the edge, and she screams, a warm gush meeting my lips as she climaxes.

I release her as she tumbles down from her ascent, quickly pulling my black V-neck sweater off and unbuttoning the gray trousers. But before I can finish removing them, she's there, unzipping the fly and yanking my pants and black boxer-briefs over my backside, freeing my erection completely. I'm not even able to finish removing them before her mouth is on my cock, her hand working the base as she unleashes her tongue on the tip. She slides the two toward each other in concentric motions until I can barely stand through the waves of pleasure.

She stops abruptly, scooting back on the bed, beckoning me to her. I mindlessly respond instantly, crawling eagerly over the covers to her waiting hands. She firmly pushes me onto my back, sitting astride me over my thighs. She hovers just out of reach, stroking me gently with one hand, licking her lips. The sight almost makes me climax on the spot.

"Who is it?" she asks.

And in my lust fog, I stare at her, confused. She laughs softly, realizing I'm not all there.

"Who threatened you?"

Through the haze, I realize she's still working me for

information. Clever, clever girl. She raises her eyebrows, squeezing me harder. I moan deeply.

"You fight dirty," I manage to reply.

She grins in agreement, releasing me, and sliding her breasts up the length of me to cover my mouth with hers. Her tongue finds mine, and our bodies meld together. I run my hands over her, itching to be inside her.

"You'll forgive me if I've had to resort to creative methods of interrogation," she whispers in my ear. She runs her tongue along its edge, breathing heavily. "Tell me, darling, who threatened you." She sits up astride my stomach, my cock tickling her backside, the slight brushing driving me mad.

"I'm not saying another woman's name while you're naked on top of me," I reply, frustrated.

Her eyes light up with understanding. She knows who I mean. My former wife. It's hard to even *think* the word in my current state.

"You're afraid of her?" she asks, running her fingernails over my nipples.

"Not at first," I admit. "But she made specific threats. And the more I learn ..." I shake my head, cursing my traitor tongue and her absolute power over me.

Serafina positions herself over my waiting erection, her hand holding me, so the tip just grazes her warm wetness. "Keep going," she encourages me.

Giving in, I grit my teeth and move to buck myself

into her, but she's ready for me. She slides back out of reach, shaking her head and smiling.

"That's not how we play, lover."

I sit up, but she's too fast for me. She descends upon me once again with her mouth and hands so feverishly that I fall back onto the bed, almost spilling myself into her mouth instantly. But she knows exactly how to back off to avoid that, keeping me right on the edge, begging for release.

"*Per favore*, Serafina," I plead.

"What did you learn?" she prompts, continuing to work me with her hand.

Sweet unholy torture. "She's not working alone. But I haven't …" I moan loudly, and she slackens her grip. "I haven't figured out who she's working with. But they've been watching me for a long time. That's all I know." I'm practically dizzy with anticipation and delayed pleasure, and I beg her silently with my eyes to give me what I need.

She smiles grimly, mounting me, and plunging me deep into her tight, hot sex. I ache inside her, needing more. I grip her hips tightly, pushing up, urging her on.

But she holds firm and still on top of me. "See, that wasn't so hard," she croons, smiling mischievously.

I huff a tortured laugh. It's abruptly cut off as she pulls my hands to her breasts and begins to ride me. I can tell she means it this time, and I'm practically weeping with relief as the sweet, wet thrusts cause the tension to ball quickly in me before erupting out into her in hot fire. I scream my release at the same time she does, and she tightens around me, extending the last small bit of what I had left in me.

Too tired to be angry that she managed to seduce the information out of me — well, some of it at least — I pull her toward me roughly, spending the last of the fire in me on claiming her with my tongue and hands.

When I'm completely spent, I bury my face in her hair, my hands cupping her backside. We lay together, sweaty and slick from sex, until we are both breathing normally again.

"I'm sorry," she eventually says softly.

I look down into her eyes. She doesn't look sorry. She looks fucking amazing, and like she knows it.

"Are you?"

She laughs. "No," she admits.

I smile down at her, despite myself.

"And now I know," she adds.

"Yes," I agree resignedly. "Now you know."

She considers me for a long while. "You followed her here, didn't you?"

It's not a question. And she's not wrong, but I don't confirm it. Though she clearly knows me well enough to glean the answer from my face or my body language.

"That's what you're doing. You're following her.

Trying to figure out who she's working with. What they can really do to you."

Again, I stay silent. She extricates herself from me and rises from the bed, and I roll onto my side to watch her walk away. She almost makes it to the bathroom before she turns to me.

"I'd just be a liability to you on this little mission, I suppose?" The anguish on her face is heartbreaking, and the picture of her standing there — naked to me in every way, with my seed dripping down the inside of her thigh — nearly breaks me. But it also reminds me how vulnerable she is, and why I must fight like hell to keep her out of this. To keep her safe.

"You'd be a liability to yourself," I correct her. "If they don't know about you — and I have good reason to believe they don't — I don't want to give them that knowledge by keeping you close for my own, selfish reasons."

She shakes her head, turning back toward the bathroom. "I'm going to take a bath," she mumbles.

I sit up on the bed. "Didn't you just shower?" I tease her.

She shoots me a dirty look over her shoulder as she turns on the taps for the huge, raised tub. "Somebody got me all dirty again," she pouts, beckoning me with a crooked finger.

I slide off the bed, grinning madly as I take her in my arms. "Temptressssss," I purr into her ear.

I kiss her soft neck, shoulders, and breasts as the tub fills, running my tongue along her nipple as she arches into me. I take it between my teeth, and suck until she's moaning. Dropping a hand between her legs, I use the wetness that still remains from our frenzied fuck on the bed to gently work her. She clings to me, clearly devoid of strength after her assault on me. I reciprocate the torture she just enacted upon me, drawing her to the brink, then pulling back just as the tub finishes filling. Watching her pant has me hardening again.

I step into the tub, pulling her with me. I lean her over the edge facing away from me, so I can enter her from behind. She sinks against me, groaning in pleasure. I reach under her and grasp her breasts in my hands, squeezing her nipples between my fingers as I use the grip to pull her onto me. In this position, I'm fully inside her, her spent cunt tight even without orgasming. It's like a silken, gloved fist and it feels like heaven. I pump into her steadily over and over, our groans of pleasure growing louder together, until I eventually feel her tightening around me even further. Knowing she's ready to climax again, I let loose, pounding into her ferociously until we're both over the edge once more. My world explodes, and my grip on her slackens as I again cry out my release. Our moans mingle as we finish, and she goes limp in my arms, clinging to the side of the tub. I sink back into the hot water and she settles into my lap, her head lazing against my shoulder.

I wrap my hands around hers, tracing small circles with my thumbs.

"Have we ever just made love once?" she asks contemplatively. "Without almost immediately going at it again?"

I laugh appreciatively at the observation. "Probably," I reply, kissing her neck. "But I'm usually far too turned on by you to be satisfied only having you once."

She turns her face to mine and kisses me briefly. "If you don't want me to come with you, I won't," she says softly. "But does that mean we can't still be whatever it is that we are?"

"Serafina," I start, turning her face back to mine. "You have been everything to me. From the moment you agreed to be mine. It's why I need to do this." She kisses me again, sweetly this time. "Please, let me do this, on my own, my way. And if I can, then I will come back to you, knowing that there's nothing keeping us apart. That there's nothing to worry about."

"Okay," she agrees.

In shock, I twist her around in the tub so she's facing me. "*Okay?*" I ask, aghast.

She shrugs. "Okay." She smiles furtively. "I can't *make* you take me along for the ride. And honestly, I don't think I'd want to go. I mean, I would, if you wanted me to.

But you don't. And while it'll be like leaving a body part behind, I'll manage, I suppose."

I look at her skeptically. "I think you could make me if you tried," I concede. "You just played me like a fiddle back there." I tip my head toward the bedroom and she laughs.

"Desperate times," she replies, grinning mischievously. "I'll try to use my powers for good, I promise."

THREE

Despite the ridiculously amazing sex and the exhaustion that followed, I find my sleep is as disturbed as it has been of late. My nightmares have been a constant companion these past months. So much so that I can feel their presence as I drift to sleep, lurking in my subconscious, waiting to torment me night after night.

They were better once, almost nonexistent even, when we were together and happy, Alessandro and me. For that brief time. Our reunion has given me a sliver of hope that we'll have that again, but it's overshadowed by the uncertainty that remains. My nightmares rip me awake once more, in the early hours of the morning.

I spring up, covered in sweat, half mad with terror as shadowy figures chase me from sleep. I press my palms into my eyes, willing the tears away. Once I'm certain of their retreat, I look around the room, now wide awake.

A shaft of moonlight glows through a crack in the drapes, casting a dim light over the room. Alessandro sleeps soundly next to me, splayed out on his back as always, looking both younger and older at once. I slip quietly from the bed and pad to the window, peeping through the drapes at the city sprawled around us.

I haven't had time for private reflection on everything I've learned since finding Alessandro last night. And while I don't have all the details, I know enough. And the way I uncovered it was surprisingly empowering. I've never used sex against a man like that, much less a man as stubborn, virile, and commanding as Alessandro is. That it worked is beyond comprehension.

But despite my reassurances to the contrary, a large part of me wants to follow him into anything if it means never being parted from him again. When he's not with me I feel less than whole. But the volatility of our relationship makes me wonder how much of that is what I want him to be, as opposed to what he actually is. If the idea of him is more fulfilling than being with him.

I shake my head in disagreement with my own doubts. Being with him, waking up with him most mornings, was the happiest period of my life. But I know even if I stay with him through this, to wherever it takes us, it won't be like it was. He'll be worried, distracted, and overbearing.

Much like he was at the height of our most contentious moments, before we were together, before we were even lovers.

I certainly haven't forgotten how insufferably insistent he can be when he sets his mind to how something should happen. How laser-focused he is on details, on seeing things through to the vision he has in his mind. I have firsthand experience of the strife that comes from getting between him and what he is pursuing.

And, quite frankly, if we ever ran across Peyton again, I'd have a hard time not beating the living shit out of the two-faced bitch. Because however she kept him in that marriage, and whatever threats she made, one day, I'll make her pay.

But that thread of anger is exactly why I need to stay out of this. This is the kind of thing I won't be able to stay cool and logical about. I can't deny that Alessandro is right — I'll just put myself in harm's way and make myself into a constant worry for him in an already stressful situation.

So, as much as it kills me, having as much information as I need in order to understand, I know in my gut that I must let him go. And hope like hell he comes back to me in one piece.

I turn from my vantage point at the window and look back at the bed. Alessandro has rolled over, his arm reaching for the spot where I slept minutes ago as if his subconscious knows I've left it. For a moment I contemplate leaving right now, bypassing another cycle of rending ourselves from each other. As amazing as it's been, it's also been like tearing open a wound where the skin had just begun to knit back together. But I know I'd suffer the pain again and again, even if those were the only terms under which I could be with him.

Some visceral part of me knows it shouldn't be this way, that I shouldn't need him so much, that I'm a perfectly whole person without him, but that small sliver isn't as strong as the rest of me. And the rest of me needs him like air, water, or food. Even now, simply standing apart from him takes conscious effort. To not go to him, and wrap myself around him, losing myself in his warm embrace. Memorizing every inch of him. Refilling my lungs with his wine-and-spice smell. I'm like a druggie. And he's my drug. Can it last? Or is it, like any addiction, doomed to consume me, body and soul? All I can hope is that I get the chance to find out.

I return to the bed and, knowing that I won't get back to sleep otherwise, proceed to wake him in a way I know he won't mind being stirred.

I WAKE TO THE SMELL OF COFFEE AND TO SUNLIGHT peeking through the drapes. Unsurprisingly, I'm alone. I slip out of bed and into the fluffy bathrobe, and tread into the living room area. Alessandro sits on the couch in only his boxer-briefs, sipping a cappuccino and reading a newspaper. A glance at the clock shows it's ten thirty-four a.m.

"Cutting it kind of close with that cappuccino, aren't we?" I tease him.

He glances up from his paper, then folds it onto the coffee table and sets down his cup when he sees that the front of my robe is open. "It's not eleven yet," he says defensively, staring at my chest. "And I slept late because someone," he gives me a pointed look as I stride toward him and settle in his lap, "disrupted my sleep with her sexy antics."

I press a kiss to his lips, lingering for a moment before pulling away. "Are you complaining?"

He smiles indulgently. "No," he admits, running a hand down my chest. He stoops and places a kiss on my nipple, which immediately hardens in response. He smiles beatifically up at me, and I can't help but laugh. His smile fades and his gaze intensifies. "How long do you plan to stay?"

I'd answered this question for myself after our predawn lovemaking, deciding that there was no point in dragging it out. For too long anyway. "This evening," I respond simply. "I'll book a flight shortly. But the room is paid for through tomorrow. You should stay."

He nods sullenly. "Thank you, I think I will. I hadn't

planned anything for today, so it works out well," he responds. "But you'll miss the fireworks."

I laugh, turning in his lap to wrap my legs around him. "We have all day to put on our own fireworks show," I promise him, covering his lips with mine.

And by the time we're done with our first "show" the cappuccino is cold, though it's well past the time any sensible Italian would drink it anyway. We opt, instead, to order in lunch, eating it while spread out naked on the bed.

As I pop a grape into Alessandro's waiting mouth, he sighs contentedly. "Let's just stay here forever," he remarks, munching on the grape.

I laugh and pop one in my own mouth. "Okay," I agree. "But don't you think they'll find us eventually?"

Alessandro shoots me a dirty look. "Way to ruin the mood," he grumbles facetiously.

I watch him eat the rest of the grapes, content in his presence for the moment. But my brain is never silent, and, while I know *enough*, I suddenly want to know *more*.

"What are you going to do? When you figure out whoever is behind this?"

He eyes me gravely, considering the question. "I've thought a lot about that," he admits. "And I suppose there's no way to know until I'm there. But I imagine there's a debt to be paid, whatever that means to them. I can only hope the price isn't too steep."

"It just doesn't make any sense," I say persistently. "Why would Peyton be involved?"

Alessandro sits up and gives me a grim stare. "That is exactly what bothers me most," he replies, rubbing his chin. "And it means they've been planning this for a long time. And it's personal."

"But who would have that kind of grudge against you?"

"It would probably take less time to guess who it wasn't," he remarks drily. "You know how it is in our business. Everything is personal." He pauses. "I never thought about it, but you probably understand better than anyone. Going through your mental list of who could hate you so much that they'd come after you in such a way. It's maddening."

"I do understand," I agree softly. "Why didn't you tell me? We should be a team."

He smiles down at me. "I'd like that," he admits. "But I didn't tell you for the same reason it's hard for me to think of us as a team, in this matter anyway. My instincts are to protect you, not thrust you out into danger alongside me."

"When you put it that way, I'm hard-pressed to argue with you," I admit.

"We've been a team before, Sera," he says. "And we will be again. Just not on this."

He's being more reasonable than I would have

expected. His defensiveness over the situation has given way almost completely to a serene but limited acceptance of my knowing just enough to go along with his decision. And in his way, even though I pushed him into it, I can tell he's now willingly trusting me with the knowledge, giving what he can while still holding on to what he needs to do.

"We're compromising," I realize suddenly, and I smile up at him.

He laughs and pushes my hair behind my shoulders. "Yes, I suppose we are," he responds, looking fondly at me. "I like it." His mouth settles into my favorite sexy, crooked smile, and a slow fire kindles deep within me.

"Someday," I say, climbing to my knees in front of him. "When there's no more danger, and we've tired of pleasuring each other all day, maybe we'll be able to live like normal people. Go out to eat. Watch movies. Take a walk in the park. I think I'd like that."

"Someday," he agrees, running his hands up my arms to cup my face in his palms. "But not today."

And the fire in me grows as it lights in his eyes, and we return to enjoying each other. Because it's just where we are. Who we are, together, in this moment. And as he takes me roughly on the bed, I happily surrender "someday" for right now.

GETTING READY IN THE BATHROOM JUST BEFORE FIVE, I lament how quickly the day has passed, and that I'll need to leave shortly to catch my seven-thirty flight back to Seattle. I take a last look at myself in the mirror, realizing suddenly that the last of the bruising has faded. That I'm healed. I smile at the appropriateness of it — there's been a lot of healing happening, and I have a seed of hope for the future.

Though as I drag my mind back to why I'm leaving, there's also a seed of fear for what Alessandro must do next, and for the separation that's coming. I leave the bathroom and find him in the living room, once again perusing the paper. I lean against the bedroom doorframe and observe him, drinking in a last private look.

His dark hair is sexily disheveled as usual, his full beard well-groomed and accentuating the sharp lines of his jaw. His dark eyes are full of life and intelligence, and he consumes the newspaper the way he does everything — with rapt intensity and total focus. His broad shoulders are relaxed, his tall and slim, but well-muscled, frame stretched out languidly, legs crossed on the coffee table. I'm a little sad he's gotten dressed.

I pull my phone from my pocket. "Say cheese," I call. He glances up and gives me his best crooked, sexy smile and I take the picture. He beckons me over and pulls me into his lap. Turning the phone around, he flips the camera and takes a picture of us. Then he turns, covering my mouth with his and snaps another. He returns my phone with a smile.

"Just in case you start to forget," he says, winking.

"I'm just sad you aren't naked," I tease. "You know, so I can remember that too." I smile slyly at him and he raises an eyebrow.

"Next time, perhaps," he replies, his voice husky.

I tuck myself under his arm and snuggle next to him on the couch, resting my head on his chest. "Will I be able to reach you?"

"I've been changing disposable phones every few days," he replies, his deep voice rumbling through his chest and reverberating in my ear. "But I set up an anony-mous email. You can contact me there, but only if you set up your own as well. I don't want there to be any way to trace my contact with you." He shifts away from me and uses the hotel pen and paper on the coffee table to jot down the email address. He hands me the paper, and I fold it into my pocket.

"Boy, you're really going cloak and dagger on this, aren't you?"

His brows scrunch together. "What does that mean?"

I smile indulgently at him. "You sound like a spy," I clarify.

He shrugs. "That's kind of the idea," he replies.

"Have you done this sort of thing before?" I ask suspi-ciously.

He smirks at me. "After a fashion," he admits. "Don't worry, Serafina, I can take care of myself. It'll be fine."

"I hope so," I murmur. I look back up at him and put a hand on his face. "I'd like to hear your voice every now and again. If that's possible."

His gaze is intense as he leans in to kiss me. His lips meet mine softly at first, but when I part mine to move with his, he slides his tongue in and wraps himself around me. Just as the heat begins to rise in me, he pulls back, leaving me wanting more.

"I'd like to hear your voice too. I'll try to call regularly, before I switch phones," he promises.

"Thank you." I kiss him softly once more before disentangling myself and rising from the couch. "I should finish packing."

He picks up his newspaper and I return to the bedroom.

When I emerge a few minutes later, luggage in tow, he is waiting to hand me my phone.

"Don't forget this," he teases me, winking, "or I won't be able to call you."

I take it from him, fighting a wave of emotion at the tone in his voice. Because I know it means goodbye. "Be careful," I reply in the same tone.

"I will," he promises, his eyes smoldering with the same intensity I feel for him right now.

I step toward him tentatively, and place a hand on his

chest, over his heart. He slides one hand over mine then grasps my chin with his other hand, tilting my face up so he can look into my eyes.

My vision blurs as tears begin to swim in my eyes. I blink, then feel them spill onto my cheeks. His face full of emotion, he gently kisses the tears away, then touches his lips to mine. And the kiss is tender, sweet, and full of sorrow. When our lips part, he rests his forehead against mine.

"*Ti amo*, Serafina," he murmurs. "I love you."

I choke back the anguished cry rising in my throat. I don't want to make this harder for either of us. "I love you too, Alessandro," I reply, my voice shaking with the effort.

He releases me slowly and nods. I take the cue and leave with no goodbye. Only love.

FOUR

I realize I may have lingered too long when I barely make it to my gate before the doors close. I thought Seattle traffic was bad, but it's got *nothing* on San Francisco. On the bright side, it gives me little time to think about staying, as I'm forced to hurry to my seat so the plane can depart.

I slide into my row, the last of first class, and note that the airplane isn't more than half full. The seat next to me is empty as well, so at least it will be a comfortable and quiet ride. I turn off my cellphone and tuck it in my bag under the seat in front of me.

Once we're at altitude, I turn it back on, thinking I'll catch up on email. But as soon as I unlock it, it opens to a video. The first, frozen frame is Alessandro's face, and my breath catches in my throat. I scramble for the headphones in my bag.

As soon as I'm hooked in, I turn the volume to max and hit play. I note that the time of the video was right before I left. He must have taken it while I was packing.

"*Mio tesoro*," his deep voice rumbles through my ears. "I wish I had a video of you, so I could hear your voice and see you smile while we are apart. But, even though I can't, I figured I could leave one for you. And," he sets the phone down and there is a flurry of motion and the sound of fabric swishing until he picks the phone back up shirtless. The tight knot in my chest unravels into a burst of delighted laughter. "As requested, at least partly, a little skin for you." He winks roguishly and laughs, and the sound sends warmth through me. "I love you, Serafina Evans. And I can't wait to come back to you and show you how much. Take care of yourself, *bella*, while I'm gone. We'll talk soon. I promise." He kisses his fingers and presses them to the camera lens. Then the video stops.

And I let the tears that follow flow until there are no more. It takes a while.

∽

On the cab ride back to my condo, I call Bryce to let him know I'm back and safe. Traffic is slow from all of the Fourth of July revelers returning home from the fireworks shows, so I have some time to kill.

"Hey, gorgeous," he answers, sounding almost like his sunshine self again.

"Hey, Bryce. I'm back," I reply.

"I know." And I can practically hear the grin in his voice. I realize he must have been tracking me and I roll my eyes, huffing a laugh.

"I should've realized you would," I chuckle.

"Are you going in to work tomorrow?" he asks.

"Maybe," I hedge. "If I can get a few things done in the morning."

"I'm sure they'll survive another day without you," he remarks drily. "Do you have time for lunch with your favorite security consultant?"

"You're not my security consultant anymore," I remind him teasingly. Not now that Sutton Developments is absorbing Evans Realty Services.

"Sera," he says, exasperated. "Just because I'm not *your* security consultant doesn't mean I can't still be your *favorite* security consultant. Though you have used my ad hoc services recently, might I remind you."

I can only assume he's referring to his detective work finding Alessandro. Even still, I laugh appreciatively. "I didn't pay you for that, so it's doesn't count," I point out.

"Touché," he responds, chuckling.

I laugh, softly this time. "Yes, let's have lunch," I agree.

"Great. The usual?" he asks.

"Sounds good," I agree.

"Then I'll see you at eleven thirty," he responds.

"See you then. Goodnight, Bryce."

"Goodnight, Sera."

I end the call, still chuckling to myself. He has to be just about the perkiest dude I've ever known. And I'm so glad he's back to his normal, annoyingly chipper self.

Given the hour, I don't try calling anyone else. I just add it to the rather long list of things to do tomorrow. And, though tired from recent events, I find I'm actually itching to get back in the swing of things — back to work. I'm going to need the distraction.

THE NEXT MORNING, I'M HOME, SITTING IN THE CHAIR pointed at the window wall. I silently watch the sky brighten with the rising sun, the city awakening beneath me while I sip a cappuccino slowly, drawing its warmth into me. Along with the reminder of Alessandro.

I watched his video as I tried to fall asleep the night before, wondering if he'd actually stayed in the hotel room or not. But either way, I dreamt of him in that gigantic, fluffy bed. Well, of *us* in that bed.

Once I've finished my coffee and it's a decent enough hour, I call Allie.

"Alison Kramer," she answers distractedly.

"Hey, Allie, it's me," I greet her.

"Sera!" she peals. "I don't know if I'm more excited that my best friend is back or my boss. I don't know how you keep this shit show running like you do! How was San Francisco?"

I don't know how to answer that, so I laugh. "It's a long story. I'll tell you when we're able to sit down face-to-face. But more importantly, how are *you*? How's the baby?"

"I'm great, now that I'm out of the first trimester and not vomiting at the sight of food anymore," she jokes. "I swear, I've actually *lost* weight since I got pregnant."

"Eek, well, I'm glad you're doing better anyway," I reply. "How is the Sutton Developments transition planning going?"

"Eh," she replies noncommittally. "There's still a lot to work out. Keith has been arguing with the attorneys constantly, and Sutton's son is a pain in the ass. We could really use you back in the office."

Sutton's son? I hadn't realized one of Charles Sutton's sons worked with him, and I find my interest is definitely piqued by the fact.

"Say no more, Allie, I'll be in after lunch," I promise.

"Really? Oh, Sera, I know you've had a lot going on, but that would be just fantastic," she breathes.

"I'm ready to get back on the horse," I reply. "Let's get all the leads and department heads in a meeting at two. And ask Maggie to schedule me for a call with Charles Sutton as late in the afternoon as possible."

"I'll do my best," she responds. "Thanks, Sera. I can't wait to give you a big ol' hug!"

We both laugh and say our farewells. Having decided to delay calling Charles Sutton until I've talked with my team, I call my mom next instead. When she doesn't answer I realize she's probably already at work, so I simply leave her a voicemail assuring her that I'm back safely from my trip, that everything is okay, and that I'll talk to her soon.

Caffeinated and squared away on calls, I stand, ready to tackle the mountain of mail, bills, and errands that I've neglected since pretty much before life got so complicated. I shake my head lightly, pushing down everything that's happened recently, good and bad, and shift my focus back to the two-week backlog of household chores ahead. Because I'm not going to get far without food or toilet paper. And if I'm going to sort out what promises to be an arduous tangle of paperwork and frayed nerves, I'm going to need to have my shit together.

BY ELEVEN-THIRTY I'M WAITING OUTSIDE THE BURGER joint that, through the few lunches we've had together, has become the "usual" for Bryce and me. I'm feeling pretty good, having tackled the important stuff, showered, and dressed in my favorite summer dress — a knee-length, muted orange and yellow short-sleeved dress that flows out in soft waves from the waist. It makes me feel oh so pretty. I chuckle as I smooth it over my hips, then tap a matched-yellow-ballet-slipper-clad food impatiently. I don't do well with hungry.

By the time Bryce is almost ten minutes late, I find myself getting downright pissy and dig my phone out of my bag to text him. As I'm typing, I see him jogging around the corner. And something about the sight of him running toward me in dark dress pants and a white button-up shirt evaporates my irritation. I try to convince myself it's because he's clearly hustling to meet me and not because I can see his muscles rippling through his shirt.

"I'm so sorry, Sera," he says breathlessly. "My dad forgot a meeting this morning and I had to pinch-hit for him. It took longer than I thought."

"It's okay, but food. Now. Please." He grins at my poor imitation of civility. "And I need to go in to the office today after all, so let's do this."

"Sure thing," he agrees as he does elevator eyes over me. I arch an eyebrow and purse my lips in disapproval. "Sorry, but you look fantastic, Sera."

"Thanks," I reply drily, ushering him into the restaurant irritably, "but save the hungry look for the food."

He chuckles but wisely doesn't respond as we get seated in a booth. Our waitress almost immediately brings water, and I don't let her leave until we've ordered. Which she doesn't seem to mind once she's had an eyeful of Bryce.

Once she's gone, I flash a mock surly look at Bryce. "Aren't you going to ask me if I found him?"

Bryce shakes his head. "Nope."

I scrunch up my face. "Why not?"

He smiles indulgently in response. "Because I know you did."

"And how exactly do you know that?"

He points his thumbs at himself and smiles. "Security consultant." Even in the face of my foul mood he still manages to stay droll. He laughs at my sour expression. "Honestly, Sera, it's not rocket science. Anything done electronically can be traced. Dinner reservations, for example. Or, more specifically, when someone *doesn't* use their credit card to pay for a meal for which they had dinner reservations. Implying that perhaps someone *else* paid for that meal. Not a strong enough indicator by itself, it's true, but when coupled with the same someone returning from San Francisco without checking out of their hotel room …" He gives me a pointed look. "Shall I go on?"

"Show-off," I reply drily. "God, Bryce, I feel a little violated."

I was joking, mostly, but his answering frown is quite serious.

"I'm sorry, I didn't mean to overstep," he responds carefully.

"It's okay," I assure him. "I know you were just trying to look out for me. Was the hotel room bugged too? Or do you want me to tell you what happened?"

He shudders. "Uh, no, I don't want to hear about that part," he says, obviously revolted.

"For crying out loud, Bryce, I'm not talking about sex," I say, exasperated. "I told you I went there to get an explanation for why he left."

"Oh. And?" he prompts.

"And I got it," I say simply.

"Well, that's good." Bryce's expression is stoic, and I can't tell if he really doesn't want to know what happened, or if something else is going on. And I realize suddenly that it might be a violation of Alessandro's trust to tell Bryce the full story anyway.

Bryce sighs resignedly. "So where does that leave things?"

"I don't know," I say honestly. "I understand why he had to leave now. I wasn't there to change his mind. So now that I know, I'm back."

"That's it?" he asks in disbelief, finally looking

honestly interested. "He's not coming back? You're not going to follow him anymore?"

"No and no," I reply succinctly, shifting uncomfortably.

"But it's not over," he guesses shrewdly. "Between you two."

I can see him holding his breath once he finishes his sentence-that's-really-a-question. Ah. I level a look at him as I realize we've hit the crux of Bryce's issue. He wanted to know, but he didn't want to know. We do so well as friends that sometimes I forget until that undercurrent of his feelings for me shows and I realize that they're still there.

"No," I admit. "It's not."

We sit in awkward silence for a moment. Long enough for the waitress to arrive with our food. Thankfully, Bryce changes the subject to work, launching into a story about the half-dozen things his dad has forgotten to tell him in the last week and how crazy it's made him having to run around taking care of missed meetings and messes. By the time we're done with lunch, the awkwardness has vanished and we're back to our usual comfortable banter.

As we leave he holds the door open for me, watching me closely as I exit into the hot July sun.

"I sure am glad you're back," he says, joining me on the sidewalk. "Hopefully, now you can put this all behind you and move on."

"I hope so too," I agree. "I'm excited to go to work for Sutton as well. It's going to be a whole new chapter."

"Look at you, on to the next thing again," Bryce says, smiling. "I'm parked this way," he jerks his thumb in the opposite direction I need to go, "but I'll see you soon?"

"You betcha," I respond. I step forward tentatively, and he opens his arms to me. Smiling brightly, I slide against him and give him a good squeeze. One that he returns in kind, and then some. I release him and step back, noting the sunshine smile plastered on his face once again. "Thanks for everything."

"Anytime," he assures me. And with a wink, he's off.

I text Allie to let her know I'm on my way in and set off to walk the few blocks to my office in hopes of soaking up as much sunshine as I can.

As I step in to the elevator and the doors close, something shifts inside me and panic rises in my throat. Having been kidnapped at gunpoint in this very elevator, I should have expected to react this way upon my return. Overwhelmed by the memory, I instinctually stop my train of thought in its tracks. *No. Deal with it.* I insist to my panicked brain. *It's over. You're fine. This is the same elevator you've taken to and from work every day for years.* I repeat the last part to myself over and over, and it works long enough to make it to my floor. But stepping out of the elevator I'm clammy and shaky. I take a moment to breathe deeply and steady myself.

Before I have a chance to recover fully, I hear shuffling and whispers. My panic almost takes back over until I hear someone whisper rather loudly, "Shhhh, she's coming!"

It's enough to snap me back to reality, and I take a moment to collect myself, since it sounds like I'm about to be on the business end of a "surprise" greeting. I try my best to suppress my amused smile and stroll nonchalantly in.

"Welcome back!" forty-plus voices cheer as I round the corner. A large banner with the same message hangs over the reception desk, and balloons and flowers adorn the desk. Allie and Maggie, my assistant, stand in the center of the crowd, beaming and applauding. I gather them both in a hug and allow the tears stinging the back of my eyes to leak out. Tears that are partly due to the warm welcome but also partly due to the lingering fear of riding in the elevator. But the former is a better excuse to be emotional and trembling.

"Thank you so much, everybody!" I cry. "I missed you guys so much." A hug-receiving line starts, and I happily embrace them all until there's nobody left.

"We missed you too," Maggie replies, lingering alongside Allie as people return to their desks.

"Apparently," I murmur, looking at the gorgeous flower arrangements appreciatively.

Allie hugs me tightly, and when she releases me I hold her at arm's length, noting that she looks softer around her midsection, fuller in the face, and extremely happy.

"You're a sight for sore eyes, Allie," I say fervently. She gives me an appraising once over in return.

"Love the dress," she remarks, "but you look like you've seen a ghost."

I press my lips together. Not much gets by Allie.

"I was just surprised," I lie.

"Mhm," she says, clearly unconvinced. "Well, in any case, you have a little more than an hour to get caught back up. Because we need the patented ass-kicking methods of Serafina Evans, Real Estate Badass, to get this thing done."

A smile splits across my face. "I'm totally putting that on my business cards," I reply.

She crosses her arms over her chest impatiently.

"Don't worry, Allie, I've already been studying up," I promise her. "But I'll get back to it, boss."

"Ugh. I'm not the boss anymore! And thank God for that," she replies, waving me away. "It was awful. Like I said, I don't know how you do it."

"What, you didn't enjoy ordering everyone around?" I joke as we head down the hall toward my office.

"It would've been more fun if they actually did what I

told them to do," she replies cynically, splitting off toward her own office. "See you in a bit."

I nod a goodbye and head into my office.

Everything looks pretty much the same. Warm sunshine emanates through the windows, making the room a few degrees warmer than the hall as well as illuminating everything with the bright glow of precious sunlight. But so much of the main area and my office reminds me of that awful night. I shake my head softly, lamenting that one bad memory can ruin all the rest.

While my laptop starts up I look around the room, briefly reflecting that at least we won't be here much longer, and I try to overwrite the horrible memories of that night with all the other good ones that have happened here. As my eyes fall on the bathroom door, behind which Alessandro and I fooled around not two months ago, even the good memories catch me off guard. And I make a note to push for the physical move to Sutton Developments as soon as possible.

THE MEETING GOES MUCH BETTER THAN I EXPECTED BASED on Allie's dramatic claims. The project management team, while a little reticent that they'll potentially expand their responsibilities into a side of the business we've not dealt with heavily, are still generally excited for the challenge.

Our brokerage is fine to move, as Sutton Developments doesn't have their own corresponding department, so it'll effectively just be more business, and thus more job security, for them. And Keith's objections to the paperwork, while completely accurate, are minor enough to be put to bed easily.

It's the property management side of things that's beginning to worry me. I had approached our lead property manager, Ana Englund, and discussed the responsibilities of running that branch completely. She seemed enthusiastic, and I have no doubt in her skills as a property manager. But her business management skills are looking to be a problem. And I'm not the only one who thinks so — our senior leasing agent, Nancy Sherwood, was apparently so unhappy with the decision that, while I was away, she quit. Fortunately, we still have four other leasing agents, which is plenty to cover the number of units we currently manage. But I'm going to have to keep a close eye on Ana and likely spend much more time mentoring her than I'd planned. And I don't think Charles Sutton will be pleased, as that was the branch of my company he was least enthusiastic to keep.

But I'll find out shortly, as our first conversation in nearly a week is only minutes away. My eyes flick again to the bathroom door, and my thoughts drift to Alessandro. It's only been two days since I saw him, but it feels like so much longer. And I can't help but wonder where he is right now. What he's doing. And if he's okay.

My intercom buzzes, and Maggie tells me Charles Sutton is on the phone.

"Sera," he greets me when I pick up the call. "I was so glad to hear you're back so soon."

"Thanks, Charles, it's good to be back," I reply. "I'm looking forward to wrapping up the paperwork and getting started on our merger."

"Indeed?" he replies, clearly surprised. "I thought Mr. Nystrom was having kittens over the contract rider."

I can't help but chuckle at the perfect description of Keith's anxious tendencies. "I assure you sir, that while I support his concerns, I think I have some wording that will work for everyone. Mr. Nystrom has already approved, and I'll pass it by our attorney first thing tomorrow."

"Excellent," he responds, pleased. "Since we will be wrapping up the paperwork soon then, we should start having daily meetings here to do some integration planning and defining roles."

"That sounds like a good next step," I agree. "Shall we begin on Monday?"

"Absolutely."

❧

Friday morning the paperwork is revised to the approval of all, with final signatures arranged for the following week. I find myself excited at the change, and I hope it's the right decision for my company. And for me.

I work a long day, diving deeply into the state of things with my teams in preparation for my discussions with Sutton the following week.

But I'm home in time to watch the sun set over Elliott Bay. Sinking deeply into my viewing chair with a large glass of wine, I watch the bright yellow fade into a mellow orange, and the mellow orange fade into a shining pink, which in turns becomes a hazy purple. As the purple begins to fade into the blue of night, and my wine glass has been emptied several times over, my phone rings.

My heart jumps, and I scramble to read the caller ID. But it's just my mom.

"Hi, Mom," I greet her.

"Serafina, darling," she trills, "I'm so sorry I didn't call you back sooner. It's been an interesting week."

Ah, the melodrama. How I didn't miss it.

"Everything okay?" I ask tentatively.

She sighs heavily. "I won't burden you with the details," she begins, and I'm already rolling my eyes because I hate when she gets like this, "but your father called."

I sit up abruptly. Now she has my attention.

"What?! When?" I demand.

"Earlier this week," she responds. "I knew you were busy, so I didn't want to bother you. And then I started thinking about whether I should even tell you, but obviously I decided to. Your grandmother told him we'd spoken. So, he called me. It was less than pleasant, but that's nothing you need to worry about."

"Then why are you telling me?" I wonder out loud.

She's silent for a short stretch. Then finally she replies, "Because he wants to talk to you. And maybe even see you."

My eyebrows practically hit my hairline. "*He* called *you* because he wants to see *me*?" I'm incredulous. After all these years, why now?

"If you don't want to, you don't have to." She sounds pleased that I seem less than eager to reconcile with him. "I'll send you a text message with his phone number. It's up to you."

"Did he say anything about why he's never tried to contact me all these years?" I ask quietly.

"He knew he'd have to go through me," my mother replies carefully. "And he didn't want to make things harder for anyone. I told him that was ridiculous. If he was a real man …"

"Mom, please," I interrupt her. "No drama. At least, no *extra* drama."

"Well, then, that's everything he said that's relevant," she says. "We didn't talk long anyway."

I take a deep breath. "Are you okay?" I ask her.

"Oh please," she responds. "I'm fine. I'm perfectly capable of handling myself."

"Of that I have no doubt," I admit, chuckling.

"Anyway," she deflects, "how did things go in San Francisco?"

I sigh deeply, trying to figure out the best way to answer her and end the line of questioning quickly.

"It went as well as can be expected," I say carefully. "I found him. We talked. I found out what's going on. We agreed that he needs some time to figure out some personal things. And then maybe we can be together. But for now, I'm back. Focusing on work."

"Well, that's good, sweetheart," she says. "As long as you're happy, that's all that matters to me."

"Thanks, Mom," I reply genuinely. Then I abruptly change the subject, and we spend the rest of our conversation catching up on less gut-wrenching topics.

Even after I bid her goodnight and hang up, I spend a long time staring at the night sky, thinking about everything.

Gabrielle Grayson aka Lucy Drummond aka my saboteur and would-be murderer. A shudder of pain and terror rolls through me. Alessandro Giordano. A shudder of bittersweet pleasure. Kent Evans. A shudder of too many emotions to name. Even remembering my father's name is odd and disconcerting, not having thought nor spoken it in years.

With everything that's happened lately, I can't say I've even fully processed the fact that my father did not, as I'd thought, choose to leave us when I was twelve years old. That he did not, as I'd also thought, with his parting words tell me that I was unlovable. Not that the truth is much better — that my mother, who'd found out he'd been cheating on her for years with another woman, whom he'd "married" and had a child with no less, had kicked him out in a rage. It was to her he directed his words — telling her that nobody could ever love her.

Any relief I felt after my mother clarified that those words were directed at her was replaced with disgust and indignation. Thinking those words were directed at me messed me up for a long time. But the truth is just as bad — and just as untrue. My mother, while a difficult woman to like, is not unlovable. She's proud, fierce, and a pain in the ass. But I love her. And I'm going to look that bastard in the eye and tell him exactly that.

FIVE

I wake on Saturday morning with startling mental clarity. Especially considering that, after I talked to my mother, I needed a considerable amount of wine to handle sifting through my mental baggage.

Unfortunately, my clarity has come with a giant side helping of anger, and I wonder if I shouldn't call Allie first to try to burn some of it off by talking it out with her. But I dismiss the idea, knowing it will almost certainly get me even more worked up. I opt, instead, to pound it out on the treadmill for a good forty-five minutes.

Afterward, I realize it was decidedly the better choice. While I'm not exactly calm, I'm in a much less hostile frame of mind. I shower and eat a quick breakfast before picking up my phone.

I take a few deep breaths and place the call.

"Hello?"

Hearing my father's voice, I freeze in panic. And I'm suddenly not sure I can do this.

"Hello?" he says again.

"Hi," I say slowly. "It's Sera." I resist adding, "You know, your daughter."

"Sera," he breathes out. "I'm so glad you called."

"You wanted to talk to me?" I ask tightly.

"Yes, I understand that your mother told you her side. Of what actually happened." He sounds as tense and awkward as I feel.

"And I suppose you want to tell me *your* side?" I respond peevishly.

"If you want to hear it," he replies quietly, "yes — I'd very much like to do exactly that."

"There are a lot of things I want," I admit. "But I'm not sure that any of it matters anymore."

"It matters to me," he asserts. "And if there's anything you need to say to me, I want to hear it."

I roll my eyes. I hate it when people say shit like that. Because ninety-nine percent of the time they're simply trying to satisfy their own need to feel like they are being the bigger person. And I know from hard-earned experience that they *don't* really want to hear it, and they definitely *don't* want to take responsibility for anything that comes from hearing it.

"Please, Sera. I'll come to you. I'll meet you wherever

you want. You can leave anytime. I just want a chance to explain. And to ask for your forgiveness. Beg for it, if I need to. Please."

My whole being screams at me to hang up. To not trust him. But my own words ring in my head, and I realize this is yet another of those crossroads — another time when I want to be able to look back and regret doing something rather than doing nothing, than walking away.

"Fine," I reply tersely. "Next Saturday. Noon. I'll text you the address."

"Thank you," he says, relieved. "I'll see you then, Sera."

"Goodbye, *Kent*," I reply. And then I hang up.

And I don't want to talk to my mother about it, but I feel I owe her a heads-up. So I text her. *Talked to him. He's meeting me for lunch next Saturday at noon. Stay tuned.*

My next move is to call Allie.

She answers quickly, perky as ever. "Hey, babe, what's up?"

"Hi," I reply in a deeply morose tone.

"Oh, dear lord," she responds. "Who died?"

I'm so perturbed that I'm long past witty banter. All I have left is bluntness. "I just talked to my father."

Whatever it was she expected to hear, it was clearly not that, as stunned silence follows.

After a few painful moments I continue. "And we're having lunch next Saturday. He wants to *explain*."

The sound — or lack thereof — of Allie's shocked silence is so entertaining that it almost knocks me out of my funk. Almost.

"I ..." Allie starts to stutter.

But I can hear David calling for her in the background. She must put a hand over the phone because I hear a muffled "Just a minute!" before she speaks to me again.

"Can you come over for dinner? I want to make sure I have enough time to do this conversation justice. And cake. There'll have to be cake."

I laugh drily. "Well, if there's going to be cake, how can I say no?"

"Good. Five o'clock okay?" she asks.

"Five o'clock? What, are we going for the early bird special at the nearby diner, grandma?" I tease her.

"There's my girl," she teases back. "But yeah, pretty much. Sorry, Sera, that's when the baby wants to eat. Gotta do what the baby says."

She's adopted a mock-serious mommy tone, and I can't help but laugh, truly and honestly this time. "Five o'clock it is, then."

"Sorry I can't talk more now," she apologizes.

"It's okay," I respond. "Oddly enough, I already feel better. But there still better be cake."

Allie laughs lightly. "Don't worry about that. Baby heard 'cake.' Now baby *needs* cake."

"I think I'm going to get along well with this kid," I joke. "See you guys then."

"Bye, Sera."

❧

AFTER A SATISFYING DINNER, WE SIT AROUND THE Kramers' dining room table indulging each in our own tiny lava cake.

As I savor a spoonful, I can't help but let out an appreciative moan. "This is *so* good, you guys," I say, and gesture with a spoon at the chocolate cream topping. "I especially like that you put chocolate on top of chocolate cake that has more chocolate in it."

Allie smiles sublimely. "What can I say? Baby loves chocolate." She gobbles down her last bite and looks contemplatively at the chocolate-smeared plate.

"Do it," I tease her. She gives David a mischievous grin and licks the dish greedily.

He suppresses a laugh and pretends to scowl at her. "In front of guests? Really?" he jokingly admonishes her.

"Sera doesn't count," Allie replies matter-of-factly, wiping a bit of chocolate from her chin.

"True story," I agree, finishing my cake. Since there's still some chocolate on it, I hand my dish to Allie and wiggle my eyebrows at her suggestively.

She laughs but instead of cleaning it herself, she takes it and stands up to bring it into the kitchen. "Thanks, but I don't want to give my poor, well-mannered husband an aneurysm," she replies.

I shrug and lean back in my chair. "Suit yourself," I respond. I release a sigh of contentment. "Thanks for dinner, guys. And for listening."

I hadn't ranted at length, especially since Allie was already up to date on the situation, but just enough to burn off some of the lingering annoyance at the situation. But I tore through those feelings and quickly got back to just not wanting to think about it any more than I have to.

"Anytime," Allie replies warmly, returning to her seat.

"What about all this merger stuff?" David inserts, changing the subject. "Does it feel weird to give up working for yourself? Having your own company?"

"*David*," Allie hisses as if he's asked something atrociously inappropriate.

"It's fine," I say to Allie. I consider my response, trying to boil down the many thoughts I've had on the topic. "I think there are parts I'll miss. But I'm not the best delegator, so having my own company was difficult. It's just more than I think is good for me to take on in the long run."

David looks at me quizzically. "Isn't your company like fifty people? What does everyone else do?" Allie grimaces at him and smacks him on the arm. "I didn't mean you, I know how hard you work."

"They do plenty," I agree, smiling pointedly at Allie. "But that doesn't mean I wasn't still all over everything, checking it, rechecking it, tweaking it. It wouldn't be so bad if things hadn't picked up so much. I just suck at turning down work. And I might have figured it out, but I realized there are other important things I want out of life. Things that take time."

Allie rubs her burgeoning belly, smiling fondly in agreement.

"What about this Sutton guy?" David persists. "Do you think you'll be okay working for him? And having your people report to him now?"

I smirk, starting to see where David is going with this. "If you're worried about how he'll treat Allie, about whether she'll still have a job if she wants it after the baby," I state, "don't. First, we're still working everything out. Second, I will *always* make sure Allie is taken care of."

Allie scrunches her face up at us. "You know, Allie is pretty good at taking care of herself," she grumbles.

"We know that," David assures her, wrapping his hand over hers. "And I guess I was asking that. But we care about you too, Sera. We want to make sure this is what you really want."

I try my best not to bristle at his use of *we* because I know he means well. *They* mean well.

"Thanks," I reply grudgingly. "I appreciate that." I take a deep breath. "I have a lot of respect for Charles Sutton, and there's a lot I can learn from him. But it will be different, and it'll be a big adjustment. Honestly though? I hadn't even thought too far into the details. It just felt right. It was a door that opened at exactly the time I needed it, and it's a fantastic opportunity. But I'm just as sure that if it doesn't pan out, I'll be fine. My employees will be fine. And everything else, I'll figure out."

"I have complete faith in you, Sera," Allie says softly.

I look up into her big, green eyes, full of love and loyalty. Blinking back tears, I rise from my chair and rush around the table to hug her.

"Thanks, Allie, that means the world to me."

And as we embrace, I say a silent prayer that I don't disappoint her.

I keep busy on Sunday with various odds and ends and a bit of work, but by the end of the day I'm heartsick and tired of my own negative thoughts creeping in on me. About everything. When my phone rings across the room as I'm cleaning up my dinner dishes, I hastily turn off the water and dry my hands, sprinting for it, hoping it's Alessandro.

My breath hitches in my throat when I see it's a number I don't know.

"Hello?" I answer anxiously.

"*Buona sera, mio tesoro.*" Hearing Alessandro's deep voice pulls on something deep inside me, and relieved, happy tears spring to my eyes as I sink into the couch gratefully.

"*Buona sera, amore mio,*" I respond, my voice thick with emotion.

"It's so good to hear your voice," he says huskily.

"You too," I agree. "I miss you."

"I miss you," he responds. "But I'm sure you have enough keeping you busy. How are things going?"

"Fine. The merger is moving forward," I say hastily, eager to move on to talking about what's going on with him. To know if he'll be coming back to me soon. "And it might be keeping me plenty busy, but I still think about you all the time. How are things going there?"

"There's progress," he admits warily. "I found her."

"That's good?" I reply, unsure.

"It was a start," he says. "But I didn't learn much before she left today. She took a flight. To Rome."

I pause, shocked, and suddenly understanding his lack of enthusiasm. "Rome?" I'm not even sure what to do with that. "Why would she go to Rome?"

"I don't know," he admits grimly. "I have my suspicions. I highly doubt she's taking a vacation but, in any case, I couldn't get on her flight. Which, frankly, isn't the worst thing. It's best if I make some additional arrangements before I go."

"You're going back to Italy," I whisper. "For real this time."

"Yes, for real this time. I'm sorry, I know it's not what you wanted to hear."

I contemplate that for a moment. I'm not sure exactly what I *did* want to hear. Short of, "Everything is fine now and I'm coming back to you this very moment." But I knew how unlikely that was to happen so soon.

"But if she's not in the country anymore, what is there to worry about now?" I ask.

"She's not acting alone, Serafina," he reminds me firmly. "There is everything to fear until I know what was behind her threats. *Who* else is behind them. And to do that, I must keep following her. This time the trail won't be cold at least. I have time to arrange to have her followed until I can get there."

I breathe out a deep sigh. "Okay," I concede. "I just can't believe it's only been four days since I've seen you. It feels like so much longer. And if you leave …"

"I know," he interrupts me. "I know. You don't think I wish more than anything that I was there with you right now? Holding you? Making love to you?"

His words send a sharp jolt straight through me. My heart races in my chest and my body aches with longing.

"I wish that too," I admit breathlessly.

"Do you?" he asks seductively. And I can tell he recognized the need in my voice. "What are you wearing, Serafina?"

A smile creeps across my face. "You first."

"I'm in bed, about to go to sleep since I have to get up early for my flight in the morning. I'm wearing what I always wear to sleep."

"So, nothing?" I bite my lip hard at the thought of his slim, well-muscled body. Of him, alone in bed, naked and wanting me.

"Nothing," he confirms roughly. "And if I were there with you, I'd be ripping off whatever it is you're clearly still wearing. But, as it is, I'm going to have to ask you to run your hands down your chest, over those gorgeous nipples of yours and touch yourself between your legs for me."

I hesitate for a moment, flushed with excitement but unsure, having never had phone sex before, if it's something I can manage.

"Please, Serafina. I'm getting hard just thinking about it."

Any reservations I'd had are dust in the wind at his erotic plea. I do as he asked, grazing an already-erect nipple over my T-shirt as I slide my hand under the waistband of my shorts, slipping a finger into the dampening flesh between my legs. As I hit *that* spot, the spot I know he wants me to touch, I let out a small gasp of pleasure.

"Good," he purrs. "Now tell me what you want."

"I want to hear you too," I reply, panting into the phone. "I want you to touch yourself."

"I already am," he admits. "Since the moment I heard your voice, it's been impossible to think of anything else." A moan passes his lips, and from its tenor I know exactly how he's working himself, as I've done so many times before. The visual of it causes me to work myself harder, and I moan too.

"I've never done this," I confess. "But Alessandro," I moan again, "I am *so* wet right now."

"Ohhh, Sera," he groans. "You drive me crazy. I wish I were inside you, fucking you harder and harder until …"

As he was speaking, I slipped two fingers into myself, and my gasping cry cuts him off. "I want you so bad right now," I breathe. I start pumping furiously, and from the low, wet slapping I hear accompanying his moans I know he's working himself just as hard.

"Yes," he encourages me. "Oh, God, yes."

I writhe with pleasure at the erogenous noises emanating from him. And, pretending it's him touching me, I sink another finger in, deepening my assault. I picture his gorgeous face, remember what he feels like on me, in me. And the tension builds inside me, my moans reaching a crescendo. Sensing my ascent, he calls out my name, and it pushes me over the edge.

I can feel myself tighten, the orgasm flooding through me, and I scream in release. Not a moment later I hear him cry out as well. Panting and only sated in a very basic sense, I slip my hand out from under my shorts and loose a sigh.

"That was interesting," I remark reflectively.

He lets out a low chuckle. "And only a shadow of what I want," he admits. "But it'll do for now." He pauses. "Are you all right?"

"I'm fine," I reply, slightly confused. "I mean, I agree, it wasn't as satisfying as getting to touch you. But it was stimulating."

"That's not what I meant, but I'm glad to hear it all the same," he replies. "I meant, how are you, really?"

Ah. He means deep down, how am I doing? Though I'm still not sure which specific issue he's referring to. Does he want to know if being back has forced me to deal with the issues from my ordeal? Or perhaps if I'm struggling with dissolving my company? Or simply with being away from him and worrying about the threats he's facing? In any case, the only option I have is to reassure him that all is well. Because he has enough to worry about.

"I'm *fine*," I reiterate. "But if you don't figure this out soon, I'm going to be forced to follow you to Rome, so I can fuck you properly."

"Hmmm, phone sex makes you feisty," he notes, clearly pleased.

"You make me feisty," I respond throatily.

He laughs a deep, melodic laugh. "I'll take that as a compliment," he replies. "I'll call again soon, okay?"

"Okay. I love you, Alessandro."

"I love you, Serafina."

SIX

On Monday afternoon, I'm on my way into Sutton Developments for our first planning meeting when my phone rings. The caller ID tells me its Bryce. I pause outside the entrance and answer.

"Hey, everything okay?" I ask abruptly.

"Hi, yeah, bad time?" he probes tentatively.

"I'm heading into a meeting. What's up?" I reply.

"It's not quick. Are you free for dinner tomorrow?" he asks grimly.

His tone worries me. "Sure, but I can do tonight too," I offer.

"It's not urgent," he responds, but continues to sound troubled nonetheless.

"What, do you have a hot date or something?" I joke wryly, half hoping it's true. For who's sake I'm not sure.

He snorts. "Yeah, with some surveillance reports. It's going to be *sexy*."

I laugh drily. "Okay, tomorrow then," I respond, bemused. "Bye, Bryce."

"Bye, Sera."

I hang up frowning. His voice was all rain clouds and gloom, no sunshine in sight. Glancing at the clock on my phone, I realize that I don't have time to wonder if has to do with me or not and enter the building.

∾

SUTTON'S ASSISTANT ANABELLE HAS SHOWN ME INTO OUR usual conference room, where I await his arrival. It's just me today, so he can break down his organizational structure and explain how he envisions folding in my employees. And myself.

I set out my folio and pen, and nervously tap the pen against the page. Finally, the door opens, and three men file in.

Charles Sutton enters first, cutting a daunting figure in a well-tailored black suit. With his dark, silvering hair and serious expression, he looks more like a well-dressed funeral director than the president and CEO of one of the most successful real estate development companies in the Seattle area.

I rise to greet him, extending my hand. As he takes it, a

small smile forms on his face, softening the harshness of his expression.

"Sera," he greets me warmly. "So good to see you." He presses my hand with both of his and turns to the men behind him.

Charles gestures to the first man, who is around my height. His shoulders are broad and his form substantial, but he nonetheless is a lean, vigorous looking man in his early forties with dark brown hair, kind dark eyes, and a wide nose and mouth.

"Serafina Evans, I'd like you to meet Suraj Singh," he says formally. "Suraj heads our research and acquisitions department."

Suraj dips his head politely as he shakes my hand. His grip is firm but not aggressively so.

"It's a pleasure to meet you, Ms. Evans," he says, smiling kindly. His voice, also, is soft and kind.

"The pleasure is all mine, Mr. Singh," I reply, dipping my head and smiling in return.

He releases my hand and steps around the table to take a seat as Charles gestures to the other gentleman, who is leaning in the doorway giving me an appraising look.

"And this is my son, Daniel," Charles continues. "He heads our development and build management department."

I extend my hand and take a step toward Daniel Sutton. He is the physical opposite of his father — barely taller than me, with dark blond hair and watery blue eyes. While clearly in his early-to-mid thirties, he has none of his father's aura of vitality and authority; rather, he has a considerably world-weary look about him. One that his sour expression isn't helping. He regards me for a moment longer before accepting my handshake. His grip nearly crushes my hand, but I don't flinch as I maintain eye contact and do my best to return in kind.

"Welcome," he says in a tone that implies anything but the word's meaning.

"Thank you," I reply sweetly. "I'm *so* glad to be here."

He finally breaks the handshake and I resist the urge to nurse my crushed digits. I watch Suraj's eyes follow Daniel until he's seated. Charles and I follow suit and take our seats.

"We will have much to cover this week," Charles starts. "What I'd like to do today is share my initial vision with you."

"I'm all ears," I reply.

Charles opens the file he brought with him and hands me a simple organization chart. I scan it briefly and flick my eyes back to his when I'm done.

"It's rather straightforward, really," he says. "Your business functions — human resources, finance, IT, contracts — fold directly into our existing structure," he indicates the leftmost column, "then you oversee our new real estate consulting services division, heading your twelve project managers," he gestures to a highlighted column on the right. "And your realty services and land use and zoning specialists will serve both your division and the land acquisitions function of Suraj's division." He points at two boxes at the bottom dotted-lined to both mentioned divisions.

Straightforward, yes. But, at the very least, it's missing a rather key piece.

"I presume," I begin slowly, "that I'll still be permitted to oversee the subsidiary property management company that will be formed from that division of my company?"

Charles steeples his fingers under his chin. "The idea was to see if it could survive on its own," he responds.

"Actually, the idea was, if I recall your wording correctly, to see if it could produce results. Without a business backbone, I don't see how that's possible," I say honestly.

"Dozens of property management companies function that way," Daniel pipes up.

I raise an eyebrow at him. His know-it-all tone rubs me the wrong way, and his statement makes it obvious that he knows next to nothing about the topic.

"And likewise, many of them fail for that exact reason," I say sharply. "It's why we weren't strictly a property management company."

"Then why did you agree to separate it?" Charles asks pointedly, though not unkindly.

"Because you said you weren't interested in running a property management company," I respond. "And you won't be. Ana Englund is perfectly capable of running the subsidiary company *from a property management perspective*. But she needs management oversight. Your proposal was to have it be a wholly owned subsidiary. Which means we have operational and strategic responsibility for it."

"A poor choice of words, then, perhaps," Charles insists. "But my intent was never to split your focus."

"It will take very little of my time," I assure him. "And it's a veritable cash cow when managed properly, which Ana *will* eventually be able to do on her own. Besides, based on your proposal, you only have me directly managing a quarter of my previous total staff. I didn't sign on to be that underutilized."

Suraj's eyebrows shoot up and a hint of a smile plays around his mouth. Daniel, unsurprisingly, looks like he's smelled something foul. But my focus is on Charles. Waiting for his reaction.

"Direct as ever, young lady," Charles replies. "My *proposal* was simply the tip of the iceberg and was merely an explanation of how I foresee the departments aligning. Yes, you will be solely responsible for overseeing and expanding the real estate consulting services department as we deem fit." He pauses and his eyes flick to his son. "However, you will also learn *every other aspect* of this business. I want you to be hands-on in each area from the get-go. And while I want you to learn, I also want your input. There is no substitute for fresh eyes. I'm going to be asking a lot of you right out of the gate. You'll have large adjustments to make transitioning your own people and learning the ropes, but I fully expect much more from you on identifying issues and helping to reshape this business."

Daniel opens his mouth in protest, but Charles puts a hand up, looking at me expectantly. Suraj looks on in polite interest. I work to keep my features calm, masking the excitement at his words.

Reshaping this business. While I knew he was interested in mentoring me while using my talents to his benefit, this was more than I could have hoped for. A small sliver of me thinks it's too much, but mostly I'm thrilled by the challenge. Especially given the shock and indignation on Daniel's face. And I don't know why I dislike him so much already, having not exchanged but ten words with him, but his reaction makes it all the sweeter.

I nod coolly. "In that case," I respond, looking each of them in the eye in turn. "We'd best get started."

We spend the afternoon reviewing the structure and operations of Sutton Developments and discussing strengths and opportunities. Suraj appears to be a kind, patient teacher, and his calm demeanor is a welcome counterbalance to Daniel's harsh and abrupt manner. But I quickly learn that both are extremely shrewd and intelligent, though in very different ways. And while my initial dislike of Daniel doesn't fade, I can tell he could be either a formidable enemy or an invaluable ally, depending on how things unfold. And despite my visceral animosity toward him, I decide to do everything in my power to purse the latter.

∽

TUESDAY FINDS ME SPLITTING MY TIME AGAIN BETWEEN ERS in the morning and Sutton Developments in the afternoon. This time I'm meeting with Sutton and his two office managers to discuss more practical matters as, with an initial understanding of Sutton's structure, I'm confident in pushing forward on integrating the companies sooner rather than later.

"How soon can we make this happen?" I begin, smiling pleasantly.

"You were right about her," Kelly Donaldson, the senior office manager, says drolly to Charles. Her round, grandmotherly appearance makes her seem inviting and warm, but she's as blunt as I am and, I suspect, all business — not someone to bullshit or trifle with. Charles gives her a small smile. She looks back to me. "We currently occupy the bottom two floors of the building. The top floor was storage that we rented out. We've arranged with the occupant to have the floor cleared by midweek."

"But," Tammy Lin, the other office manager, interjects, "it will really depend on what you're bringing with you."

I spread my hands in front of me. "We can bring it all, or I can arrange to leave any or all of it behind," I offer agreeably. "Whatever works best."

Tammy nods, her dark bob bouncing on her shoulders, and makes a note. "Good. Then we can move everything over the weekend and be ready for your team to join us on Monday."

"Just like that?" I ask, a little shocked at how easy it sounds.

"Pretty much," Kelly laughs. "We'll have to iron out the details this week, but I think it's doable."

"You ladies are miracle workers," I reply. "I'll put you in touch with my admin, Maggie, so we can get started."

I look at Charles and he raises his eyebrows and smirks at me.

"I'm sorry. Too fast?" I ask self-consciously. "It is, of course, up to you."

He waves me off mid-sentence. "Not at all," he replies. "I'm just a little surprised. We don't sign the contracts until tomorrow, yet here you are, ready to go."

I offer a small smile and a shrug. "No point in wasting time."

"As usual, we're on the same page," he agrees. And he gives me a *real* smile. A warm, genuine, fatherly smile.

And as much as I've been trying to play it cool, composed, and businesslike, I can't help but smile back in kind. And for the first time in a long time, I feel optimistic. It feels good.

∞

THE FEELING CARRIES ME THROUGH THE DAY, AND WHEN I go to meet Bryce for dinner at someplace a little more upscale than our usual, I'm still riding the high on the promise of good things to come.

But seeing Bryce enter the lobby looking like a train wreck abruptly brings me back to earth. He's still his usual towering, ruggedly handsome self, albeit in a slightly-more-wrinkled-than-usual navy button-up shirt and tan khakis. But his disheveled shock of thick, chestnut hair gives away that he's been running his hands through it constantly. And his face is more serious than I've ever seen it, with absolutely no trace of his usual upbeat manner. He looks somber and tired, and I'm immediately worried again.

"Hey," he greets me with a sigh.

"Hey," I reply unsteadily. "You okay?"

His mouth tightens in a thin line and his nostrils flare as he releases another huffed sigh through his nose. "Nope."

I lay my hand on his arm and look up warily into his

eyes. "We can skip this," I gesture to the restaurant. "Go someplace quieter. Or rain check. Whatever you want."

He gives me a small, joyless smile. "Thanks, Sera, but I'm starving," he replies. "Let's just eat."

"Okay," I reply skeptically. "But let's sit at the bar. You'll get food faster that way."

He nods and follows me into the bar. Since it's a Tuesday night, it's pretty empty and there are several options. Bryce heads for a small booth opposite the bar. I pull menus out of the caddy on the table and hand him one.

A waitress comes to take our order quickly. I order a chicken salad. Bryce orders steak and whiskey. As the waitress leaves I raise an eyebrow at him.

"Rough day, huh?" I tease him. Bryce runs his hands over his face and nods. "Dish, Hoyt. Get it off your chest."

He drops his hands and looks me squarely in the eye.

"Your boyfriend went back to Italy," he responds dully.

I pull a confused face. "I know," I reply slowly. "But that can't possibly be what you're upset about."

"You know?" he asks incredulously.

"He called me on Sunday night. To tell me he was going to Rome," I respond.

"Oh," he replies quietly, leaning back. "I thought for sure it'd spook you."

"Nope, not spooked," I assure him. But he doesn't

look reassured. "You're starting to freak me out over here. What's going on?"

The waitress drops our drinks on the table, and Bryce downs half his glass before he responds.

"My mom insisted that my dad get checked out by a doctor. She's noticed him forgetting things too," he finally says contemplatively, swirling the remaining contents of his glass. "They think it's stress, but they're running more tests. He's been told not to work until they can figure out what's causing his memory issues."

"Ah," I say softly. "You're worried about your dad."

He shrugs. "Of course," he agrees, "But he also left a huge fucking mess." I blink hard. I can't recall ever hearing Bryce curse. It's weird. "Whatever is going on with him, it's been going on for a long time. And shit is hitting the fan constantly now, and I'm having to clean it all up." He pauses, silently fuming. "I'm *angry*. Angry at him for covering this up for so long. For doing this to me. And my mom, and my sister." He shakes his head and drains the rest of his whiskey.

I stare blankly at Bryce, unsure of how to respond. Not because I don't want to reassure him, but because it's like I'm staring at a completely different person. The absence of joy on his face has changed his appearance enough. But I just don't know what to do with the foul mouth, hard drinking, and anger coming from him.

And for once, even after a prolonged, awkward

silence, he doesn't apologize for his outburst like he normally would. He simply goes to the bar to refill his whiskey.

Not that I think he needs to apologize, but it bothers me because the Bryce I know would feel like he needed to. Like he'd somehow inconvenienced or scared me with his vitriol. Finally, something slowly clunks into place in my brain as he sits back down, sipping his whiskey once more.

"You thought I was going to run after Alessandro," I realize. "That I'd leave. One more pile of shit hitting the fan."

He looks up at me grimly, and the answer is apparent in his appraising look.

"Bryce," I say sadly, catching his eye. "I wouldn't leave you at a time like this."

He sets his glass down firmly, the amber liquid sloshing dangerously close to the lip of the glass, and gives me a hard stare back.

"Wouldn't you?" he demands.

His tone is so accusatory that all I can do is look at him in shock as our food is delivered. Not that I'm hungry any longer. But he dives right into his steak, stabbing at it angrily.

"No, I wouldn't," I reiterate firmly.

He snorts. "Sure you would, Sera. If *he* asked you to,

you'd go running," he states, popping a bite of steak and mashed potatoes into his mouth.

And I feel like I've been slapped. My gut instinct is to protest, but I have to stop and ask myself if that's true. If Bryce needed me but Alessandro wanted me, would I abandon Bryce for Alessandro? *Yes, probably,* says a little voice in my head.

But, no. NO. After all that Bryce has done for me, I wouldn't. He saved my *life*, for fuck's sake. I have to think I wouldn't be so weak, so awful a friend as that. And it occurs to me, ultimately, that I'm *not* being asked to choose. I'm not making a wrong decision. Bryce is shit-stirring because he's angry. He's *trying* to pick a fight with me.

"Well, he's not asking, so do you want me here or not?" I snap. I realize as soon as the words are out of my mouth that it was the wrong thing to say to him while he's in this mood. Not that I'm sure there was a right thing to say. In any case, the harsh look in his eyes already tells me what he's going to do. He's going to keep pushing until I leave. My heart drops in my chest before he even speaks his next words.

"Do whatever you want," he says dismissively, finishing his second whiskey. "I don't care." He leaves the table briefly for another refill.

When he returns, I clench my jaw and prepare to take the high road. "I'm sorry you're upset, Bryce," I say, carefully controlling my anger, "but I'm not your enemy. And I don't appreciate being treated like one."

Bryce downs his whiskey in one go and slams the empty glass down hard enough on the table that I flinch. Even the bartender looks up in surprise. "You want to talk about treating people poorly, Sera?" he hisses. "Let's talk about it. I'm just a fucking joke to you. You know how I feel and you let me fawn all over you, so you can feel good about yourself when your boyfriend's not around. And occasionally you mix it up by using me so you can find him and get back to fucking him. Who is treating who like shit here?"

"You're drunk," I whisper, my face bloodless, tears pooling in my eyes. "And you're upset. I've never been anything but completely honest with you. And I've never, *never* treated you the way you're treating me right now."

He leans back in his seat, pushing his half-eaten food away. "You can't be honest with me, Sera. You can't even be honest with yourself."

"What the fuck does that mean?" I ask with deadly calm.

He laughs mirthlessly. "It means you ignore shit you don't want to deal with. Like the fact that you don't seem to give a flying rat's ass about what it does to me to be friend-zoned so I'm always second to an asshole that lies to you constantly. Or that you have feelings for me too, but you're too preoccupied with abandoning your dreams so you can be ready for whenever the asshole decides to waltz back into your life to notice. Or maybe, that you were just fucking held at gunpoint two-and-a-half weeks ago, but you like to pretend like it didn't happen. Like ignoring it will mean you don't have to deal with the fact that you're *terrified*."

A look of realization dawns on his face, causing him to pause his rant, but not for long. "Well, there's an epiphany! That's probably why you chase after that prick. Because he'll never really be there for you like I am. So you don't ever have to really be in a real relationship that requires real trust and intimacy. Because God knows *that's* terrified you for *years*."

When he's done, he crosses his arms over his chest smugly, staring me down as if daring me to respond. But I'm beyond words at this point, my jaw on the floor. Even the bartender is openly staring, a half-dried pint glass and rag frozen in his hands. I look from Bryce to the bartender and back.

And with the heat of the moment passed, the smile starts to slip off Bryce's face. And in this moment, he's no longer the charismatic, gorgeous man that unfortunately still couldn't distract me from the man I was already falling in love with. As if I'd had a choice. Because if I did, I have no doubt that I would have chosen Bryce. Until now.

I stand, shaking, and pull a twenty-dollar bill from my purse, placing it on the table.

"I don't know who you are," I manage to say, my voice husky and full of rage and tears. "But if my friend Bryce ever shows back up, tell him to give me a call."

And then I walk away without looking back. I don't get far before the tears begin to fall.

SEVEN

I only manage a few, fitful hours of sleep that night. I can't help but lie awake, weighing Bryce's words. Wondering how much merit there is in them, or if they were just the tired, drunken ramblings of a man going through something awful.

In either case, I still can't stop thinking about it. Have I really treated him so poorly? He's right, we've always walked that line between friends and more. But even when we dated, ever so briefly, while Alessandro and I were apart, I have to admit I've never thought I could feel for Bryce what he feels for me. Not because he isn't worthy, but because I was already in love with someone else when I met him, even if I didn't want to admit it to myself yet. But was continuing to be his friend anyway so awful? I'd always thought of it as his decision. Because while I do care for him, I've made sure he knows where he stands with me.

Yes, I decide, it was his choice to be my friend. To help me when I asked for it. Even if I needed more from him than I was able to give back. But I *was* already falling in love with Alessandro when I met Bryce. There just wasn't room for both in my torn and tattered heart. But as I learned to trust Alessandro, I think it healed me. And paved the way so I could start trusting others again too. I can't regret falling in love with Alessandro over Bryce, however problematic it has been. Because of it, I was able to be whatever I am with Bryce. But our once-easy friendship is now a complicated mess.

I also can't help but wonder, would it have been different if I'd met Bryce first? I shake the thought out of my head. There's no point in speculating. That's not how it happened. And no amount of wishing it were some other way will change what is.

Even after the awful things he said, though, I don't want to abandon Bryce to whatever he's going through. But I can't help but be terrified by that person in the bar. It really was like the man I knew was gone. Utterly and completely. I never even dreamed Bryce capable of saying those kinds of things to me. Possibly even of *thinking* those things. It's like his super-ego had an arm wrestling match with his id and lost horribly, allowing his id to run his mouth *and* his brain. But then, most men are often controlled by the primitive reactions and desires on the id's level. I just hope it doesn't keep running the show for long. Because I miss *my* Bryce already.

∽

AS I ANNOUNCE OUR MOVE DATE IN A TEAM MEETING ON Wednesday, I try to inject the enthusiasm I felt yesterday into my voice to cover the exhaustion and disappointment that replaced it after id-Bryce's appearance at dinner. Not that it matters much anyway, as most everyone is wrapped up in their own reactions. Allie, not surprisingly, corners me after the meeting.

After everyone has filed back to their desks, she closes the conference room door. She takes a seat next to me and leans forward on the table.

"What happened?" she asks tolerantly.

I shake my head sullenly. "God, am I that bad an actress?" I grumble. "Did I just totally freak everyone out?"

"Not at all," Allie reassures me. "None of them know you like I do." She pauses. "Is it Alessandro? Did something happen to him?"

"No, he's fine, as far as I know," I breathe. "It's Bryce."

Allie raises an eyebrow. "Did you two …?" She looks at me suggestively.

"No!" I protest vehemently. "We had a fight. At dinner last night. Or, rather, he said some awful things to me and I left."

"Bryce?" Allie asks in disbelief. "What did he say?"

Once I've rehashed the conversation and told her everything, her look of disbelief has devolved into abject shock and horror.

"Yeah," I affirm. "That's pretty much where I'm at. It took me most of the night to pick my jaw up off the floor."

"Wow, Sera," she finally says. "I'm so sorry."

I wave a hand in the air dismissively. "This, too, shall pass."

"You know none of that is true, right?" she asks, looking at me inquisitively. "It's his problem if he expects more. You've done nothing but tell him exactly how it is the whole time. I don't know where he gets off blaming you for his following you around like a puppy."

I bark a short, cynical laugh. "I don't blame myself, either," I agree. "But I still don't like having contributed to where he's at right now."

"I get that," she allows. And then, after a pause. "Do *you* think you only fell for Alessandro because you knew it couldn't go anywhere?"

I sigh heavily. "How could I possibly have known that?" I ask, irritated. Not at Allie, just at the continued emotional toll it's taking on me. "Sure, he had a reputation. But I didn't fall for him because he's gorgeous, or because he's fantastic in bed. I fell for *him*, for who he is. *Despite* everything else."

"I know," she replies confidently, and I look over at her in shock. She smirks. "I just wanted to make sure you knew that too." She rises from the table and gestures for me to follow her. "Come on, we have work to do."

I look at her questioningly. "What, exactly, are you referring to?" I ask suspiciously.

"We're going to plan a party," she replies. "A farewell party for the office. Because I think we can both agree that everyone around here," she looks pointedly at me, "could really use to let loose for a while."

I follow her, grimacing as I try to think of how I can explain to her that that's part of the reason I'm even doing this. Because as the boss, it's almost always completely unacceptable for me to let loose.

"Then you better be scheduling an after-party," I reply as we reach her office. "Because I'm not going full drunk-girl-dancing-on-a-bar in front of everyone here."

"Eh, we're a little too old for that anyway," she replies, smiling and rubbing her pregnant belly.

"If you say so," I reply. "Then what did you have in mind?"

She smiles mischievously and closes her office door behind us.

I ARRIVE EARLY ON FRIDAY MORNING TO HELP ALLIE enact her farewell party vision. As a catering company sets up a lavish breakfast spread in the conference room, Allie and I work together to assemble a photo booth, swag bags, and several "awards" selected from submissions the previous day. She won't show me what they're for until it's time to give them out, and my curiosity is piqued. But she shoos me off to "whip up a speech," as if that's how I operate. I give her a wide berth nonetheless, snagging a pastry from the conference room and retreating to my office for a few quiet minutes before everyone arrives.

As I enjoy my breakfast, I sit in my big, comfy chair and kick my heels up on the credenza under the window to stare one last time at the view of Seattle and the bay. Even at this early hour, I can see boats cruising the water and throngs of tourists swarming the streets. It's the first time I've felt comfortable in my office again, like the shadow of past events — good and bad — no longer holds sway on the cusp of our departure.

I remember, suddenly, that I'm supposed to meet my father for lunch tomorrow, and my mellow mood sours. I consider calling my mom for a moment before I realize she's at work. My circle of support has drastically dwindled between Alessandro being gone, Allie being preoccupied growing a human being, and id-Bryce's appearance. I'm mostly on my own to deal with everything. I polish off the bear claw I was eating and suck the sticky sugar off my fingers. At least the food is good. And, with a smirk, I step out of my office to join the festivities.

As I stroll through the office, I note that during my short break everyone has arrived, and the party is already in full swing — people are snacking, socializing, and snapping goofy pictures with the wide variety of photo booth props. I lurk around the small clusters of those saying their goodbyes to each other or discussing what the new company might be like. I engage little, mostly just absorbing the upbeat excitement floating in the air, happy that everyone seems to be mostly ready for this change.

Before I know it, Allie pulls me up on a makeshift podium in reception to say a few words. As I watch everyone gather, I can't help but get a little emotional at the finality of the moment. When everyone is present, I take a deep breath and gather my thoughts.

"Thanks for tearing yourself away from the pastries," I greet the crowd. A small ripple of laughter flows through the room. "I started Evans Realty Services more than four-and-a-half years ago in the hopes of finding the best and brightest to bring my vision of a full-service real estate company to life." And I can't help it, my voice is thick with emotion. I clear my throat a bit and steady myself. "Thanks to you all, I've surpassed even my wildest hopes and dreams for this company. And together we've done *amazing* things. So even though things are changing, it's because I know we're ready for the next big thing.

Through Sutton Development's established channels, we will get to work on bigger, more exciting projects than ever before. You'll *all* be exposed to new parts of the industry and get opportunities we wouldn't have had access to otherwise. This is truly going to be the opportunity of a lifetime — for all of us." I hold each of their gazes in turn as I speak. My eyes finally land on Allie next to me.

She steps up next to me lightly, as if sensing the wave of emotion that's about to overtake me. "And while we have exciting things on the horizon," she interjects, "We also wanted to take a few minutes to look behind us." She holds up a stack of certificates. "I reviewed your submissions yesterday and selected three in particular to receive awards." She hands the first one to me. "Sera, will you please do the honors?"

I look down at the certificate in my hands and bite back a laugh. "The first award goes to Melissa Thomas," I announce, grinning. "For the funniest property management moment — 'tenant submits application citing occupation as *sperm donor*.'" The crowd bursts into appreciative laughter as Melissa steps up and takes a bow, accepting her certificate, along with a larger swag bag that Allie hands to her.

Allie hands me a second certificate and, once again, I have to suppress my reaction. "The second award goes to Mark Hamilton," I announce. "For the most awkward leasing agent moment — 'having to show a unit to a friend's wife, who showed up hoping to rent the place with the boyfriend neither of us knew about.'" On cue, the whole team groans sympathetically. Mark bounds up with a grin to accept his goodies.

As I read the third certificate, I give Allie a look. "You're killing me here, Allie," I gripe.

She laughs and motions for me to read it out loud.

I sigh dramatically. "And finally, to our one and only head broker, Frank Ignacio," I continue. "For the *grossest* real estate agent moment — oh god, Allie, do I really have to read this?" Frank laughs in the back of the room. "'That time a very famous, wealthy client wouldn't be deterred from taking a shit in a nonworking toilet.'"

And everyone, including me, absolutely loses it as Frank accepts his award. Finally, when the noise subsides, Allie announces that she's pinned the rest of the submissions to the conference room wall. Everyone eagerly heads to peruse those that didn't land awards, and I manage to snag another bear claw before they've all been claimed by the crowd taking one last pass at the breakfast bar while they chuckle over the other crazy stories.

As the party dies down, Allie announces that everyone is welcome to stay and polish off the food, but that they're also free to leave early. Cheers erupt all around, and people start heading out, taking a smaller swag bag each. I hover in reception, assuring them each that I'll see them soon.

Once they're all gone, including Allie, I return to my office. Everyone else already packed yesterday, but I left it for today. I wanted to be alone, knowing I'd need room and time to come to terms with the end of an era.

～

Late that evening at home, I lean against the glass wall in the living room, the coolness against my forehead soothing the dull aching in my skull. Watching the cars below is surreal, their tiny lights snaking through the streets like glowing ants in a black maze. I nearly jump out of my skin when my phone rings in my pocket.

"Hello?" I answer nervously.

"*Ciao.*" I release my breath. Alessandro. He's okay. I hadn't had much time to worry this week, but he's never been far from my thoughts.

"I'm so glad it's you," I say. "How are you?"

"I don't know, Sera. It's strange, being here. Seeing her here."

"Have you learned anything?" I ask.

He sighs. "Where she's staying. What she does each day. But nothing of use yet," he admits. "There is someone else in the house with her, but I haven't laid eyes on them, much less figured out why she's here. I'm tempted to just go knock on the damn door and ask her."

"I doubt she'd tell you," I respond, "and from what you've implied, I don't think that's the best idea."

"I know, Sera, I wasn't being serious." He's frustrated.

I try to change tactics. "Why is it strange, being there?" I ask curiously.

"I left almost six years ago now," he replies thoughtfully. "And I didn't leave under the best of circumstances. I didn't think I'd ever come back."

"Why did you leave?" I ask, suddenly realizing that, oddly, we've never discussed it before.

"There wasn't one reason," he replies carefully. "The company I was working for was a dead end. I was one of the few who knew what they were doing. And I had a mentor. At first, he was amazing. But he quickly became very strange and limiting. There were family problems too …" he stops himself as if he didn't mean to say it. "It was just a mess. It was time for me to move on."

I'm suddenly suspicious that we'd never discussed it because clearly there are parts of the story he doesn't want me to know. "And you had to leave your country, your home, to do that?" I ask skeptically. The more I think about it, the more I realize something about his explanation is definitely lacking.

"It's complicated," he replies cryptically, sounded

exhausted even though I know it's morning where he is. "I'm sorry, I really can't go into it right now. Suffice it to say I burned a good number of bridges when I left. So, there are a several people that I can think of that she could be working with. But I can't find *any* connection she would have had to any of them, so I'm just going to have to keep at it. I'm tapping my contacts as minimally as possible. I don't want it widely known that I'm here. And that's not making it easy."

I mash my lips together tightly, unwilling to press him on the issue, but also unsure of how to help. And I certainly don't want to push him into action when I have no idea what he would even do or the cost of trying to force answers. I wish I was on better terms with Bryce right now or that Alessandro and Bryce were somehow closer. Because he's the only person I can think of that could help. The distance from both men I care for most stings sharply in my gut.

"I'm sorry," Alessandro murmurs. "I'm not in the best of moods. And I'm sure you want to go to bed."

I slump to the floor, pressing my head against the glass wall once again, staring up at the stars this time.

"All I want is you back, safe," I reply, feeling every inch of the distance between us. Physical and otherwise.

"Then I'd best get back to it."

A single tear slides down my cheek. "Okay. Thanks for calling," I murmur.

"*Ti amo*, Serafina."

"I love you too, Alessandro."

After he hangs up, I realize I still haven't told him about anything that's been going on with me. And that this time he didn't ask.

∽

I'M STILL NOT IN THE BEST OF MOODS AS I GET READY TO meet my father for lunch. As if he weren't already starting out at a disadvantage. I've chosen a rather nice bistro, mostly since it's on the north end of downtown, where I rarely venture for any reason because it's much more touristy.

I choose a simple, light blue shirtdress and flat, braided leather sandals, as the mid-July heat is in full effect. I quickly pull my hair into a messy bun, not bothering to apply any makeup. I'm not exactly trying to impress him.

On the drive, I stick within sight of the water as it's always had a calming effect on me. Something about imagining what lurks beneath its surface, in depths that can't be seen, puts everything in perspective. It reminds me that we are all just small fish in a very big pond.

I arrive early, so that I can be seated and ready to order when he appears. And when he does, I almost don't recognize him. I'm more surprised than I should be, considering I haven't seen him in more than fifteen years. And much as I misunderstood things I heard through my childish ears, my childish eyes remember a much different man. He's less than my memory of him. Not short, at around six feet, but he no longer inspires any of the fear or awe I had of him as a child. His thinning brown hair, once so close to the same shade as mine, is muted and dull with age. Even his still-sturdy frame seems less large and imposing, though the air about him remains austere and daunting. I'm not sure if time has simply worn him down, or if my memories of him made him more. Probably a bit of both.

I make no move of welcome once he spots me through the crowded restaurant and begins moving toward me. How he recognizes me, I'm not even sure as he hasn't seen me since I was an awkward, overweight, pimply teenager.

He stops politely beside the table. "Hello, Sera," he greets me seriously.

I nod in greeting. "Kent," I say, my tongue crisp on my teeth as I say his name. I gesture for him to sit and he does, slowly and carefully as one would around an animal that might claw their eyes out as soon as they make one wrong move.

"Thank you for meeting me," he says. "I half expected you not to come."

I try not to register the tinge of insult I take from his likely innocuous supposition as he picks up a menu, scanning it while keeping measure of my expression.

"I said I would," I reply, bristling slightly despite my

determination to remain impassive. "And *I* don't break *my* promises." It's a cheap shot, I know. But I just can't help it.

He folds his menu onto the table and sighs. "I guess I deserved that," he allows.

A waiter appears and takes our orders, whisking our menus away with him as he departs.

"Why don't you say what you came here to say," I suggest, folding my hands in my lap, "and we can decide what you deserve later."

A smile tugs at the corners of his mouth and he leans back in his chair, crossing his legs.

"Very well then," he agrees. "I'm sorry, Sera. I wish I'd been more involved in your life after I left. I never wanted to abandon you, and I let my issues with your mother get in the way of having a relationship with you. I've regretted that for years. But once you were an adult, I didn't know whether you'd even want to hear from me anymore."

"So you just didn't bother checking?" I ask bitingly.

"I was a coward," he admits. "And I didn't know what your mother had or had not told you."

"I see. You're sorry you didn't try harder to see me, but you're not sorry you had another family. Another child. One that, clearly, you did see."

He leans forward, putting his arms on the table so he

can wring his fingers together while he formulates his response.

"No," he finally says. "I'm not sorry I had another family. I *am* sorry for the pain it caused you and your mother. But I don't owe you an explanation for what happened between your mother and me. As your parent, however, I *do* owe you an apology for not being there for you. I wish I had a better excuse for it, but I don't. All I can do is try to show you how terribly sorry I am."

"Say I believed you," I humor him. "What then? What do you want from me?"

"I just want to know you," he replies, dropping his eyes to his hands. And his tone, his look, his countenance, are all consistently sincere. He flicks his eyes up to meet mine. "Can you forgive me?"

I sigh deeply. I've never been one to hold grudges. But forgiveness and trust are two very different things, not that I'm inclined to hand over either. With everything that's happened lately, I find myself running short on both. I'm quiet for a long while before I answer his question. He fidgets under the long silence but doesn't dare to break it.

"I don't know," I finally reply honestly. "Probably. But I don't have much bandwidth for, well, anything right now. I've got a lot going on." And while it's the truth, it's also a shield. I don't know if I *want* him to know me.

He shifts uncomfortably in his chair. "I understand," he replies. "I didn't mean to barge into your life and demand anything." He pauses thoughtfully for a moment. "Let's just have lunch."

Since we're already doing exactly that, I simply nod in response. An awkward silence ensues as we wait for our meals. But another benefit of having run my own company is that I'm fairly used to awkward business lunches, so using those skills we manage to make it through the meal fairly well. I offer little, and he spends most of the time telling me about what he does and asking about mundane things like our old house, how my mother is, and so on.

He mercifully doesn't try to tell me "his side of the story" or ask me anything terribly personal. And at the end, he even pays for lunch.

"I'm glad I got to see you," he says as we stroll through the door into the bright day.

I consider him thoughtfully for a moment. "You know what? Me too," I admit.

He beams at my response. I realize I do feel relieved, and even like there might be some part of me that needs to deal with this part of my past. Maybe, going slowly, I could do this.

"Would you …" he hesitates, clearly nervous. "Would you want to do it again sometime? You could even meet your brother. If you want."

I chew on my lip for a moment before responding. "I'll think about it."

"That's fair," he replies slowly. "But I'll be out of the

state on a business trip for most of August. How about we plan to do lunch again in two weeks, before I go? And if you decide you want me to, I'll bring him along."

Despite his attempt at nonchalance I can sense that, for whatever reason, it's important to him that his children meet. And, admittedly, I am curious. But I'm still not even sure I want to see my father again so soon, much less the brother I only recently learned exists.

"I'll think about it," I repeat, and I can't help but smile a little at my own stubbornness.

My father laughs. "Some things never change," he says, smiling. "I never could make you do anything you didn't want to do."

I offer a small shrug in response and he laughs again.

"I'll give you a call that week. Take care, Sera."

"Thanks for lunch," I respond. And with a small wave, we part.

As I walk back to my car, I call my mom, knowing she's likely been on edge and waiting for a report. I keep it brief, as I just don't have the mental energy for much more than summarizing everything that happened. She's quiet and doesn't offer much resistance to my ending the call quickly. Thankful, I start the short drive home, so I can collapse into my favorite chair with a bottle of wine.

EIGHT

The rest of the weekend and the following week pass in a blur. The former of sullen drinking, the latter of moving, reorganizing, and settling in to our new home at Sutton Developments, though I spend a good portion of the week going back and forth to the ERS offices, coaching Ana and helping her find a new office space more suited to the reduced team size. But overall, I'm happy with her progress up the learning curve, and I'm confident that I won't need to coddle her much longer.

At Sutton Developments, Charles has arranged for us to have everything we need to settle in, and almost every member of his staff welcomes us with open, helpful arms. Except Daniel, of course. But thankfully, aside from seeing him in the bevy of meetings I've started attending to get up to speed, he mostly just avoids me. Even with my own steep learning curve to tackle, I'm still able to focus on balancing the relocation and meeting our regular weekly commitments to our current clients. Charles has helped there too, mostly by agreeing not to add any new work to our plates until things calm down. It's no small blessing, as between those few main tasks I'm swamped.

I'm so fully occupied, in fact, that it's not until the end of the week that I realize I still haven't heard anything from Bryce. While I can't help worrying, I'm not exactly clamoring for another encounter with id-Bryce and decide it's still best to let him come to me.

And yet, on Saturday as I take care of all my usual errands, I almost call him. That one spectacularly awful dinner aside, I miss him. More than I want to think about.

As I finish dinner, with all my errands done I don't have much else to do besides sinking back into my favorite chair with more wine. As I cradle the empty glass in my lap, I realize who else I miss. *What* else I miss. Though it's only been two-and-a-half weeks since we parted, and little more than a week since I've heard Alessandro's voice, I want *more*. As I stare sullenly out the window, a deep longing washes over me. The physicality of the week hasn't helped. My muscles are tense, aching to be soothed.

I refill my wine glass and wander upstairs to the raised tub, filling it with piping hot water and bubbles. Stripping my clothes, I sink gratefully into the comforting heat. It calms the worst of the restlessness, and I sip my wine in hopes that it will help with everything else. Never having been one much for self-pleasure, I'm considering it briefly nonetheless when my phone rings.

Setting my wine glass down, I reach for the phone on the counter. My breath hitches in my throat seeing the international number.

"Hi," I answer, my voice low and breathy.

"*Ciao.*" His voice alone is enough to make me ache, but its low, rough tone is off somehow.

"How are you?" I ask delicately.

"I've had better days," he responds morosely. "How are you?"

"Missing you," I admit. "Naked. In the tub."

"Is that so?" He sounds wary but intrigued, so I push a little more.

"Yes, and as a matter of fact, I was just wishing you were here with me. I miss you in *so* many ways," I purr.

"I miss you too," he replies, but his tone is still odd — guarded. "You have no idea."

"I think I do," I say, remembering how he initiated our first telephonic encounter. "What are you wearing Alessandro?" I start skimming my free hand down my chest, the heat between my legs rising.

But he doesn't respond for long enough that I self-consciously stop as my hand comes to rest between my legs. Though even the light touch of my fingertips has me biting my lip, eager for his response, and a small sigh escapes my lips.

"Please," he finally begs, and for a moment I think he's ready to play. "Don't." His response is a bucket of ice water over my libido, and I shrink back into myself, mumbling an apology.

He lets out a low growl that surprises me.

"What's wrong?" I ask meekly.

"I'm sorry, Serafina. I'm just too distracted. There's too much at stake," he says, his frustration clear in the hardness of his voice. "I don't have anything concrete to tell you. Just suspicions."

"Of what?" I press.

"I can't, not yet," he replies.

And now my own frustration is no longer just physical. "How are we right back to this place?" I ask testily. His unresponsiveness is so like when he left me that I can't help but be reactive.

"Because we're right back to it not being safe," he responds just as testily.

"Then why did you call?" I snap.

"Because I said I would," he sighs. "And because I wanted to hear your voice."

"Well, you've heard it," I retort.

"Yes," he agrees. "I'll go now. I'm sorry, Serafina."

"Goodbye, Alessandro." And I hang up before I can say what I'm really thinking.

❧

THE WORKWEEK BEGINS ONCE MORE, AND I'M HAPPY FOR the distraction. I barely slept after I spoke to Alessandro, and I was in a foul mood all Sunday. I do my best to lose myself in re-establishing a rhythm and try not to take out my continued personal frustrations on my team, or on anyone else at Sutton Developments, for that matter.

When Allie calls me into her new office on Tuesday afternoon, I'm bracing myself for a lecture, assuming the unpleasantness stewing beneath the surface unknowingly spilled over when I wasn't paying attention and somehow triggered her finely tuned Sera-needs-a-talking-to radar.

But when I arrive, I find her and one of my project managers, Heather Irving, sitting quietly in wait. Sensing the tension, I close the door behind me.

"Hey guys, what's up?" Allie looks up at me from under a furrowed brow. Heather shifts nervously in her chair. As I sit down in the chair next to Heather, I note her anxiously fidgeting with her long, black braids, her full, dark lips set in a firm frown.

When it's clear that Heather isn't going to speak, Allie does. "Ms. Irving is submitting her resignation," Allie explains from her seat behind her desk. "I asked that she tell you personally."

I raise an eyebrow and turn to Heather, a slight, dark-skinned girl in her mid-twenties, though she has the air of someone much younger. She's always been on the quiet side but is sharp and has already been a valued contributor to our team in the six months or so that she's worked for me.

"I'm so sorry to hear that," I tell her honestly. "Is there anything we can do to change your mind?" She shakes her head so violently that I'm a bit taken aback.

"I mean, no, thank you," she amends in her quiet, girlish voice. "I just want to pursue other opportunities."

I glance at Allie and she shrugs imperceptibly.

"If you've been offered another position, I'm happy to see what we can do to match the pay or job description," I offer, feeling her out.

"It's not that," she replies reluctantly.

I consider her for a moment. She looks, quite frankly, rather terrified.

"Heather, did something happen that we should know about?" I ask gently.

The slight widening of her eyes tells me that my instincts are right. Something happened here. But she doesn't want to say what.

"If so, I'd like to know. Anything that is enough to drive away a valuable employee is something I need to know about. And if it's something to do with our new situation, it's especially important that I have that information. Because we still have time to call this off if there's a serious issue."

"No," she offers quickly. She clears her throat. "Nothing happened that you need to be concerned with. I just think it's time for me to move on."

I don't need to look at Allie to silently agree that we've just been lied to — the mistruth hangs thick in the air. Even Heather looks ashamed of it. But I know pressing her won't help, either.

"Okay," I respond. "But please, if you decide there's anything we should know, please don't hesitate to call Allie or myself."

Heather swallows hard and nods. "Thank you, Ms. Evans."

I rise and round the desk, grabbing a pen and sticky note from the corner of Allie's desk. I scribble a note to her. *Standard severance. Let's talk when you're done.* I slide the note to Allie and she looks at me questioningly, and I know it's because we've never given severance to an employee who quit. I give her a hard look in return that clearly says, *Just do it.* With a last, concerned look at Heather, I say goodbye and return to my office to wait for Allie.

∽

Not twenty minutes later, Allie steps into my office and closes the door behind her. She shifts a box out of her way and drags a chair in front of my desk, plopping down tiredly.

"I hate this part of the job," she says.

"You didn't fire her," I point out. "She quit."

"I know," Allie muses, "but it's still awkward as ass."

I shrug. "Comes with the territory. Did she give you any other hints as to what might have driven her to quit so suddenly? Obviously, it has to do with all this." I gesture to the office and boxes around me.

Allie rubs her belly thoughtfully. "No, not really. She just seemed *scared*," she admits.

I press my lips together grimly. "I had no idea," I admit. "I've been so busy this past week. Everyone seemed to be doing rather well, I thought."

"I thought so too," Allie agrees. "And I've been keeping my eyes and ears wide open."

"Well, keep it up," I encourage her.

We're interrupted by a knock on the door, followed by Maggie's head popping in. "Mr. Sutton wants a quick word on a potential new client for our team," she says.

My eyebrows jump in surprise. "Tell him I'll be right there," I instruct her.

Allie gives me a look. "And so, it begins," she murmurs.

∾

With Charles Sutton's grace period seemingly over, several new requests for proposals hit the team at once, and we untiringly dive into the new work. So far, it's nothing out of our wheelhouse, but it keeps me at work late on Tuesday and Wednesday. When I drag myself home on Wednesday night, I'm not pleased to hear my phone ring just as I'm about to pass out on the bed.

I glance at the phone and note that it's just past nine p.m. And it's my father calling. Begrudgingly, I answer.

"Sera, I'm not calling you too late, am I?"

"It's fine, I'm still up," I reply, trying to sound perkier than I feel. "I assume you're calling to confirm for Saturday?"

"Yes," he responds. "And to see if you wanted me to bring Hunter."

Hunter? I guess I hadn't heard my half-brother's name before. Interesting.

"Sure, yeah, that's fine," I hear myself say through a tired fog.

"Oh! Okay, well, then I guess we'll see you Saturday at noon. Same place?"

"Sounds good." I'm barely awake.

"Good night, Sera."

"Good night, Kent." I end the call and turn off the light, surrendering to exhaustion.

∽

It's not until the next morning, as I drink my first cup of coffee at my desk, that I realize what I'd agreed to. I shake my head at my own stupidity for answering the phone when I should've ignored it and gone to sleep. Oh, well. That ship has sailed, and I had to meet him sometime. Maybe his presence will even make things slightly less awkward.

I shake my head, trying to refocus on the notepad in front of me. I have a meeting with Charles, Suraj, and Daniel to prepare for. They want to hear my first impressions and concerns, so I settle in to organize my meeting notes.

∽

That afternoon I enter the conference room to find everyone already seated and in the middle of a discussion. They all look up as I enter, and I can feel the heat on my cheeks. Charles is at the head of the table, as usual, with Daniel on his right and Suraj on his left.

"Am I late?" I ask tentatively, taking a seat next to Suraj. Suraj smiles at me warmly and shakes his head.

"Not at all," Charles assures me. "We were in a meeting before this that ended early. We've just been discussing our performance metrics as we approach the end of the month."

"Don't stop on my account," I reply, quietly opening my notes and pretending to absorb myself in reviewing them. But I'm laser-focused on their discussion as they continue to debate the cause of disappointing operational indicators.

"There's no one root cause," Daniel insists. "Each project's numbers are solid. We're just not growing our revenue streams quickly enough."

"I agree," Suraj says. "We're running more or less to estimates, except on a couple larger add-ons. It's just the market. Things aren't as hot as they have been the past couple of years."

I snort involuntarily, then freeze. I slowly look up to see all three men staring at me.

"You disagree?" Daniel asks archly.

I close my notepad. "No," I reply carefully. "I agree that the market is stagnating. But you're also picking your projects poorly."

Daniel bristles visibly. As head of development, he's typically the one to identify potential projects, so I'm not surprised that he takes it as a direct insult.

"Elaborate," Charles requests succinctly, steepling his fingers under his nose.

I take a deep breath and press my lips together. "Okay," I agree. "I've reviewed your performance metrics.

They're an amalgamation of the metrics of each individual project with aggressive short-term goals for each. And most of your projects fall under one of three categories — large luxury townhouse and condo developments, large luxury retail development with luxury condos built over them, or standard to luxury retail spaces."

"And your point?" Daniel asks in a curt tone.

I eye him evenly. "My point is you're too niche," I reply. "Too entrenched in high-end spaces, large builds. It takes too long to sell out those kinds of spaces, so you don't see great results in your shorter-term metrics. You need to diversify into other areas that sell faster to balance out your revenue. Hot areas. Ecologically sustainable builds. Efficiency housing. That sort of thing."

"We've looked into ecologically sustainable builds," Daniel says, waving a hand dismissively. "Sourcing the materials is too difficult and costly."

"Then you haven't accurately balanced against market prices, reduced maintenance costs, and long-term ROI," I insist. "Not to mention economies of scale. Have you done a full analysis based on a specific project proposal? Or series of projects? There is always a sweet spot. It's a whole untapped market."

Charles turns to Daniel, waiting for his response. Daniel shifts uncomfortably in his chair and fights to keep a scowl off his face.

"Not exactly," he begrudgingly admits. "My suppliers said …"

"Only what is in their own interest," I interject. "Surely you know better than to take their word as law?"

"I'm not accustomed to being interrupted," Daniel retorts sharply.

"She has a point," Suraj says softly. "Perhaps it's time to revisit the issue more fully."

"Be my guest," Daniel replies, rising from the table. "I'm afraid I need to get back to work. I wouldn't want to leave things alone too long. My suppliers might start walking all over me, after all."

We all stare at him as he goes.

"Don't worry about him," Charles assures me gruffly after the door has closed behind Daniel. "He's not used to being put in his place, especially by a woman."

I raise an eyebrow. While I can absolutely see Daniel being a sexist pig, Charles didn't so much strike me as the type. But perhaps the two are more alike than I thought? Regardless, Charles' words concern me.

"What Charles means to say," Suraj offers, "is that we are very glad to have a fresh voice. Especially one that isn't easily intimidated into silence."

I turn my head slowly toward Suraj and consider him carefully for a moment. I initially took his calm manner and genial smile as comforting traits. But I do wonder what he *really* thinks. If he's simply projecting what he wants me to see, but underneath is just as bad as Daniel. I mean, why would he put up with it otherwise?

I shake myself a little, mildly ashamed of the unfounded negativity. Suraj has been nothing but kind to me. And only time will tell what I've really gotten myself into.

"I'm glad to hear it," I finally reply. "Shall we discuss efficiency housing then?"

Charles and Suraj exchange a look and both men uncharacteristically burst out laughing. I press my lips together to suppress my embarrassed smile, but I'm also secretly pleased that they seem delighted by someone standing up to Daniel. It means, at least, that they're not fond of his antics, either, and I try to take heart from that.

"Yes," Charles says after he calms down. "Let's."

NINE

I start the weekend with extremely mixed feelings. I'm thankful to get a break from the dagger-stare and silent treatment Daniel bestowed upon me for the rest of the week, but the impending lunch with my father and half-brother isn't exactly a thrilling prospect, either.

I know next to nothing about Hunter. My father was extremely careful to avoid talking about him at our first lunch, for which I was grateful at the time. But now I'm not sure what I'll say to him.

I stick to my usual coping tactic — distraction — by spending the morning thoroughly cleaning the condo. Just as I'm about to hop in the shower, my father calls.

"Sera, I'm so sorry to do this, but we're not going to make it," he greets me.

"Um, sure, okay," I reply, confused. "Thanks for letting me know. Is everything all right?"

He lets out a foreboding sigh. "I'm afraid I was overly optimistic about Hunter's feelings toward meeting you."

My eyebrows shoot toward my hairline. "And you waited until now to tell me that?" I ask incredulously.

"I made the mistake of not checking with him first," he replies carefully.

And in the background I hear someone grumble, "It's called an ambush, Dad."

I mash my lips together in a hard line, suppressing annoyance and anger. Annoyance at being cancelled on at the last minute, and anger because, well, who the hell is *he* to not want to meet *me*? I mean, seriously, how was he the wronged party in this whole mess?

"I see," I finally reply tightly. "Some other time, perhaps."

"Yes," he agrees. "Take care, Sera. I hope to talk to you soon."

"Have a good business trip," I respond. "Bye."

"Goodbye, Sera."

I chuck my phone onto my bed and storm angrily into the shower.

As the hot water courses over me, yet fails to soothe the tension in my limbs, I wonder why I'm so bothered. I wasn't exactly looking forward to lunch anyway, so shouldn't I be happy that it was called off? Except I realize it feels like yet another thing going wrong in my life. Another rejection. And I just wish everything didn't have to be such an uphill battle.

∾

But on Sunday afternoon, I get a call that wipes my petty complaints off the map. The moment I see David's name flash on my phone, as if a sixth sense kicks in, I know something is horribly wrong.

"David," I answer, tense. "What's up?"

"Sera," his voice is thick and hoarse. "It's Allie. She's lost the baby."

I feel like someone has punched a dagger through my chest as pain radiates through me. Tears stream from my eyes, and I want to beg him to tell me it's not true. But as I struggle to master myself and respond, I realize if I feel this way, I can't even imagine how David is feeling. How *Allie* is feeling.

"Where are you?" I finally manage to ask.

"Harborview Medical emergency room," he replies throatily. "But, Sera ..."

"I'll be there as soon as I can," I interrupt him, choking back a strangled sob.

"Sera, she doesn't want to see anyone," he continues. "She's out of her mind."

A fresh wave of tears spills across my cheeks, and my

heart breaks open for my best friend, for the agony she must be going through.

"I'm coming anyway," I insist.

He sniffs loudly. "I knew you'd say that. But don't say I didn't warn you."

"Can I bring you anything? Do you need anything from home? Or food?" I ask.

"No," he replies. "Maybe later. I can't even think about anything else right now."

I stop myself from saying, "I understand," because I know I really can't, but instead settle for, "I'll see you soon."

As I enter the emergency room, I do my best to compose myself. My own devastation can wait. It's time to be here for Allie and David. I text David a short message — *I'm in the waiting room.*

A few minutes later, he emerges through the double doors behind the check-in station. His wavy dark blond hair is all over the place, and his usually clear blue eyes are stormy and rimmed with red. He embraces me somberly, and I wrap my arms around his shaking torso. He lets out one, sharp sob and gives me a squeeze before releasing me.

"I'm glad you're here," he says. "They want to take

her in for a D&C, but she's refusing. They've given her a few minutes to calm down, but they need to do it. She's bleeding too badly."

The hurt in my heart spears through my body once more. "Can I try talking to her?"

He looks at me warily for a moment. "Since I can't seem to calm her down enough to convince her, it's worth a shot," he finally agrees. "She won't be happy that I called you. But at this point I'll try anything. I'd rather avoid them having to sedate her while she's like this."

I nod, understanding. If Allie didn't want something to happen, she'd fight it with every fiber of her being.

I don't ask if he's called Allie's mother. I know she's in Nebraska, so it wouldn't do much good in any case. And outside of family, I've known Allie the longest anyway. I put on my brave face and let him lead me to her room. I can hear the hysterical sobs before he even opens the door.

"Al?" he asks tentatively, poking his head around the door.

"Go away," I hear her shaking voice respond from inside before it devolves back into the heartrending bawling I'd heard as we approached.

"Let me try," I whisper to him.

He shrugs and steps back from the door, sinking despondently into a chair on the wall opposite her room. I enter quietly and close the door behind me. In the dim light I see Allie's shaking form under a thin hospital blanket, her back to the door.

I lick my dry lips and approach the bed, clearing my throat to announce myself. Allie's head swings wildly toward me.

The utter desolation etched into her fine features almost cracks my careful mask, but my presence surprises her enough that her cries subside to low, tortured gasps as I round the wide bed and settle on the edge facing her, one leg propped up on the side so I'm sitting next to her. She stares at me, eyes wild, as if barely recognizing me.

Without a word, I open my arms to her. She shifts her head onto my lap and clings to my leg, sobbing. I silently lean in to her, resting my head on hers and wrapping my arms around her back. And I let her cry as my tears slip silently into her hair.

After a time, I hear her sobs subside and her breathing even out, and I know she's fallen asleep, overtaken by the exhaustion of her despair. I continue to hold her until sometime later, when David quietly enters, a nurse at his back.

The nurse steps around him. "They're ready for her in surgery," she says apologetically.

"Give us just one more minute, please," I ask quietly. The nurse nods and steps outside, where I can see her hovering in the hallway.

I look down at Allie and sigh, stroking her hair back

from her face. "Allie?" I prod gently, rubbing her back. Her eyes open slowly, and she sniffs loudly. "Allie, the doctors need to take care of you. Please," I plead, "please let them."

She starts sobbing quietly, but after a moment she nods. I nod in turn to David, who steps out to fetch the nurse. And, with David and I on either side of her, holding her hands, she finally allows them to prepare her. We promise to be there when she wakes, and they sedate her. Mercifully, she quickly dissolves back into the oblivion of unconsciousness, and David and I numbly shuffle to the waiting room.

As we settle tensely into seats facing the doors, David takes my hand. A single tear rolls down his cheek as he squeezes it tightly. "Thank you," he whispers.

I nod, unable to form words through my sorrow, and squeeze back. And we wait quietly, our hands clinging to each other for the small sliver of comfort it lends.

Not more than fifteen minutes later, the surgeon steps into the waiting room. David releases my hand and rises to meet him.

"Mr. Kramer?" he asks, and David nods. "Your wife's procedure went just fine. Given her level of distress, we've decided it's best to keep her sedated so that she can rest and recover overnight. You'll be able to take her home tomorrow, but she should still take it easy for another day or two after."

"Thank you, doctor," he responds.

And with a curt nod and sympathetic look, the surgeon returns through the doors. David slumps back into the chair next to me.

"Tell me how I can help," I say to him. "I can stay here if you need to go home. Or I can bring you anything you need. Or I can just stay with you and keep you company. Whatever you need."

David gives me a thin, forced smile. "Thanks, Sera, but Allie won't be awake until tomorrow, and I think I just need some time to process all of this. I can get some food in the cafeteria, and I'll sleep on the bench in her room. You can go home."

I fight the urge to insist on helping, and simply nod. "Okay," I breathe. "But call me if you change your mind. I'll take care of things at work. Just let me know if she needs me. I'll call after work tomorrow."

He gives my hand one last squeeze, and I know it's a dismissal. I take the cue and rise, but I have to force my feet to move. Leaving feels wrong, but I know there's nothing that's going to feel right.

TEN

onday dawns after a sleepless night, and I relay Allie's excuses to her new department head. I resolve to go see her after work rather than simply calling, but the visit is more troubling than reassuring. Allie barely speaks and, while she thanks me for being there for her, asks me to give her some space while she deals with things. I return home that evening, disturbed and more than a little concerned for my friend.

It's not until I'm heading to bed that I realize I hadn't heard from Alessandro over the weekend, per his usual routine. I'd be concerned, but after our last conversation, I imagine he's going to avoid calling again until he has something he can share to avoid another fight about his withholding things from me. And I still haven't heard from Bryce. Trying not to feel friendless and alone, I surrender to my exhaustion.

∽

THE REST OF THE WEEK BRINGS FURTHER STRUGGLES AS I start to notice Daniel undermining me subtly. It starts in little ways — a thinly disguised put down in a staff meeting. Interrupting me on a phone call with Charles and a potential new client, which I wouldn't have even noticed had he not made such a big deal the week before about how rude it is to interrupt someone.

It doesn't take long before he starts accelerating his campaign of interference and nasty comments, and by Friday I'm pretty fed up. When I learn he's bumped my team meeting out of our conference room, citing a pressing meeting with a client, I'm more than a little irked. Still, I suppress the urge to confront him, knowing it will do no good. But the immaturity of it all grates on me. And as I head home, driving much more angrily than usual, I'm once again faced with the feeling that everything is just so much harder than it should be right now.

I eat a light dinner at home but have little appetite. For food, anyway. Wine, however, I've definitely been drinking more than my fair share of these days. I can't help but wonder if everything that has happened is a sign. That I'm pursuing all the wrong things: Alessandro, this merger, a relationship with my father. Maybe those are all the wrong choices for me. I feel like I'm losing everyone I care for and making enemies of everyone else.

I sigh, finishing yet another glass of wine, and admit to myself that I'm probably being a tad overdramatic. I'm not a great mental processor. I'm used to working things out verbally, preferably with someone who knows me well. But the only person that's an option with at the moment is my mother and, while our relationship is vastly better than it once was, we're not yet quite to the heavy, soul-deep stuff that I currently find myself mired in.

As darkness falls over the city, I slow my drinking and stare out the window wall at the few visible stars in the sky, feeling small and alone in the universe. I palm my phone, pulling up my address book, contemplating. My mental math tells me it has been more than three weeks since I saw Bryce.

Fuck it. I place the call. And immediately panic. I end the call as quickly as I can, hoping it didn't have time to ring through. I'd resolved not to call him. To let him call me, just as I'd spat at him as I walked out that night. I'm just tipsy, and weak, and shaken up from everything. I take a deep breath and push myself out of the chair, determined to put my slightly drunk self to bed immediately when my phone rings. It's Bryce, calling me back.

"Bryce," I answer, careful not to let the alcohol affect my voice. "Hi. I'm sorry, but I called you by mistake."

"Did you?" His voice has a sharp, alluring edge to it. I don't respond. "Well, either way, I think it's about time we talked."

"Is it?" I ask, attempting nonchalance.

"Or I can talk, you listen," he allows. "But it's more fun if you talk too." His deep voice is notably missing its former sunshine and ease, but the edgy playfulness that has replaced it is bewitching.

"I'm not sure I have anything to say," I counter. "But then, I guess that all depends on what you want to talk about."

He chuckles, and even his laugh is different. It's hollow. "I've been meaning to call you," he says. "But I wasn't sure you'd answer after what happened."

"Mmmm," I reply noncommittally.

"Exactly," he responds. Then I hear him take a deep breath. "I want to apologize. I shouldn't have said those things to you."

I cock an eyebrow, reading between the lines. "But you meant them," I assert.

"Yes, I meant them," he agrees. "But that doesn't excuse the way I behaved."

"No, it doesn't," I concur.

"I'm sorry, Sera. Can you forgive me?" He sounds sincere, and just hearing his voice reminds me how very much I miss him.

"Yes," I admit readily. "I accept your apology."

"Seriously? That's it?" he asks incredulously.

I laugh. "Yes, that's it," I confirm. "You're lucky I happen to be badly in need of a friend right now."

"Excuse me?" he responds indignantly. "Are you serious right now?"

I bite my lip, realizing that I implied I only forgave him because I was desperate for someone to listen to me whine.

"I'm sorry," I say hurriedly. "Fuck. It's been a shit few weeks, Bryce. And I've missed you. That's all."

"Sera," he says tensely, "I don't want to be an asshole again, but I need you to realize I'm not a consolation prize. I'm not the guy you're going to turn to anymore when you can't be with whoever else it is you'd rather be with at the moment."

"That's completely fair. But for what it's worth, you've never been a consolation prize to me. But I understand if you feel that way," I admit, chagrined. "Does this mean we can't be friends?"

He sighs impatiently. "I don't know," he replies. "I'd like to be your friend, but I'm not sure I can."

"Wow," I respond softly. "Okay, well, thanks for the apology anyway. Take care, I guess?"

"This isn't happening the way I wanted it to," he groans, clearly frustrated. "I mean I'm not sure I can *just* be your friend. I want to. But the dynamic we had is not going to work for me anymore."

"I don't know what that means," I admit.

"Me neither," he agrees, laughing. "But we'll figure it out. I miss you too, Sera."

Relief washes through me, followed by exhaustion.

"Let's leave it there for now then," I say. "And hopefully we'll talk again soon."

"Okay," he agrees. "Goodnight, Sera."

"Goodnight, Bryce."

That night, for the first time in a long time, I sleep soundly.

∽

OVER THE WEEKEND I ATTEMPT TO CONTACT ALLIE, BUT she ignores my calls and texts. Taking the hint, I leave her be and bury myself in work and errands.

The following week, things continue to be a low level of nasty between Daniel and me. Well, mostly from him, and I spend my time reminding myself not to rise to the bait.

But on Wednesday, I learn through procurement that Daniel cancelled a software order I'd placed. Mystified and fed up, I storm into his office.

He looks up disinterestedly as I close the door loudly behind me and approach his desk, fuming.

"What?" he asks sharply, barely glancing at me as he types at his laptop.

I toss the procurement form at him. "Why did you cancel this order?"

He glances at the paper and adds it to the trash bin besides his desk.

"You don't need it," he replies, continuing to ignore me.

"Actually, I do," I retort. "And who gave you the authority to cancel my orders?"

Daniel sighs dramatically and looks up from his screen.

"You already have project management software, and so does my project management team. We don't need a third set," he explains condescendingly, ignoring my question.

I squeeze my hands into fists, my nails digging into my palms. "Our software is out of date. We needed to upgrade. And your system is even worse."

He shrugs nonchalantly. "I think it works fine."

"Thankfully, your opinion in this matter is irrelevant," I insist. "I am ordering the software. And if you have an issue with something I order, or with anything else, for that matter, please discuss it with me *first*."

Daniel leans back in his chair, eyeing me speculatively. "That's exactly your problem," he drawls. "You think you have authority here."

The cold glint in his eye is, frankly, rather terrifying. I

suppress my anger and fear and respond as dispassionately as I can.

"I don't work for you," I remind him coolly. "And if you're unclear as to what powers I'm allowed, perhaps we should discuss it with Charles."

Daniel rises from his chair and walks around me to the door, blocking my exit and glowering at me. I freeze, unsure of his intentions.

"Listen carefully," he hisses ominously. "If you think some know-it-all cunt is going to waltz in here and take over my family's business — *my* business — you must be even stupider than I thought you were. If you don't do exactly as I tell you, and stay the fuck out of my way, you're going to regret it."

My jaw drops open in shock before I can stop it. "I'm going to do my job," I insist tightly, my voice quavering with anger. "If you have a problem with that, I suggest you take it up with *our* boss. And if you threaten me again, *you're* going to regret it." I push past him and grab the door handle, but he's too fast for me.

He slams against the door violently with one hand, his other hand rising and curling into a fist. Wide-eyed with shock and fear, I instinctively recoil. My reaction stops him in his tracks and he drops both arms to his sides.

"You've got a big mouth, you know that?" he says softly, menacingly, as he advances on me. I stand my ground, though terror rips through me as he stops inches from me, looking into my eyes threateningly. "I don't put up with stupid bitches who don't know their place. And if you say anything about this to anyone," he looks me up and down, leering, "I'll have to find another way to show you who's the *real* boss around here."

My terror melts once again into anger. "How *dare* you speak to me like that?" I seethe. I make to move around him and he blocks my path. "Get the fuck out of my way right now, or I'm going to scream."

He shakes his head and laughs, then leans dangerously close so our faces are almost touching. His watery blue eyes are ice cold as they lock on mine. "I don't think you will. Because then it will be my word against yours. And do you really think my father is going to believe you or his own son when I tell him that his new protégé came on to me in my office and threatened to lie about me if I refused her advances? After fucking that Italian client of yours, everyone knows you're just a horny little ..."

Even I'm surprised as my hand flies out of nowhere and strikes him across the face, hard. He runs his fingers over the red mark spreading across his cheek and chuckles.

"Lucky for you, I like it rough." He pauses. "Say a word about this to anyone and I will ruin you," he promises. "Your career, your employees. And then I'll return that little smack a hundred times over." He steps back and opens the door.

I can see his assistant peering around the corner from her desk. Not knowing what else to do, I leave without a word, pale as a sheet. I return to my office, closing the door behind me. Leaning against the back of the door, tears of shock, rage, and horror start streaming down my face. I wrap my arms around myself to stop the shaking. It's minutes before I'm able to breathe through the initial trauma and calm myself.

As I sink into my chair, it occurs to me that this merger may have been one of the worst mistakes of my career. Because even if I go straight to Charles and he believes me, the fallout would be awful for everyone.

I sit in my office motionless and overtaken with indecision for the rest of the afternoon. By the end of the day I still can't decide whether to say something. Or whether to stay or call off the merger. I realize I don't have to choose now. But, for good measure, I document my full conversation with Daniel in an email and send it to myself before I go home. In case I need the proof later.

I OPT TO IGNORE DANIEL FOR THE REST OF THE WEEK AND, for once, he seems happy to do the same. On Friday I get a text from Bryce. *Lunch tomorrow?*

Relief courses through me, and not just because Bryce is talking to me again and wants to see me, but because I realize he's the perfect person to talk to about Daniel. I pause at the thought, wondering if that's crossing the line of leaning on him too hard. I decide it's worth broaching the subject, at least.

Love to. When and where? I respond. His return text comes swiftly. He chooses a Japanese restaurant over our former usual. And not our usual time either. My gut twinges a little at the clear message — it's a new era, no more "usual" Bryce and Sera.

BRYCE IS EVEN AT THE RESTAURANT ALREADY WHEN I arrive, waiting at a table. Also, not the usual. He stands to greet me, and I'm taken aback by the changes to his appearance. His hair used to be long enough to run his fingers through, curling gently around his collar, but now it's closely cropped and styled, highlighting the sharp angles of his cheekbones. The cheekbones are new too, or at least I'm certain they didn't used to be that well defined. He's clearly lost weight. Not that he was in any way heavy before, but he's obviously lost body fat and possibly gained even more muscle mass. The sinews and veins of his huge biceps pop against the cuffs of his white polo shirt, and his thick thigh muscles strain his fitted khakis. He looks *hot*. He smirks at my open-mouthed shock. I snap my jaw shut and lean in for a brief hug. He even *smells* hot. Like summer sky, wind, and evergreen.

I clear my throat as I take a seat. "It's good to see you," I say. I'm having a hard time tearing my eyes away, in fact.

His blue eyes sparkle knowingly as he returns my gaze. "You too," he replies, clearly amused.

"You look good," I say, attempting nonchalance and failing miserably.

He smirks again and shrugs, opening his menu. "I've started lifting more seriously, watching what I eat. It helps with the stress," he explains simply.

I flip my menu open too, and we both peruse in silence for a few moments. I choose quickly and close my menu, considering him as he makes his selection. "How's your dad?" I ask softly.

His eyes flick up to mine and hold my gaze for a moment before returning to his menu. He finishes choosing and closes it, tossing it away from him toward the edge of the table.

"Not great," he admits. "He won't eat unless someone feeds him, and he barely talks anymore. He has around-the-clock care now." He leans back in his chair, running his hands over his head. I try not to notice his arm muscles flexing as he does so, or the tightening in my body in response.

"What's the prognosis?" I press.

He shakes his head. "They don't really know. It's progressing faster than typical dementia." He looks like he really doesn't want to talk about it.

"I'm so sorry, Bryce."

"Don't be. It is what it is."

I close my eyes and take a short breath before I reopen them. "But I imagine that's been hard on your family," I say obviously, unsure of what else to offer.

"My mom most of all," he agrees. And after a pause, "It hasn't been a picnic at work, either." He doesn't say any more.

I fidget in my chair, deciding whether to try to draw more out of him. He's certainly less verbose than he once was.

"I can imagine," I reply vaguely. I tear my eyes from his and try to forget my own struggles at work, but a small sigh escapes me.

"Sounds like I'm not the only one with work troubles," he observes.

I huff a small laugh as the waiter approaches to take our order.

When he leaves, Bryce leans forward on his arms, knitting his fingers together nervously.

"Tell me about it," he prompts quietly.

His cool manner is a little disconcerting. It has none of the serenity and calming power it once had. In fact, if anything, it's unnerving. Like he's subtly interrogating me or something. I can't quite put my finger on it.

"Okay," I agree, leaning away from his intensity. "Charles Sutton has a son — Daniel — that works for him. Turns out Daniel doesn't like me very much. It has made things uncomfortable."

Bryce cocks his head to the side. "That's unfortunate," he replies. "But I've never known you to be cowed by anyone. Not even when you should be."

"No," I agree with a smirk. "And while he does scare me a little, I'm not going to let him intimidate me. I'm just not sure how to handle him."

"He scares you?" Bryce's sharp tone, while so unlike the sweet protective one he used to use, still has the same tenor of concern.

And I realize I'll need to be careful not to give away exactly how disturbing my conversation with Daniel was. Because the Bryce I knew would be ready to tear Daniel limb from limb if he knew exactly what went down.

And while I suspect Bryce is now trying to be less involved in my life, I'm not interested in unleashing him on an unsuspecting Daniel. So I couch our encounter in carefully chosen truths.

"You know how men can be," I say flippantly, waving my hand. "They don't realize being physically bigger can be a little daunting to a woman during a heated conversation. He's just threatened by me. He thinks I'm trying to steal the legacy he intends to inherit from his father."

"Are you?" Bryce asks with a hint of amusement.

I look up at him sharply. "No," I reply firmly.

Bryce runs a hand over his hair again, as if he enjoys the feel of the short, fuzzy cut. "What about Charles Sutton?" he asks.

"What about him?" I respond drily.

"Well," Bryce starts, "it did sound like he wanted to groom you to help run his company."

"*Help* being the operative word," I point out.

Bryce looks me in the eye, and it's like his gaze pierces straight through me. "Is this guy threatened *by* you, or did he threaten *you*?"

"How did you know that?" I gasp.

Bryce chuckles and leans back in his chair. "I know the type," he replies. "And I'm guessing you're telling me all this because you want my help."

I frown but can't keep the guilty look off my face. "I'd happily take any advice you have," I concede.

His response is quick, automatic. "Dig up some dirt on him. Threaten him back. Or hold onto it and, if he really pisses you off, use it against him."

I'm surprised at both the glib tone and the calculating malice of his advice. "Do you always fight this dirty?" I ask. I'd meant it teasingly, but as the words come out of my mouth, they hang in the air with a meaning I hadn't meant to imbue them with.

Bryce raises an eyebrow at me and considers me carefully. He rolls his bottom lip through his teeth and I can't tear my eyes from it.

"Yes," he finally replies. "Welcome to my dirty side, Sera. I'd gotten a little tired of playing nice all the time." His low voice is laden with suggestive tension. He takes a sip of his water, breaking the spellbinding eye contact, but I still find myself unable to speak. Or breathe properly.

And this time when the food is delivered, I've lost my appetite for entirely different reasons.

∾

Lying in bed that night, I replay the lunch in my head. While there was a shadow of my Bryce in there, so much about him was changed, the events of the last weeks hardening him, body and soul. I should mourn the loss of my cheery friend, but the cool, sure manner that has replaced it is equal parts enticing and terrifying. And I find I don't mind the combination.

I drift off to sleep, remembering our parting. The way he looked down seriously into my eyes before stepping forward, his scent and the heat rolling off him wrapping around me, to place what should have been a chaste kiss on my cheek before leaving. Except that it was all I could do to stay still, to not turn my face and capture his lips with mine. And I know he was just as aware of the tension between us as I was. I want to chalk it up to it having been nearly six weeks since I've had sex, but I can't help worrying that it's something more.

But my tense flesh and the heat between my legs betrays me. I dream of him. Of us. Naked, my own soft curves entangled with his long, muscular frame. Of his head between my legs, his tongue working with his fingers to pleasure me. And while I'm somehow aware that it's a dream, that it's not actually happening, the orgasm that rips through me, pulling me from sleep, is absolutely real.

ELEVEN

The dream was so lifelike, and the release that followed so undeniably real, that I find myself preoccupied on Sunday morning with wondering whether I'd just cheated on Alessandro. But I know it's silly, because it wasn't real. And even if it *had* been real, would it be cheating? Not that I have any plans to live out that fantasy, but it does make me realize that we hadn't exactly made any promises to each other.

But deep down I know Alessandro wouldn't be with anyone else. And the thought makes me feel even guiltier. Both for having those thoughts about Bryce and for giving Alessandro such a hard time on the phone when we last spoke. And in trying to remember exactly what I'd said, I realize it has been more than three weeks since I've heard from him. I've been so preoccupied with things here, I hadn't realized that it had been quite so long.

Unease starts to unfurl in my stomach. I pace the living room for a while, considering the reasons he might not have called. But none of them calm my increasing anxiety. And some of them lead me into downright panic. I'm on the verge of booking a flight to Rome when I remember the email address. The one he gave me to contact him if I needed to.

I scramble desperately for the scrap of paper I'd tucked in the inner flap of my folio. I sigh with relief when I find it, and type out a short email on my phone, too rushed to wait for my laptop to start up.

Haven't heard from you. Getting worried. Call me or at least let me know you're okay. Ti amo. I stare at the blank subject line for a minute and, unable to come up with anything, send it anyway. Rather than feeling better, I feel a new tension as I realize I'm going to be on edge constantly while I wait for a response.

And while I wait, I figure it's time to check on Allie. The phone rings and rings, and I think she's not going to answer when, finally, I hear her voice.

"Hi," she greets me simply, her voice sounding tired and morose.

"Allie," I breathe, relieved she answered. "How are you doing?"

She's been out of work for two full weeks, so I know

clearly she's not doing great. And I feel stupid for even asking, but I'm not sure what else to say.

"I'm all healed up," she replies in the same dead, even tone. "But I still can't …"

"I know," I say quickly to spare her having to explain. "I'm glad you're better physically, at least. Are you ready for a visit? Can I bring you anything?"

"I appreciate that, Sera, but I just still need to be alone. I'm sorry."

"Oh, Allie," I reply, tears welling up in my eyes. "You don't have to apologize to me, babe. You just take all the time you need."

There's a long pause before Allie finally replies. "I am. I don't think I'm coming back to work, Sera."

"You mean this week?" I ask

"I mean ever," she clarifies.

My heart sinks in my chest.

"I don't understand," I whisper. And my brain really has stopped in its tracks, unable to process her statement.

"I just can't. I can't face any of it right now," she replies. I can hear her sobbing quietly. "I'm sorry, Sera." Over the phone I hear fumbling and receding sobs.

"Allie?" Thuds. More fumbling.

"Sera," David's voice comes on the line. "I'm sorry. Allie is having difficulty dealing with things."

"That's an understatement," I reply heatedly.

"I know," he agrees. "I've never seen her like this. I've asked her to get help, but she's just not ready."

"I don't care if she's ready," I say angrily. "You need to get her back to the doctor. *Now*. Don't let this fester, David. Something is wrong."

"She lost a child, Sera, of course something is wrong," he snaps. "You think I don't know that?"

I instantly regret not being more tactful. Because clearly David is still struggling too.

"I know you do," I reply, taking my tone down. "I know this is hard for both of you. What I'm trying to say is that there is still something *physically* wrong with Allie. It's normal to be upset. But this is way beyond that. Depression isn't just mental, David. She's not just going to snap out of this. She needs help. Whether she wants it or not."

A loud sniff tells me that David is in tears. I made David cry. *Could I be any bigger of a shit?*

"You're right," he finally replies thickly. "You're right. I'll take her to the doctor first thing tomorrow."

I breathe a huge sigh of relief. "Thank you. Let me know if you need anything, okay?"

"Okay. Thanks, Sera," he replies.

"Anytime, David. I love you both so much. Hang in there. Get help. I'll talk to you soon," I promise.

BUT I'M SPARED CHECKING BACK IN AS BARELY A DAY passes when I hear from David on Monday afternoon. He tells me Allie is napping after reluctantly seeing the doctor, but he is reassured as her symptoms were, in fact, diagnosed as depression. Because with a diagnosis comes the promise of help — a dim light at the end of the tunnel. But it will be a tough battle and, after much discussion, Allie and David have still agreed that it's best if Allie takes a leave of absence from work.

While I'm sad at still being without my closest friend and confidant by my side, especially given my ongoing struggles with Daniel's attitude toward me, I'm more relieved that she's getting the help she needs to heal. And I know even without Allie to confide in, I'll navigate these issues, but I still selfishly wish that she were here. It's just not the same without her.

Daniel continues to treat me with cold indifference, but others are starting to pick up on the tension. But nobody, not even Charles, breathes a word about it. And without anyone to talk to, I'm afraid it's becoming my new norm. And that thought scares me almost as much as facing it alone.

∾

I'M DISTRACTED ENOUGH BY MY CONCERNS ABOUT ALLIE and work that I don't even think of Bryce until midday

Tuesday when my phone rings and his name flashes across the display. I gladly accept the call, pleased with anything that will interrupt the tension of my day.

"Hey, Bryce, what's up?"

"Sera," he breathes my name, and I instantly suspect something is wrong. "Are you busy?"

"Never too busy for you," I assure him. "Are you okay?"

He sniffs loudly, confirming my suspicions. "My dad passed away this morning." His every word is laced with sorrow, and my heart crumbles for him.

"Oh, Bryce," I reply, tearing up. "I'm so sorry. What can I do?"

"There isn't much to do at the moment," he replies thickly. "My mom wanted to be alone with him until ..." He chokes back a sob, unable to finish his sentence.

The thought of Bryce crying throws me because despite everything we've been through, I've rarely ever seen him more than a little upset about *anything*. My heart aches for him, and the sadness that's lurked under the surface lately hits me full force.

"Where are you?" I ask softly.

"Home. Just processing. I don't know what else to do right now. I just thought you should know," he replies, clearly struggling to keep it together.

I decide instantly that this is one person in my life I'm not going to leave to their own despair. And I might need the comfort of his presence as much as he needs mine.

"I'm coming over," I reply in a firm tone. "Stay put."

There's a long pause on the other end of the line.

"You don't have to do that," he responds. But I can tell he wants me to.

"I know. I'll be there as soon as I can," I assure him.

"Thanks, Sera." His relief is palpable.

As soon as I hang up I gather my things and poke my head in Charles' office. He's chatting idly with Daniel, whom I do my best to ignore. Charles stops speaking and looks at me inquiringly.

"Sorry to interrupt. I need to take the afternoon off," I inform him. "So I won't be able to make our meeting. I'll catch up with you first thing tomorrow?"

"Everything okay?" Charles asks, subtly probing for a reason.

"I'm fine," I assure him. I debate how much to reveal. Somehow, I don't think "a close friend's father died" will go over well. But I can't think of the distress in Bryce's voice without wanting to run to him. And if I'm being honest, I'm not exactly sorry to be leaving. But I shove the latter observation deep down. "It's just an emergent one-off personal issue that needs to be dealt with right away."

Charles considers for a moment, but as I've been nose to the grindstone for a full month, he's not exactly in a position to begrudge me an afternoon.

"Well, thanks for letting me know," he finally replies. "We'll see you tomorrow."

I smile joylessly and take my leave.

~

WITHIN A HALF HOUR I'M AT BRYCE'S DOOR WITH A bottle of whiskey in one hand and a bouquet of white roses in the other. I ring the doorbell and hide the bottle behind my back.

He opens the door, his eyes rimmed with red and his face stained with tears. Before I can utter a word, his arms wrap around my waist and he pulls me into him, burying his face in my hair. I can feel his anguish in the tight grip he has on me and the cool moisture on his cheek where it touches my neck. We stand for a moment, half in his apartment, half out, as he takes what solace he needs from the warmth of our bodies pressed together. When he finally releases me, he wordlessly plants a kiss on my forehead and steps back to allow me in.

I offer the roses as he closes the door behind me. "It's not much, but I had to bring something," I explain.

He nods grimly as he takes them. "Thanks." He brings them into the kitchen. While he rummages in the cupboards, presumably looking for a vase, I glance around, realizing I've never actually been inside his apartment before.

It's a typical bachelor pad — sparse, with dark utilitarian furniture and little decoration. But it's tidy and clean, and it smells like him. As I turn back toward the kitchen, I realize he's putting the flowers into a large plastic mug.

"No vase, huh?" I tease gently.

His answering smile is dull and lifeless. "No, but this'll do."

"You look like you could use a drink," I reply, setting the bottle of whiskey on the counter next to the flowers.

He gives a dry laugh and nods. "You read my mind," he responds. "Want one?" I nod, and he retrieves two glasses and pours a generous amount for each of us.

He saunters into the living room, dropping defeatedly onto the large, leather couch. I perch in the matched chair adjacent to him, but he shakes his head and beckons me to sit next to him with his free hand. I comply silently, still unnerved by his overall quieter manner.

I slide into the corner of the couch, facing him, with one knee touching the side of his leg. I touch his arm gently as he sips his whiskey. "You can talk to me," I say softly, encouragingly.

He gives me a speculative side-eye glance and sets his glass down on the coffee table. I follow suit, my drink untouched. He slides his arm onto the couch behind me and crooks his knee up as he turns to face me.

"I don't feel like talking," he replies. His eyes rove

over my face, and I look down, tugging my dusty pink shirtdress over my knees self-consciously. When I find the courage to meet his gaze again, his eyes are a stormy grey-blue and aren't so much focused on me as they just happen to be fixed in my direction. I can tell he's retreated deeply into his own thoughts.

His gaze is so lost and forlorn that, before I can stop myself, I reach a hand out to touch his cheek and bring him back to the present moment. But before my fingertips can make contact with his face, his head snaps back and his fist closes around my hand. He sits up, his eyes wide.

"I'm sorry," I apologize, blushing to the roots of my hair. I make to pull my hand from his grip, but he tugs it gently toward him.

"It's okay," he assures me. "You just startled me." He lowers his hand into his lap, taking mine with it, and gently strokes his thumb over my palm. The touch sends tingles up my arm, and I can feel my cheeks still flushed with heat.

I swallow hard and lick my lips, willing myself to find words again. "Clearly. You've obviously got a lot to deal with right now. I can go if you want. I just wanted to see you and to let you know I'm here if you need me. But I don't want to make this harder for you."

He continues absentmindedly stroking my hand and it takes all my effort to focus my eyes on his face. "I said I don't feel like talking," he responds, his voice low and tired, "not that I didn't want you here. I'm glad you're here."

When his eyes meet mine this time, I see the conflict. The old Bryce, filled with longing for what could have been between us, warring with this new, harder Bryce. And I don't know under what terms he had hoped to restart our friendship, but I can see his struggle with his grief for his father, and his desire to be comforted.

And I know suddenly without a doubt that I'm more than capable of being whatever he needs me to be right now without crossing any lines, if that's what must be done. And not just because he's been there for me more times than I care to think about. But because I care for him deeply, and it's what he needs.

I open my arms to him, and he doesn't even hesitate before falling into me, tucking his head against my heart and wrapping his long arms around my torso. As I feel his body shake with tears and sobs of grief, I slide down into his embrace, resting my cheek on the top of his head. With one hand, I stroke the back of his head, the other I wrap around his quivering shoulder. I tuck my knees into his midsection and he sinks deeper into my chest, his warm tears rolling over our entwined arms.

As I hold him through his anguish, I banish all my own heartache, focusing on rubbing slow circles on his back, and on honoring his unspoken need for someone strong enough to unconditionally console him through this ordeal.

At some point we must have drifted off, tangled together, because I open my eyes and note several hours have passed. I can't see Bryce's face, but his body is still, his breathing even and heavy. I loathe waking him, but my biological needs are pressing, and I don't think I can disentangle myself while he's unconscious, as his torso has me completely pinned to the couch.

"Bryce," I prompt softly, my voice cracking from disuse. I tug gently on his arm.

He stirs finally and sits up languidly. "What time is it?" he asks hoarsely, rubbing his eyes.

"Almost five," I reply. "Where's your bathroom?"

He gestures vaguely down a hall I hadn't noticed, and I shoot off the couch.

When I return to the living room, our glasses have been cleaned up and Bryce is standing near the door, keys in hand.

"I need to pick my mom up from the hospital," he explains.

I gather my purse and meet him at the door, frowning. "Are you okay to drive?"

He gives me a deeply impatient look. "Sera, I had half a drink, hours ago. I'm fine."

I push his shoulder lightly. "I wasn't talking about the alcohol," I retort. I stop short of reminding him of the leaky, blubbering mess he was earlier this afternoon, but clearly the look on my face says enough. I can tell I'm annoying him, as he mashes his lips together and his nostrils flare.

"I'm fine," he repeats.

"All right," I relent. "I'm just concerned about you. You'll let me know if there's anything I can do to help?"

He takes a deep breath and runs a hand over his head. "Of course," he replies finally, opening the door.

I move toward it and he grabs me by the hand, pulling me into a gruff hug. I breathe in his scent, my fingers trailing over the taut muscles of his chest, and press out of his embrace after a moment. He releases me, and I know from the closed look on his face that we're back once more to our new tightrope walk, the comfort of our closeness this afternoon at an end.

But as I walk away, I can feel his eyes follow me down the hallway. And I'm bothered by how much that pleases me.

TWELVE

On Wednesday morning I step out of Charles' office and head downstairs to meet my team. As I round the corner into the open cubicle area that holds not only my team but most of the other project-management-related functions, I run into Daniel.

"I see you decided we were worth your time today," he remarks snidely, blocking my path. I make to go around him, but he shifts, making that impossible. "What, you can't even be bothered to speak to any of us anymore?"

I see a few heads peering over the low cubicle walls at his purposely loud, attention-grabbing comments.

"Hello, Daniel," I reply shortly. "It's so nice to see you too. Now if you don't mind, I need to meet with my team."

He folds his arms over his chest. "I do mind, actually.

Care to share what exactly was more important than your job yesterday afternoon?"

"I do mind, actually," I reply mockingly. "As it's none of your business."

He is distracted by my response, so I take the opportunity to push past him.

"Having to pick up your slack *is* my business," he replies loudly to my back.

I stop and whirl around. "Oh, *please*," I say hotly, not bothering to keep my voice down. "As if I left anything that required your immediate and precious attention. And if there was anything so urgent, you could have called me. But I can see instead of using common sense, you'd rather be a passive-aggressive asshole to try to make me look bad in front of the entire office." More heads pop up over cubicle walls. "Next time, I'll make sure my loved ones know that all deaths and other family emergencies should be after business hours, so you aren't inconvenienced."

A low "ooooh" erupts amongst the crowd of onlookers. If my words weren't enough, their response leaves Daniel completely at a loss. His face turns beet red, his eyes shifting nervously between me and the spectators, realizing his attempt at humiliating me has backfired spectacularly.

"That's not ... I didn't ..." he sputters. His confusion quickly turns to rage. "Everyone back to work!" he barks.

All heads duck back down, and Daniel storms off before anything more can be said.

I can't help but give a small, satisfied smirk as I head to my meeting.

∾

THE REST OF THE DAY IS GLORIOUSLY FREE OF DANIEL-related drama, as his mortification keeps him from being near me unless absolutely necessary. And even then, while he's unable to contain his furious glares, he doesn't speak a word to me or interfere in any of my affairs. In the absence of his usual campaign of taunts and undermining me at every turn, I manage to have an exceptionally productive day.

Early that evening I'm feeling especially motivated. Or perhaps I'm antsy, having checked my email for the millionth time with still no response from Alessandro. I've resolved not to worry, as there's literally nothing I can do. Even if I wanted to go after him, I wouldn't know where to begin. And there's no way in hell I'm broaching that subject with Bryce.

At that thought, I realize I need to check in with him. He answers on the first ring.

"Hey, gorgeous," he answers distractedly. I'm taken aback at his former usual greeting, and my heart melts a little at the emergence of that small sliver of what we were.

"Hey," I reply, controlling the emotion in my voice. "Bad time?"

"No," he assures me. "No. I'm at my mom's, but I can talk for a few minutes."

"How is she doing?" I ask.

Bryce sighs deeply. "She's devastated. My sister, my aunt, and I are all trying to help her plan the funeral, but it's rough. Practically every decision sends her into hysterics. And there's so much other shit to take care of. It's rough going all around."

"Your father's estate plan didn't cover final arrangements?" I ask the question before I even consider that it might be insulting. Surely, they'd have already thought of that.

"I don't know," he replies. "I hadn't looked into it. We're still kind of in react mode."

"I get it," I say. "This is unimaginably huge, for all of you. When is the funeral?"

"Sunday," he responds distractedly.

"As in this Sunday?" I'm incredulous. They clearly haven't even looked into Bryce's father's final wishes and they're planning to hold a funeral in not quite four days?

"Yes," he replies. "Mom wants it over with."

"Bryce, text me the address," I demand. "I'm coming over to help. Now."

"Sera …"

"Don't start that 'Sera' shit with me, Bryce. This is what I do. I organize things. I make things happen. Now, I'm coming over there to get as much of this taken care of as I possibly can, so you either give me the address or I'm going to use my real estate agent powers to find your parent's house, so help me God."

Bryce's answering chuckle brings me back to earth a bit. I didn't realize how angry I'd gotten all of a sudden.

"Okay. I'll send it to you as soon as I hang up," he agrees.

"Damn straight. See you soon." I hang up before he can respond and whip into action, gathering everything I'll need.

As promised, my phone pings with Bryce's text before I'm even done. And within minutes, I'm on my way to their house in West Seattle.

⁓

"HEY," BRYCE GREETS ME AT THE DOOR, LOOKING rumpled and weary in jeans and a T-shirt. He gives me a quick side hug and escorts me into the huge, ornate foyer.

"Hey," I reply softly, looking up at him. I don't have time to say anything else as a woman my age pops into the room looking a little more enthusiastic than I'd expect under the circumstances. I look back up at Bryce expectantly, and he releases me from his side.

"Sera, this is my sister, Emily," he says. "Emily, this is Serafina Evans."

Emily's blue eyes, so like her brother's, sparkle at the introduction. She is around my height but slender and wild-looking, with the same thick, wavy chestnut hair as Bryce cascading down her back. She rushes forward and embraces me tightly.

"It's so nice to finally meet you," she says. "Bryce won't shut up about you. I'm just sorry we didn't get to meet sooner, under better circumstances." She steps back and smiles sadly at me, and I realize she's excited because of *me*.

I shoot Bryce a surprised and pointed look.

"Em, don't embarrass me," Bryce mutters, blushing furiously.

"It's okay," I assure him. "It's nice to meet you too, Emily. I'm so sorry for your loss."

"Thank you," she replies sincerely, grabbing my hand. "Come on, you should meet my mom too."

I look at Bryce again, checking to make sure he's okay with her pulling me into the living room. He shrugs and follows.

I barely have time to register the lavish décor of the living room — with its light grey walls, thick grey-and-white damask curtains, finely carved upholstered wood furniture, and arrangement upon arrangement of white flowers of all kinds displayed on every surface — before Emily has pulled me to a stop in front of the largest greyish-blue settee where two older women sit.

Both women have the same hair and eye color as Bryce and his sister. But Bryce unmistakably looks like the older of the two. Bryce seats himself next to her and folds his large hand over hers.

"Mom, this is my friend Sera," he says to her gently. "She's here to help with the funeral arrangements."

The tenderness in his voice and countenance bring tears to my eyes. I can practically feel his love and concern for her radiating off him. She places her other hand over his, squeezing his palm.

"Mrs. Hoyt," I say, my voice catching. I clear my throat. "I've been thinking about you ever since I heard. I'm so sorry for your loss. This must be so hard for you."

"Rebecca, please," she replies, gesturing for me to sit on the smaller couch opposite her. "And thank you. It has been much more difficult than I thought it would be. Even when you know it's coming." She presses a handkerchief to her eyes.

"I didn't know your husband, Rebecca, and I want to hear more about him sometime. But for now, I'm here to take as much of this off your shoulders as I can," I offer.

Bryce's eyes meet mine, and they are filled with love

and sorrow. My breath catches in my throat, surrounded as I am by all the emotion in the room.

Rebecca nods thankfully as the tears slip down her cheeks, clearly unable to speak. The other older woman offers her hand.

"I'm Rebecca's sister, Charlotte," she offers. "Thank you for coming."

I lean forward and gently squeeze her hand in greeting. "I'm glad to be able to help," I admit.

"Well, we need lots of it," Emily chimes in. "We've been trying to get things together, but there's just so much to do."

I rise from my chair, slinging my bag over my shoulder. "I'll need to know what you've done so far, where your father's important papers are, and the contact information for his attorney. Leave the rest to me."

Emily arches an eyebrow at Bryce. "You weren't kidding about her," she says. Bryce huffs a small, dry laugh and shrugs. "This way."

With a brief farewell, I take my leave and follow Emily down a long hallway into what is unmistakably a man's study.

"Where can I set up?" I ask tentatively.

Emily points to the large desk that was clearly her father's. "It's the best place," she replies, noting my hesitation. "Really, it's okay. I'll pull up a chair and get you what you need."

Reluctantly, I settle into the giant black leather seat behind the desk. It smells of aftershave and cigars. The desk is neat and tidy, with no personal effects other than a framed picture of the family. Bryce's father was nearly as tall as he was. I can see that Emily looks more like him though, with her sharp features and willowy frame.

"What was his name?" I ask softly, embarrassed that I'd never asked, as Emily pulls her chair next to mine.

Emily looks longingly at the photograph for a moment before responding. "Landon. Landon Jeffrey Hoyt."

∾

EMILY IMPARTS EVERYTHING THAT'S BEEN DONE SO FAR which, as it happens, is actually not very much, and I ask her a few questions before getting the contact information I need and dismissing her. What I don't share with her, nor had I with Bryce, was that I've handled exactly this situation not once, but twice in the last five years when both of my mother's parents passed away. It's a struggle to suppress those memories as I work through the list I've drafted, but for Bryce's sake, and his family's, I do.

By the end of the evening I've spoken to the family lawyer, located the estate documents in a filing cabinet, and have a good handle on what needs to be done to pull everything off by Sunday. Thankfully, there are precious few details that Landon Jeffrey Hoyt didn't leave instructions for.

When I emerge around ten p.m., Rebecca has already gone to bed and Bryce, Emily, and Charlotte are sitting in the living room talking in hushed tones. As I approach, I swear I hear my name, but their conversation ceases and their heads whip toward me as I enter the room.

"I have good news," I start. They all look at me expectantly as I take a seat next to Bryce on the large sofa. "I've located the estate documents and spoken with the family attorney, in a general sense of course, as he couldn't discuss any of the details with me."

"And?" Bryce prompts expectantly.

"And your father has already paid for a family-only private funeral at a nearby funeral home. One of you needs to contact them first thing tomorrow to set up a time slot for Sunday. Everything has already been selected — casket, flowers, music — it's all done."

Bryce sinks back into the sofa, clearly relieved.

"I can do that," Emily offers. "I have the rest of the week off."

I hand her the sheet with the funeral home information and summary of arrangements.

Bryce nods. "Me too," he adds. "What can I do?"

"While the funeral will be small, his final arrangements also stipulated for a large wake after, here at the house." I hand Bryce the relevant pages. "He was pretty specific about the guest list, décor, music, food, you name it.”

Bryce skims the list, a sad, wry smile appearing on his face. “That’s Dad. He was almost as organized as you are,” he says fondly. He glances up at me. “I can take care of this.”

“I can help too,” I assure him. “I still have to work the rest of the week, but I’m all yours this weekend.” I think I see Emily and Charlotte share a look, but I ignore it and press on. “The attorney needs to speak with you, Bryce. About the company. He says you haven’t returned his calls.”

Bryce frowns, folding the paper in his hand nervously. “I know. I just can’t deal with it right now.”

I suppress a sigh. “Unfortunately, there are a few pressing matters that need your attention now,” I insist. He looks at me defiantly, and I can read his unspoken message. “And you can’t send someone else. It has to be you. There are things you need to sign. It won’t take long, Bryce, and you’ll feel better once it’s done.”

He twirls the page in his hands a few more times. “Fine. I’ll do it first thing tomorrow,” he concedes.

“Good,” I breathe, relieved. “Your mother will need to talk to him eventually too, but that can wait. For now,” I produce the final sheet, “I think she’s the best person to proof his obituary. He wrote it a couple of years ago, so it shouldn’t be too much work. But it'll probably be very difficult for her to do alone."

Charlotte plucks it from my hand. "I'll help her," she responds.

"Then that's it for this week. But if your mother needs help with any of the estate paperwork afterward, I'm happy to help," I offer. "I've been through it more than once, and most lawyers suck at making sure you really understand what you're signing and everything that needs to be done."

Charlotte looks at me sadly. "Who did you lose, dear?" she asks kindly.

I blush softly and blink back tears. "My grandparents," I admit.

Bryce gives me a strange look, then pulls me under his arm and kisses the top of my head. The look between Emily and Charlotte is unmistakable this time.

"I'm sorry to hear that," Charlotte murmurs. I brush away the tears and disentangle myself from Bryce's embrace.

"Thank you," I respond. "I should really be going now. But I'll check in with you, Bryce, after work tomorrow."

"I'll walk you out," he agrees.

I say goodnight to Emily and Charlotte and let Bryce lead me to the door. He steps out onto the front porch into the warm August night. I let him wrap me in another of his warm hugs and try not to think about how much I enjoy it

— how good he smells, or the feel of his tall, muscled frame against me, or the tenderness in his embrace.

As I drive home, I tell myself it's just loneliness and sorrow and empathy that are stirring whatever emotions that I'm feeling for Bryce. I also try to suppress the guilt when I realize I hadn't thought of Alessandro nor checked my email all evening. And when I get home I'm too tired and overwhelmed to do so, and opt instead to fall asleep fully clothed on top of the covers.

AT BRYCE'S INVITATION, I REJOIN HIS FAMILY ON Saturday afternoon to set up for the wake the following day and to stay over so I'm on hand to help with final preparations in the morning. Even between the five of us — well, four mostly, as Rebecca is still too distraught to do much — it still takes all afternoon and into the evening before we're able to settle in for a late dinner.

We eat in relative silence, the impending activities too somber for words. When we're done, Bryce leads me out into the back yard, to a small swing on the patio. It's barely big enough for us both, and I'm forced to sit up against Bryce, his long arm slung behind my shoulders. We sit quietly for a few minutes, staring up at the stars.

I formulate several sentences and chicken out, unsure of what to say. While Bryce has clearly needed the physical comfort, he's still so much quieter than he once was. But given the weight of all that he's been dealing with, it's understandable. Still, I don't want to unbalance whatever tenuous equilibrium we've achieved.

"I'm glad you're here," he finally says, breaking the silence. "I didn't want this to be confusing, but I also didn't realize until just now how much I needed someone to lean on this week."

"I did," I admit. "And I'm glad I could be here for you. You've been …"

Bryce shakes his head in a silent plea to not go there. I stop immediately, looking down into my entangled hands, blushing. No talking about feelings. Message received.

A rough finger pulls at my chin, breaking the spell of my self-flagellation. Bryce tilts my head to look up at him. His eyes glitter in the darkness of the night, searching mine for something. His finger stays on my chin, holding me so I'm unable to break his gaze. Not that I could if I wanted to. Whatever passes between us in this moment is something I can't even put into words. It's beyond attraction, beyond sorrow. It's a tug on my heart that I can't deny.

I lift my head up further toward him and part my lips. He sucks in his breath sharply and runs a rough thumb over my bottom lip, leaning in slowly until he's merely inches away.

"If I didn't know better, I'd think you wanted me to kiss you," he murmurs, his breath warm on my face.

My heart thunders in my chest. "Maybe I do," I whisper, unable to lie to him.

His lips settle into an amused smirk, and I can't tear my gaze from them. He leans in, touching his nose gently to mine. If I moved forward even a little, my lips would be pressed against his. My stomach tumbles at the thought, but I remain perfectly still, waiting to see what he does.

"Well, maybe I will sometime," he murmurs.

He releases me and returns his gaze to the stars. The butterflies in my stomach turn to lead, and I don't know how to react. Or what I really feel for him. And whether I should be feeling it at all.

But for now, maybe I'm just relieved. Because that part of me that still belongs to Alessandro squirms uncomfortably at whatever just almost happened between Bryce and me. Though admittedly, that part is undernourished and unsure. It's been four weeks since I've so much as heard from the man who claims to love me but still left me. And the more time passes, the harder it is to remember why that was for the best. Because on top of not having made any promises to each other, it's starting to look more and more like I may never hear from him again. In fact, I have to work to pull the memory of his face, his voice, to mind.

But I also know I can't overwrite the ache and uncertainty of Alessandro's absence with something I may only be feeling because of the unfortunate passing of Bryce's father and the tumultuous events in my own life. And I know Bryce once had feelings for me, but his need for me now is clearly mostly based in his grief. To start something now would, at best, be a small comfort to us both. At worst, it could obliterate any hope of keeping him in my life. My gut twists painfully, and that thought stops whatever yen had started to grow in me this past week, hardening my resolve to put anything I feel aside and focus only on being there for Bryce, and trusting that once it's all behind us things will be clearer. Easier.

My resolve is tested again sooner than I'd thought when Bryce walks me to my guest room.

"If you need anything, I'm two doors down," he says, leaning against the doorframe and looking down at me. "The bathroom is the first door."

Looking up into his face, I nod, not trusting myself to speak. Because despite the war in my heart, the sight of him towering over me — tortured, sad, and exquisitely handsome — I realize I'm only human. And I want to touch him, to make love to him, to wipe away his worries with flesh on flesh.

I'm suddenly thankful we're having this conversation by the light of the moon filtering into the room, because if the lights were on I'm sure he'd see the flush in my face.

As it is, I'm having trouble keeping my breathing even from the desire welling in me.

It's just the situation, I tell myself, willing my body into submission.

"Thanks," I finally manage. "I'll see you in the morning."

He regards me stoically for a few more moments before turning to leave. "Goodnight, Sera."

"Goodnight, Bryce."

Once he's gone, I check my phone. I have a missed call from Allie. Another sharp pain tugs at my heart. Knowing it's too late, I vow to call her back tomorrow and make my way to bed, overwhelmed by the emotion of the day.

THIRTEEN

Bryce

I'm lying awake in bed when my alarm goes off at five. I shut it off absentmindedly, still brooding on the events of the previous evening. Kicking myself, really, for not giving in to the come-hither looks Sera was throwing me last night. But being close to her this week, needing to be close to someone, has thrown everything into chaos as it is.

Ignoring the tension in my groin, I roll out of bed and throw on running clothes to work off the strain by pounding the pavement instead. Even though I almost never run on Sundays. But that's how worked up I am.

An hour later, I'm dripping with sweat but still tense as ever. I down a protein shake in the kitchen as the first light of day creeps over the horizon. The house is quiet, everyone still clearly abed. Though I'm sure, like me, nobody slept all that well.

Stripping off my sweat-soaked shirt, I head to the bathroom to shower. The heat of the shower wraps around me like an old friend, but just the thought of Sera sleeping in the next room has me hard again. I grit my teeth as I work myself, imagining my hand is her hand, her mouth, her sex. I explode quietly under the stream of water, both momentarily sated and frustrated that she's still forefront in my mind at moments like this, despite my determination to stop thinking about her like that.

Done with the shower, I wrap a towel around my waist and head to my room. As I'm opening the door, Sera's door snicks open and she slips into the hallway. She's so preoccupied with being quiet that she doesn't notice me at first and I'm able to get a full look at her. And I'm reminded why it's so hard to stop being attracted to her. Her long, wavy brown hair is in complete, sexy disarray, and she's wearing an oversized shirt that clearly shows her full breasts are free of a bra. The shirt hangs just below her crotch, putting her shapely legs on display. I can't help but gawk a little and be thankful that I just abated my erection in the shower. Because it would be hard to hide in this towel.

After a few steps she looks up and her eyes meet mine.

She freezes. I give her a small smirk as I watch her eyes travel to my lips, then chest, then down.

"Good morning, gorgeous," I say before I can help the words. I curse internally at my second slip. I swore to myself I'd stop calling her that. But I'm not exactly as in control of myself as I'd like to be these days.

"Hi," she squeaks, clearly unnerved. "I'm just going to …" she points to the bathroom and slips inside quickly. I step into my own room to dress for the day, the black clothes I'd laid out on the bed a reminder of what's to come that sobers me considerably.

∽

I'M STANDING IN THE KITCHEN DRINKING COFFEE WHEN EM joins me. She looks like hell, but I don't say anything.

"Why do you look so much better than I feel?" she grouses at me.

"If it helps, I feel like you look," I counter. She glares at me as she pours a cup of coffee for herself.

"It most certainly does not," she replies haughtily.

Aunt Charlotte appears and catches us feigning stink eye at each other as she starts preparing breakfast. "Your mother will be down shortly," she warns us. "Behave, please." As if we're still children to be scolded.

Mom and Sera enter the kitchen together shortly after, engaged in quiet conversation. The sight of them together makes me nervous in a way I can't quite explain, and I clear my throat. Their heads snap up.

Their tête-à-tête broken, my mother moves to help Aunt Char with breakfast and Sera takes a seat at the dining room table, eyeing me nervously.

In true Sera form, she's wearing a black shirtdress, cinched at the waist with a black belt. I realize everyone is already dressed in their finest blacks, myself included, and the thought adds to the somber tone of the day.

"Coffee?" I ask Sera.

"Yes, please," she responds.

I pour her a cup and drop in cream but no sugar.

She looks at me inquisitively as I set it down in front of her and plop into the chair next to her. "I didn't realize you knew how I take my coffee."

I wave my hand, brushing it off. Like hell I'm going to confess that I've catalogued her every preference. I'd explain it's years of training in observing people, but I know if I say it out loud it will probably sound like something more than it is.

"We have to leave in an hour for the funeral," I remind her. "It'd be a squeeze in Aunt Char's car, so we can drive separately if you want."

She looks up at me like a deer frozen in headlights. "I hadn't assumed I was invited to the funeral," she admits. "Since it's family only. I thought I'd stay here and make sure everything is ready for the wake."

Em and Aunt Char share another of their looks that they think nobody notices. I ignore it as usual, but I can tell Sera sees it too.

Mom pauses flipping the bacon. "Sera, dear, you're more than welcome. In fact, I insist," she says warmly. "I don't know what we would have done without you this week."

For the first time since it happened, my mother sounds strong again. And I have no doubt that it's, as she says, in no small part due to Sera's efforts and her authoritative presence that leaves you confident that everything is going to be taken care of. I look down into my coffee, tears burning in my eyes. For so many reasons. When I've mastered myself, I look up to find Sera staring at me. Silently asking for confirmation.

"I want you there," I admit, in a quiet tone that will reach only her ears.

She gives a small nod of understanding and, when nobody is looking, reaches out to give my hand a gentle squeeze.

∾

When we file out of the funeral home two hours later, everyone is in tears. The ceremony was short and simple, but exactly what we needed. No frills, no fanfare. Just enough time to see him, remember him, and say goodbye. Aunt Char and Em hold each other as they walk ahead, and my mother is tucked under my left arm, sobbing quietly into my chest as we exit. Sera walks on my right at a respectful distance.

My father's still form flashes through my mind again, and more tears silently find their way down my face. In the presence of others, I suppress the lifetime of memories threatening to reduce me to the mess I was earlier in the week. I can only hope I'm strong enough to save that for later, when I'm alone once more.

Just when I feel like I'm going to lose that battle, Sera's warm hand slips into mine and she gives me a strong squeeze. I look over at her, her hazel eyes brimming with the tears and anguish I'm sure is reflected in my face. I squeeze her hand back, grateful not to be the sole pillar of strength in our miserable party.

∾

WE MAKE IT BACK TO THE HOUSE WELL AHEAD OF THE start of the wake. Sera heads to start preparing, but I pull her aside into the living room. Without a word, she opens her arms to me, and I gratefully fold myself around her. Her quiet strength calms me, which is exactly what I needed, and I release her once I'm sure I'll be able to manage on my own for a while. I watch her walk away, concentrating on making my mind blank and numb.

As people start to arrive, I position myself at the front of the house to act as a buffer so that my mother has time to prepare herself for the steady stream of well-wishers that are arriving.

And arrive they do — well more than a hundred of them over the course of two hours. I barely see any of my family members as I let the wave of mourners flow through and over me, their kind and well-meant words drops in a tumultuous ocean of grief. I both hear them and don't as I surrender to the experience.

By the time people have stopped arriving, I feel like a broken shell and seek out the solitude of the patio. I'm not there long when a hand holding a plate of food drops in front of me. I look up to see Sera's face, full of concern. I accept the food gratefully, and she hands me a generous glass of whiskey to go with it. I don't realize my hands are shaking until I take it from her.

"I should bring some food to your mom," she says softly. "I'll be back as soon as I can, okay?"

I nod mutely, unable to even voice my thanks. I feel as though talking will unleash the dam holding back the pain of it all. But she disappears, not needing me to say anything. Grateful, I concentrate on eating.

Once I've finished my food I realize I should go in and check on my mom as well, so I rise reluctantly, dropping my dishes in the kitchen. Feeling ever so slightly stronger for the food and alcohol, I find my mother in the living room leaning on Aunt Char and listening blankly to one of dad's golf buddies extend his condolences. Sera sits next to her with a plate of untouched food.

I touch Sera's arm to get her attention. "I've got this," I assure her, taking the plate and her place.

She rests her hand on my shoulder and squeezes it reassuringly. "Let me know if you need anything," she responds, and retreats to the kitchen.

It doesn't take but a look at my mom to realize she's about to pass out, so I manage to convince her to have a few bites of food between conversations. Once she's looking less peaked, I take the empty plate back to the kitchen to find Sera leaning against the counter, looking uncomfortable.

"You okay?" I ask her as I get myself more whiskey.

She gives me an incredulous look. "I'm fine," she replies impatiently. "How are you holding up?"

"Trying not to think about any of it. Failing miserably," I admit.

She bites her lip and visibly restrains herself from reaching for me. I lean back into the counter behind me, encouraging the distance between us.

"What's bothering you the most?" she asks.

Her question catches me off guard. And it's an interesting one.

"I'm now the president of Hoyt Corporate Services," I admit.

She looks confused. "That's a bad thing?" she asks.

I sigh heavily. "No. Yes. I don't know," I reply, frustrated. I regroup to come up with the shortest possible explanation. "I knew it would happen someday. I just didn't think it would be so soon."

"You're worried you're not ready?" she guesses.

I stare down as I swirl the whiskey in my glass. "I know I'm not ready," I admit. I look up at her. She bites her lip again, and I look away.

"The Bryce I know can handle anything," she says softly but confidently. I huff a snort of disagreement and down the rest of the amber liquid. "You may doubt yourself, but anyone who knows you can see how capable you are."

I meet her gaze. "I know I'm capable. But there was so much I wanted to do before I took on that kind of responsibility," I clarify. The alcohol warms me and enhances the relaxing effect of the first glass.

"Like what?" she asks.

"Fall in love. Travel. Get married. Have kids. I don't know, take your pick," I reply, watching her closely.

She looks deeply conflicted, and I hope it's because she's having doubts. About the Italian prick. Her feelings for me. All of the above. And I'm just out of my mind enough to want to encourage those doubts, against my recent determination to keep her at a distance, as a friend. But she hasn't been making that easy. As usual.

I set my glass down and slowly push myself to a standing position.

"Can't you restructure? Distribute the responsibility?" she suggests, warily watching me as I slowly advance on her.

"I suppose I could," I agree. "But like I said, I've been trying not to think about it. I've got enough on my mind right now." I stop inches from her, looking down into her face. It's all I can do to let the heat between us simmer, to see how she responds, to see if she asks for it again this time.

She's no longer casually leaning against the counter but is tensely gripping its edge with her hands. "I can imagine," she murmurs, looking up at me like she's hypnotized. Her lips part slightly and my gaze drops, watching them expand and contract slightly with her labored breathing. My mouth dips slightly toward hers like it has a mind of its own.

She straightens up and presses a hand on my chest. "We shouldn't," she says softly. But the desire in her eyes betrays her.

I slide my hands around her hips and pull her gently toward me. I run a hand lightly up her back. "That's not what you said last night," I murmur.

Her eyes widen in surprise, and I can't help giving her a devilish smirk as I lower my face to hers, the wide chasm of pain in my gut overriding my good sense and resolve. I can feel her melt into me as I reach for her lips with mine.

"Shit," a voice exclaims from the doorway. Glass shatters.

Startled, we jump apart, breaking the spell. I look over and Em is standing in the doorway, a broken tumbler of dark liquid at her feet. Sera rushes to grab towels to help clean up the mess.

Emily makes a hasty retreat once things are put to rights, and Sera glances nervously at me.

"We should probably get back to your mom," she says. And I know the moment has passed. I nod and follow her into the living room.

And I'm not sure if I'm more annoyed at myself for knowing better, or relieved that she seems as confused as I am.

WE SPEND TIME IN THE LIVING ROOM WITH THE REMAINING smattering of guests, Aunt Char surreptitiously continuing to feed mom.

As the wake winds down, I'm surprised to hear the doorbell ring again. Em leaves the room to answer it. But even I'm not prepared for who she returns with. Holding a bouquet of flowers, Madison Connolly stands before the assembly. All eyes turn to her, and not just because she's a late arrival.

Madison has always been stunning. The perfect five-and-a-half-foot-tall beauty queen that she is, her long blond hair perfectly styled, her bright blue eyes expertly outlined to stand out in her heart-shaped face, she wears a black minidress that can only be described as outrageously sexy. The halter cut pulls her small, firm breasts into pleasing cleavage, and the clingy fabric outlines her tiny waist and narrow hips.

She looks the same as she did a year ago when we painfully decided to end our relationship of three years. I'd only just managed to get over her when I met Sera. Or maybe because I met Sera. My heart thuds uncomfortably in my chest.

"Madison. What are you doing here?" I ask sharply. It's not much of a greeting, I know, but she wasn't exactly invited, and I'm completely thrown off.

"I saw the obituary in the paper today," she replies in her breathy, feminine voice. "I had to come pay my respects." She approaches my mother and offers the flowers. My mother accepts them, but almost immediately hands them off to Aunt Char. "I'm sorry for your loss."

"Thank you, Madison," my mom replies formally. "Do sit down."

Madison takes a seat beside me on the sofa opposite my mother. I shift toward Sera, almost unconsciously.

Madison takes clear note and leans forward, extending her hand to Sera.

"I'm Madison Connolly," she introduces herself.

Sera glances at me nervously and takes her hand. "Serafina Evans," she responds. While everyone else in the room has gone back to their conversations, my family is tensely watching the exchange between the two women. "How do you know the Hoyts?" Sera's tone is polite, but clearly as mystified as I am at Madison's sudden appearance.

"Bryce and I were together for years," Madison replies, dropping a hand on my knee. I'm too stunned to react. "I adored his father. I was so sad to hear the news."

"I see," Sera replies, eyeing Madison's hand as it subtly strokes my knee.

"And you?" Madison asks, eyeing Sera.

"I'm a friend of Bryce's," Sera replies hesitantly.

Em huffs quietly in her corner. I throw her a pleading look, but she avoids my gaze, clearly unwilling to interfere.

"How nice," Madison replies, then turns her attention back to me. "Bryce, darling, does this mean you'll be taking over the family business now?"

"I …" before I can even formulate a full response, Sera excuses herself and ducks into the kitchen. I try to go after her, but Madison squeezes my knee gently, drawing my attention back to her, looking at me expectantly for a response. "Yes, I already have actually."

She engages me sympathetically on how difficult that must be, and by the time there's a polite break in the conversation, Sera has rejoined the crowd in the living room, chatting with Em in the corner. So I continue to talk to Madison as the afternoon wears on, becoming more absorbed in the conversation.

And after a while, I actually find it a relief to talk to someone I've known for so long, who knows me. I don't have to explain my fears to Madison. She remembers them all and is a good listener. And while our breakup was devastating and necessary, I can tell she still cares for me. I'm not sure how I feel about her, but it's an unexpected comfort. It feels nice to just talk to a woman I'm not interested in.

It's nearly dinner time when Sera gently interrupts. I look around, surprised to see that besides us three only Aunt Char is still in the room.

"Can I talk to you for a sec?" she asks, eyeing Madison guardedly.

"Sure," I reply. "Please excuse me, Madison." Madison nods understandingly, and I step into the kitchen with Sera.

"Everything's all cleaned up. I'm going to head home," she says, fidgeting with her belt.

I realize I've been ignoring her for the better part of the afternoon, and I suddenly feel like a world-class ass.

"I'm so sorry, Sera. I hadn't seen Madison in so long, I just got absorbed in catching up with her. If you stay we can …"

"No," she interrupts. "Don't apologize. You looked happy talking to her. You should go back in there."

I'm silent as I try to figure out if she's sincere. Because I know I didn't misinterpret what almost happened in this very room earlier today.

"It's surprisingly nice to see her, but she's my past, Sera," I explain.

Sera contemplates me for a moment before responding. "There are things you need right now that I can't give you." The unspoken implication that Madison can give those things to me is simple but powerful.

"You've given me more than enough," I correct her. "Thank you. For being here for me. And my family. You're a good friend." I open my arms to her and let her come to me. I breathe a sigh of relief when she does. "It's going to be a crazy week, but I want to see you next weekend, okay?"

She nods into my chest. I kiss the top of her head.

"Walk me out?" she asks, pulling away from my chest and smiling up at me.

"Of course," I reply.

A few minutes later as I wave her off from the porch, Madison appears by my side.

"Do you love her?" Madison asks.

I turn and give her an impatient look. "What do you want, Madison?" I ask tiredly. I can't help but wonder why she reappeared now. Because I know it's not just to pay her respects to my father, whom she barely acknowledged when we were together.

"She loves you, you know," Madison asserts.

I glance over at her. Her expression is open and sympathetic.

"Not like that," I reply. I walk back into the house and Madison follows. Everyone else has gone, and it's only us in the foyer.

"You're wrong," she replies nonchalantly.

I shake my head and run a hand over my hair. "She's in love with someone else," I mumble.

"It's possible to be in love with two people at the same time. Besides, what could the other guy possibly have that you don't?" she asks coyly.

I smile wryly at her. "She was with him first," I reply.

"Was? She's not now?" Madison asks.

"It's complicated," I respond.

Madison rolls her eyes. "If they're not married, you still have a shot," she encourages me.

"It doesn't matter anymore," I say with a note of finality. I'm over talking about this with the woman who wouldn't commit to marrying me. "What are you doing here?"

"I thought you might need a friend," she says suggestively. I eye her speculatively. "You look good, Bryce. A little too good, considering."

"Don't be fooled. I'm a fucking mess," I reply angrily.

Madison steps closer. Close enough that the smell of her perfume wraps around me. She runs a finger down my chest. "Need a distraction?" she asks softly, peering up at me from under her eyelashes.

I look down at her stoically, unsure of how to respond. She takes the opportunity to unhook the fabric behind her neck. And with a shimmy, her dress falls to the floor, revealing her naked body underneath.

Despite myself, I feel my cock harden as I take in her lithe form. "Goddammit, Madison, my mother could come downstairs any minute." She always was an exhibitionist.

"Then you'd better take me to your bedroom," she whispers invitingly.

My chest aches, my heart unable to expand enough to contain all the emotions I've felt this week. I close my eyes to block it all out. Madison takes the opportunity to lift my hand to her breast. My eyes fly open in surprise as she strokes her pink nipple with my thumb and moans softly.

My control slips and my baser needs take over.

"Fuck." I grab her dress from the floor and shove it in her arms, lifting her by the waist.

She wraps her legs around me as her lips find mine and I stride purposefully down the hall. Our tongues wrestle in a practiced dance as I close the door behind us and drop her onto the bed.

All the angst, all the tension coils like a spring inside me as I relieve myself of my clothes and pounce on the naked beauty in front of me. Sensing my acute need, Madison opens her legs to me, guiding me into her. It's been so long and the sensation is so overwhelming that it takes all of my strength to adjust to the tight, wet grip of her around me.

She lifts my head in her hands and stares into my eyes. "Stay with me, big boy," she breathes.

I nod and bury my face in her hair once more, moving slowly and deliberately. There was a time that I enjoyed nothing more than looking into her eyes as we fucked, watching every look of pleasure pass over her face, but now, after everything, I just need to imagine she's someone else.

But even that is too much, and I'm overwhelmed with emotion and sensation. I pull back, needing to regroup. Before she can question me, I drop between her legs. If I can't keep my shit together, I can at least pleasure her until I can.

I spread her wide open, and run a finger down her

seam, parting her for my mouth. I gently flick with my tongue, and she tightens under the assault, writhing and moaning. With a smirk, I slide a finger deep in her, causing her to arch off the bed. It pleases me to watch — I've always enjoyed the controlled response of this act. As I work my tongue over her with increasing intensity, I add another finger, curling them toward me inside her. Her hips buck off the bed and I suck her sensitive flesh into my mouth to keep locked onto her.

Her moans escalate, and I unlatch my mouth, sliding my teeth gently over her most sensitive part as I pull away.

"Shhhh," I admonish her. "They'll hear you."

She nods and bites her lip hard, her fingers gripping the sheets, so I renew my assault in full force, pumping and curling my fingers furiously as I suck her back in with my lips, flicking my tongue rapidly. A stream of curse words whispers through her teeth as she tightens around my hand and finishes as quietly as she can.

I relent, using the moisture on my hand to stroke myself as I climb back onto the bed between her legs. Feeling more in control, I lift her to me and slide in slowly. She's still tight from her climax, and I focus on keeping it together. When she's expanded to accommodate me, I hold her legs astride my chest and pump slowly, fully in, fully out, and over again.

I close my eyes, surrendering to the sensation. Her hips rise to meet me as I increase my pace. I feel her fingertips graze my cock as she works her clit to our rhythm. I rest one of her legs against me and reach a hand down to grasp the tip of her breast. She arches into my touch and my hips as all her most sensitive spots are stimulated simultaneously.

I lean forward into her, deepening my assault, increasing the pounding to a frenzy, our hips slamming into each other. She's controlling her moans like a good girl, and the only noise in the room is our labored breathing and the arousing sound of skin slapping on skin.

Her breathing accelerates again, and she whimpers, and I know she's close. Falling on her completely, I rock myself into her madly, the tension coiling in a crescendo. It's not long before we both shatter under the pleasure. I let out the low groan I've been holding back as the last hot lick of gratification ripples through me and come to a rest, quivering over her small frame, her legs wrapped tightly around me.

My face buried in the bed beside her head, I relish the feeling of release and the sticky, sweaty, realness of our entwined bodies. And I realize it's probably for the best that Sera and I didn't end up here. I wasn't lying to Madison. I'm a fucking mess. And I needed this, even though I didn't realize how much. But I think Sera might have. And while part of her might have wanted to give it to me, it's just better for everyone if we didn't go there. Because, at the end of the day, I feel like I just don't have anything real to give right now.

Madison pushes a small hand against my sweaty shoulder, bringing me back to myself, and I roll off her obligingly. We lay quietly as our breathing returns to normal. I'm not sure what to say, or what she expects.

"Thanks," I finally say, awkwardly. She gives me an incredulous look and bursts out laughing. And to my immense surprise, I join in until tears are leaking out of my eyes.

When the fit of laughter has passed, she rolls onto her side to face me. I put an arm under my neck to prop my head up, so I can meet her gaze.

"You're welcome," she replies. She traces a finger down the center of my chest. "You really do look amazing. Why'd you wait until we'd broken up to get this ripped?" I give her a disbelieving smirk.

"I've always been this ripped. I just padded it over with a solid layer of burgers and beers," I respond drolly.

She groans. "Men. I swear. You cut out a few burgers, eat a few vegetables and you get the V," she says, running her fingertips along my hip.

I shrug nonchalantly. "If I knew that's what did it for you, I would've cut them out a long time ago," I tease. It was a joke, but suddenly I realize it sounded way more serious than I meant it.

Thankfully, she doesn't seem to take it all that seriously. She simply shrugs back and smiles. "I don't know a woman alive who could resist this," she replies, running her palm over my six-pack.

It feels nice, but I'm so spent it gets zero reaction. "I know one," I murmur.

Madison raises an eyebrow. "Has she seen it?" she asks disbelievingly.

I chuckle. "This morning, actually, after I showered," I reply.

"Well, make sure she sees it a few more times, and I promise it'll work its magic," she says confidently.

"Heh. Well, I'm not above fighting dirty these days," I admit, "but I'm not exactly in a magical place right now."

Madison gives me an appraising look. "Are you sure about that?" she asks shrewdly. I sit up and pull my pants back on.

"I don't really want to talk about it," I deflect. Madison shrugs and rises from the bed, slipping into her dress.

"Suit yourself. It was good seeing you, Bryce."

I eye her speculatively as she heads to the door. "That's it?" I ask skeptically. She flips her hair over her shoulder and smiles at me as she opens the door.

"That's it," she replies. And with that, she's gone. And I'm alone with my grief once again.

FOURTEEN

I t's not until lunchtime on Monday that I realize I'd forgotten to call Allie back. But calling her only dumps me into her voicemail. I hang up without leaving a message, making a note so I remember to try again after work. And then I return to the same fog I've been in since I left the Hoyts' house yesterday.

For what feels like the millionth time, the mental image of Bryce in that towel distracts me from everything but breathing. And even that is difficult. The smooth curve of his massive pecs flowing into the tight muscles of his abs and the defined, dark trail of hair leading down the perfectly taut plane of his lower abdomen were so head-spinningly distracting that I still don't know how I managed to look him in the face for the rest of the day.

Knowing he was built was one thing. Seeing it was another.

Almost as distracting is remembering Funeral Barbie showing up and capturing Bryce's attention for the bulk of the day. On top of her being exactly the kind of woman I imagined he'd be interested in, it was more disturbing to watch him pour his heart out to her for hours while I took care of, well, pretty much everything. It just reinforced the feeling his unnerving silence had given me all week — that he's not interested in being anything more than friends. Despite our almost-kisses. And even those, I know, were likely just borne of the confusion of the grieving process.

But I'm carefully refusing to acknowledge the hot boil of jealousy in my gut and the implications of it. Because I know torturing myself wondering whether Bryce grief-fucked Madison isn't going to help anything, so I bury myself back in work.

⁓

THE REST OF THE DAY PASSES MORE SLOWLY THAN I EVER thought possible, but I battle my way through. Finally home, I sink gratefully into my favorite chair and call Allie.

"Hello?" she answers.

I'm beyond relieved to hear her voice. "Allie, I'm

sorry," I breathe. "I had a rough weekend. I meant to call you back yesterday and I completely spaced. I'm so, so, so sorry."

The line is silent for so long that I'm starting to think she's not there anymore when she finally responds. "It's fine." Her words are tight, and its obvious she doesn't really mean them.

"It's not fine," I admit. "You've been going through so much, and I haven't checked in in a week. I feel just awful."

A heavy sigh issues across the line. "You should."

I can't help but chuckle. "You're right. What can I do? Bring you chocolate? Booze? Do you need to shop? Mani-pedi?"

"Yes, to all of those. Eventually. I'm still working on things."

"Tell me about it," I prompt.

Reluctantly, Allie explains her therapy and the side effects of the antidepressants they've put her on, and that she's still struggling with the basics — eating, showering, talking. But the more she talks, the lighter her voice sounds. It's difficult, but I simply listen. At so many points I want to interject, reassure her, or even be there with her to hug her. But having been through depression myself, I hang back, allowing her to set the pace and level of conversation.

I don't mention Daniel, Alessandro, or Bryce, or my

mixed-up feelings. But when she's done, I do ask her when I can see her again. We make a lunch date for Sunday, and I hang up, near tears. I can't decide if they are happy tears for my recovering best friend, or simply tears from all the emotions that have raged in me lately. In either case, I take care of a few things and retire early, exhausted in every way possible.

On Tuesday, I stop by the grocery store on my way home. In the bread aisle I spot a familiar set of long, black braids. As I approach, I realize it is, in fact, Heather Irving. My project manager who abruptly quit under dubious circumstances.

"Heather?" I place myself a respectable distance away so as not to startle her.

She looks up from reading a cracker box in surprise. "Ms. Evans," she replies. "How are you?"

"Heather, you don't work for me anymore, call me Sera, please," I insist. "I'm okay. We've missed you. How are you doing?"

She puts the cracker box back on the shelf and chews on her lip. "Making do," she replies. "I got a job at a broker's office in Fremont. It's not the same, but it's okay."

"Well, I'm glad to hear you were able to find something so soon," I respond. "Maybe put in a good word for me." I meant it as a joke, but her eyes widen seriously. "I'm kidding. It's just a little more difficult at the new office than I thought it would be."

"It's not …" she trails off, looking like she wants to say something. I prompt her with silence and open body language. "It's not Daniel, is it?" She practically whispers the question.

My heart drops. "Well, yes, actually," I admit. "He's …" I pause, searching for the word until I notice the tears in Heather's eyes. "Maybe you know what he is."

Heather glances around nervously, licks her lips and nods. My throat constricts, and I try to think of a way to get Heather alone without scaring her in hopes of getting the full story.

Taking a gamble, I step toward her and lean in a little, so I can speak quietly.

"Why don't we get some sandwiches and go sit in Pioneer Square and talk about it," I suggest. Heather looks terrified and unsure. "Please, Heather. If he's treated anyone else like this, I need to know."

"Okay," she says, barely above a whisper.

I step back and nod, leading her out into the warm evening air.

∽

A SHORT WHILE LATER, WE'VE MANAGED TO SNAG A BENCH with our food, and I'm quietly munching while Heather's food sits beside her, untouched. I let the silence prompt her once more, and I'm not disappointed.

"The afternoon of the day before I quit, Daniel invited me into his office," she starts, picking at a piece of shredded lettuce. "We'd flirted a little during the move, and he said he wanted to get to know me better. To see how my skill set might be used more widely in the company." She pauses, twirling a braid absentmindedly as she sips her soda. "We talked shop for a while, and then he got up and closed the door. It made me a little nervous, but he sat back down, and we talked about our personal lives for a bit, so I relaxed, figuring he thought it was a conversation best had privately. We were talking about books we'd read recently, and he asked if I'd ever read those popular ones — the ones with BDSM." She blushes furiously, and I drop my food, my stomach already roiling at what I suspect is to come.

"What did you say?" I manage to choke out.

"I told him I had," she admits. "He asked if I enjoyed them. I told him I liked the idea that love could give you the strength to change who you are. But the other stuff is not really my scene."

"He was disappointed," I guess.

She throws me an uncharacteristically sharp look. "He was angry," she corrects me. "All of a sudden. Like he was a different person. He got in my face and demanded that I admit that I was just …" she chokes on the words and tears well in her eyes again, "a dirty little whore that needed to be punished."

"Oh, Heather," I gasp, grabbing her hand and squeezing.

She squeezes back and wipes the tears away with her other hand, and signals that she wants to continue.

"I tried to push him away, but he hit me. Told me to shut up. That if anyone heard me, he'd destroy me." Her voice is barely above a whisper as she angrily wipes tears from her eyes. I dig a tissue out of my bag and hand it to her, giving her a moment to collect herself. "It was late by then, and I was pretty sure everyone had gone home. I told him I wasn't going to fight him. To just do what he wanted. I just wanted to get it over with. To get out of there. I didn't know what else to do. It was my fault. I should have said no. I should have fought."

The fury that unfurls in me at her words is like nothing I've ever felt before. And it takes every ounce of my not inconsiderable self-control to say my next words in a measured enough tone not to scare Heather, not to make her feel as if my anger is in any way directed at her.

"It was *not* your fault," I hiss. I want to grab her face and make her look at me. "Heather." Her eyes slowly slide to mine. "It was not. Your. Fault."

She shakes her head. "I shouldn't have gone in there

alone, and I …" I close my eyes and hold up a hand for her to stop, reining in my rage again. I take a deep breath and open my eyes.

"He told you it was your fault, didn't he?" I seethe.

She nods miserably. "He said I wouldn't have come into his office if I didn't want it. And if I told anyone what happened they'd never believe me anyway. And if I did that he'd make sure everyone knew what a slut I was. That they'd never believe he did anything wrong. It was my word against his."

"You should know that he said similar things to me. But our conversation happened in the middle of the day, and I was lucky enough to get out before he could touch me," I say. My admission sends Heather over the edge, and she starts sobbing uncontrollably. I offer my arms to her and she collapses against me gratefully. I run my hand over her hair, murmuring to her over and over, "It's not your fault."

Eventually her sobs subside, and she uses the last of my tissues to wipe away her tears.

"Thank you for telling me all this, Heather," I tell her. There's an ache in my chest that's suddenly grown exponentially. I can't even begin to imagine how she must feel. And why so many bad things are happening to the people I care about.

"I'm sorry I didn't tell you before. I could've stopped him from …" she starts, until I shush her.

"It doesn't matter. What matters is what we do next. Can I tell you what I think we should do?" I ask carefully. Heather nods meekly. "Good. I want to take you to the police station. Right now. I think you should report this."

Heather looks terrified. "But when he finds out he'll come after me," she whispers.

I shake my head vehemently. "I will *not* let that bastard hurt you again," I promise her. "If it's okay with you, I'm going to call a friend and ask him to come with us. Do you remember Bryce Hoyt?"

Heather nods. "Your security consultant," she says.

"That's him. He's got friends at the police department. I'd like to ask for his help, if that's okay with you," I reply.

Heather stares into the distance for a bit, sniffing loudly.

"Okay," she finally agrees.

I let out a sigh of relief and pull out my phone. Bryce answers immediately.

"Hey, Sera, what's up?" he asks curtly.

"Hey," I reply, steadying my voice. "I need you to meet me at the police station. How soon can you do that?" I can almost hear the deadly calm on the other end of the line.

"Give me fifteen minutes," he replies. "Are you okay?"

"I'm fine," I promise. "I'll explain when I see you."

He hangs up before I can say goodbye, but I'm not offended, only thankful he's understood the urgency.

I offer a hand to Heather as I rise. "I'm going to be with you as long as you need me," I promise.

She takes my hand and rises. "Let's go."

HEATHER AND I AREN'T WAITING AT THE POLICE STATION long when Bryce strides through the doors, obviously straight from work, in tailored black pants and a black short-sleeved button-front shirt, a gun holstered under his left arm and looking admittedly rather angry and terrifying. Heather shrinks into me a little, and I give Bryce a wary look. His body language immediately softens, sensing the fear of the quaking girl half-hidden behind me.

"Thanks for coming," I greet him, gripping Heather's hand. "This is Heather Irving. She used to work for me. And she needs our help."

"Hi, Heather," he says in a soft voice. "I don't know what happened, but I'll do whatever I can, okay?"

Heather slinks out from behind me and nods. "Thank you," she whispers.

"Who do we need to see?" he asks me.

"Do they have a special officer who deals with sexual assault?" I ask carefully.

Bryce's mouth hardens into a thin line. "They do," he

responds tightly. He leads us to the information desk and he checks in with the officer on duty. The officer retreats down a long hall and Bryce turns back to us. "It'll just be a minute."

As promised, little time passes and a slender Latina officer emerges with the desk officer. She approaches us.

"Natalie," Bryce greets her. She nods in acknowledgement. "Heather, this is Officer Natalie Ramirez. She's going to take your statement. Do you want Sera or I to come with you?"

Officer Ramirez gives Heather a warm smile. Heather glances sidelong at me. "I'd like to go by myself, please," she replies, just above a whisper.

I give her hand one last squeeze and let her go. "We'll be right here waiting, okay?" I assure her.

She nods and lets Officer Ramirez lead her away. And I'm left wondering what she left out of her story that she didn't want me hearing when she gave her statement.

As soon as I'm sure she's gone, I collapse into the reception room chair behind me, burying my face in my hands. Bryce sits next to me and rubs my back soothingly for a minute while I collect myself.

"Heather quit a month ago. Right after we moved to Sutton Developments. Wouldn't say why," I explain.

"Let me guess. Daniel Sutton?" he asks. I shoot Bryce a shocked look. He shakes his head and leans back in his chair. "You told me he threatened you. You must have known I'd investigate the guy."

I understand the implication immediately. "He's done this before?" I ask incredulously. I'm so shocked that my voice is barely audible.

"He's been accused of sexual harassment before, yes," Bryce admits. "But the case was ultimately dropped. If you think for one second that I'd let you keep working with someone who was convicted of sexual misconduct, you obviously don't know me very well."

I'm so overwhelmed, I don't even bother scolding him for thinking he could "let" me do anything.

"I need to share something with Officer Ramirez when they're done," I say.

Bryce is so silent I have to glance up at him to see if he's heard me. And when I do I can tell he absolutely has. His gorgeous face is contorted into an unrecognizable mask of cold fury.

"Explain, please," he hisses.

"He didn't touch me," I assure him, resting my hand on his arm. "The things he said to Heather were very similar to things he said to me. Threats he made. If it could help them establish a pattern or lend weight to her story, I want to go on record."

Bryce's hand clamps over mine, almost to the point of pain. "Tell me what he said," he demands.

I'm torn. If I tell him, I know he'll be furious. Both at

what Daniel said and for my downplaying it in the first place. But if I go on record, he'll probably find out anyway.

"He told me to stay out of his way or I'd regret it. And then he said if I told anyone he threatened me, he'd tell them I came on to him and he rejected me, so it's just sour grapes. And then it would be my word against his," I pause, trying to remember what other venom he'd spewed to make me slap him. "And he knew about me and Alessandro. He said everyone knew that we were fucking, so nobody would believe I wasn't trying to fuck him too. I slapped him for that."

Bryce gives a small laugh. "That's my girl," he murmurs.

Heat flushes my cheeks, and I try to ignore it. "He promised to ruin me. And to beat me if I told on him," I conclude.

Bryce runs a hand over his hair, but his fury has abated, and he's not reacting as poorly as I thought he would. "We'll get Heather somewhere safe until they're able to press charges," Bryce assures me. "If Heather's story has those same elements, along with your statement and the original charges, I think they'll have what they need."

I consider that for a moment. "What if Heather doesn't want to press charges? What if Daniel won't admit to anything? It's been a month, I'm sure there's no physical evidence left," I protest.

"The state will probably do it anyway. Anyone who sees how scared that girl is will know the truth," he points out.

I find a small relief in that, until something else occurs to me. "What about me, Bryce? Is it safe for me to go back to work tomorrow? I'm not even sure I can, knowing what I know," I say, shuddering.

"He won't have any idea you're involved," Bryce replies. "But I, for one, am not really thrilled about the prospect of you being near that guy. Though I don't think you're in any immediate danger. And I'm always a phone call away."

I look at Bryce as the truth of his words sink deep into me. Bryce *is* always a phone call away. Even when we weren't talking, I think I knew that. That he'd always be there for me. We've been through so much together, it's hard to imagine it any other way now. It pains me in a way I can't quite name, until it clicks. *If only I could say the same for Alessandro.*

Bryce's eyebrows shoot up, and I realize I must have actually said the words. I can feel my face flush again. "I didn't mean to say that out loud."

"He's not answering your calls?" Bryce asks resignedly.

I shake my head. "I don't even have a phone number

for him. I tried to email him, but he didn't respond. I thought about trying to find him," I admit.

"As in, going to Italy?" he asks. I nod, embarrassed by how stupid it must sound to him. "I don't think that's a good idea."

"Me, neither," I sigh. "But it's been a month and I'm beyond worried. I know it would be pointless at best, dangerous at worst. But what else am I supposed to do? Maybe it'd be a good excuse to take off work, so I don't have to deal with Daniel."

Bryce runs a hand jerkily over his hair. "I'll make a call," he finally says. "I'll see if I can get a bead on him." The sorrow and gratitude that washes over me causes a lump to form in my throat. Sorrow for putting Bryce through this. Gratitude for answers. Or the hope of answers. Finally.

"Thank you," I breathe. "I feel like I've been hanging over a precipice this whole time."

He gives me a look that tells me it explains a lot. "You're welcome," he replies. "Besides, you don't want to leave in case Heather needs you. And you might want to clue Charles Sutton in on what his son has been getting into."

I realize he's right. And I wonder whether Charles will be surprised. There's only one way to find out.

FIFTEEN

I insist on seeing Charles first thing on Wednesday morning. Perplexed, he cancels a call and sees me into his office, shutting the door behind us. I have a brief moment of pause at the act but am almost immediately embarrassed at the thought. Charles has been nothing but good to me. It's Daniel who's the monster.

"What can I do for you this morning?" Charles opens, looking at me kindly and with concern from behind his desk. His large hands are folded loosely over his dark grey suit jacket in a gesture of complete comfort and trust.

I feel bad for the hell I'm about to unleash. "I need to tell you something," I start. "And it needs to be kept in complete confidence."

Charles frowns and leans forward. "I would hope by now you know you can trust me," he says sternly.

"I do, but this is different. I considered asking someone from HR to join us as well, but I wanted to give you this news first," I explain.

His eyebrows shoot up. "You have my word," he agrees solemnly.

I take a deep breath and prepare to just say it. Like me, I know Charles isn't one for suspense or beating around the bush. "Do you remember the young woman who used to work for me who quit right after we moved?" Charles nods, acknowledging that he recalls. "Last night she filed sexual assault charges against Daniel. It's the reason she quit."

Whatever he was expecting, it clearly wasn't that.

"She claims my son sexually assaulted her?" He is incredulous.

"He groomed her, after a fashion. Then raped her in his office. Then threatened her."

Charles steeples his fingers under his nose, shaking his head and clearly deeply troubled. "And I take it that you believe her?" he asks.

"Without a doubt," I reply emphatically. "He made similar threats to me."

Charles looks up, very surprised now. "And what exactly is it that you would like me to do, Sera?" he asks, stone-faced.

"I ..." I stutter and stop. I'm at a loss. It's almost a nonresponse, though I'm not sure what I expected. "I just thought you should know. The police will likely be questioning him shortly. And I intend to go to HR after this to provide them with the same information. But I wanted to tell you first."

Charles leans back in his chair, grim faced. "If you had come to me right away, I would have told you to do exactly that. This is not the first time something like this has happened. But the other times there were always questions. Uncertainties. And it was nothing quite as serious as this."

I don't miss that he said *times*. As in more than once. But that's not my biggest issue with his response.

"You won't take the word of my employee that he raped her, but you'll trust mine that he threatened me?" I ask heatedly. I don't know if I should be flattered or disgusted, but I'm leaning heavily toward the latter.

"I didn't mean that at all," he responds. "This young woman's allegation is an escalation from past events. And a very serious one. But since I don't know her at all, yes, your experience and assessment of the situation lends a great deal of weight to her claim. But I would have believed your story with or without hers." Charles pauses for a moment, looking seriously conflicted about whatever he plans to say next.

"I didn't intend to put you in a position to explain or defend his actions," I offer. "And, ultimately, the police will take it from here. There is truly nothing more you need to say."

Charles dips his head in acknowledgement. "Nonetheless, I want you to know that I love my son. But as his father, I am aware of his shortcomings. Perhaps more acutely than anyone. Part of what has made him so successful is his aggressive tendencies. But throughout his life that same quality has also gotten him into a great deal of trouble. It is up to him to deal with the consequences of his actions and choices. I think he has known and resented that I have no tolerance for his inadequacies for some time. So I believe it will come as no surprise to him when I make no move to shield him from whatever is to come."

"Meaning?" I press.

"I have long since decided that Daniel will not be my successor," Charles replies matter-of-factly. "It's in large part why I decided to take you on. I see that potential in you. I haven't openly shared that decision with anyone until now. And I trust that you will keep *that* in confidence." He looks at me pointedly over his steepled fingertips.

"Yes, sir," I agree. I had suspected something along those lines, but nothing of the magnitude to which he just admitted.

Bryce was right: Charles has been grooming me to take over his empire. And I'm sure even though he didn't know for sure, Daniel sensed the threat. His actions toward me certainly speak to that.

"Thank you," Charles replies softly. "Then, if we're done here, I believe you have something to discuss with Mrs. Harris in human resources. I'd prefer that she was prepared before law enforcement arrives."

I nod, rising. "I appreciate your response to all of this. Truly," I tell him sincerely.

Charles smiles pensively, and I turn and leave before my emotions get the better of me.

∽

BY LUNCHTIME DANIEL HAS BEEN SUSPENDED PENDING internal investigation and sent home. It's an obvious move to get him out of the building so nobody sees the cops bringing him in for questioning. But, through Bryce, I know that that's exactly what happens on Wednesday afternoon. Thankfully, Heather was also able to relocate to stay with family for her safety, and Officer Ramirez and Bryce helped her get a restraining order started for added protection. It leaves me nervous and wondering where my added protection is.

I know I can call Bryce if I need to, but between helping me with Heather and managing the transition to full responsibility for Hoyt Corporate Services, not to mention still mourning the loss of his father, I can hear in his voice how stretched thin he is. So I swallow my fears, pretend everything is fine, and return to work on Thursday like nothing has happened.

But the atmosphere at work is no better than before Daniel was suspended. The flurry of office gossip is all off-mark, as the only three people still at the company who know the true story — Charles, Brooklyn Harris, and myself — sure as hell aren't going to share what's really going on. To evade conversation about it, I must isolate myself all day, and by quitting time I'm ready for some hard alcohol from the strain of it all.

But with Allie out of commission, Bryce overtaxed, and Alessandro still far away and unreachable, I can't think of anyone to call. And drinking alone just seems too sad. I'm scrolling through my address book when I'm reminded that Emily had programmed her number in at the wake and told me to call her sometime to get together. And it actually seems like a pretty perfect solution.

∾

"I'm so glad you were available," I say to Emily, sipping my margarita.

She smiles fondly at me from across the table. "I'm glad you called," she admits. "I was going to check on you soon anyway."

"That seems a little backward. I should be the one checking on you, considering," I reply.

Emily shrugs. "Thanks, but I'll be all right," she assures me. I give her a disbelieving look. "Really. I think at some point it might hit me hard, but I'm strangely okay right now."

"Well, that's good?" I hazard. She chuckles. "So what made you think you needed to check in on me?"

Emily gives me a pointed look. "Oh, you know, the short, blond bitch who stomped all over my brother's heart back to torture him by scaring off the best thing that's ever happened to him?" she replies glibly.

As someone who doesn't usually embarrass easily, I find myself blushing an awful lot these days. And I wonder how much Emily knows about the complicated situation with Alessandro, Bryce, and me. And how much she has guessed about my feelings for her brother. But mostly I can't even process her referring to me as the best thing that's ever happened to Bryce. Because how things have unfolded between us has been one of the most challenging situations of my life. And that's saying something.

"Bryce can take care of himself," I mumble. "And I'm going to need empirical proof that I've done anything but take advantage of his giving nature."

"Well, I'll give him that now," Emily admits. "But he used to be a huge doormat. Especially where Madison was concerned. Lately, though, not so much. Not even for you.

But meeting you brought him out of the epic funk he was in for months. He was back to his normal, chipper self for a while there."

"And now he's not, also thanks to me," I sigh. I take a big gulp of my drink and find Emily looking sympathetically at me. "But I'm kind of relieved to hear his mood swings are an established pattern. I thought I broke him."

Emily laughs loudly. "Oh, honey, no," she chortles. "I think he's finally exactly where he needs to be."

"You think? It's not too much? His taking over your dad's company? He's still so young," I respond, concerned.

"He'll manage," she assures me. "I meant he's finally in the right headspace. Neither doormat nor asshole. I know you guys weren't talking for a while, but when he went full asshole on you it took him a couple weeks to realize what a jerk he was being. To everyone, by the way, not just you."

"Yeesh. I'm so sorry for unleashing that," I reply, cringing.

She waves a hand dismissively. "In case you hadn't figured it out, that was *not* your fault. A lot of things pushed him to that point. But he needed to get there, and then get through it. And he'll get through this too, but I'm finally seeing signs that he's on the right path," she says.

"Good. I want him to be happy," I respond. I stare down into my drink, blinking back tears.

"You make him happy," she informs me gently. I snort derisively. "Think what you want. But why else can't he stay away from you?"

"I don't think he wants that kind of relationship with me anymore," I reply. Voicing it, I realize that I feel disappointed. "But it's better that way. Things are complicated for me right now too."

Emily cocks her head to the side. "Tell me about it," she replies, taking a sip of her Long Island iced tea.

So I do. We talk for hours, and it feels good to get it all off my chest. And through it I manage to learn a bit about her too. When I head home around ten, while it may be my decently drunk state, I feel lighter. And like I have a new friend.

I WAKE, STILL MILDLY BUZZED, IN THE DEEPEST DARK OF night to a cacophony of sound. I have trouble functioning for a moment, unsure of what hell has broken loose in my condo. When I finally come to enough to connect that my security system is alerting me of an intruder, I bolt upright in bed, instantly terrified. I reach under the bed for the baseball bat I keep there and clutch its grip tightly with both hands as I slither out from under the covers.

My eyes flit to the nightstand and note the absence of my phone. *Shit.* I left it on the kitchen counter when I got home last night, tipsy as I was. The closest security panel is in the hall at the top of the stairs. It will tell me where the breach was. But the alarm also automatically alerts building security and the police, so after a moment of frantic thought I opt to stay where I am.

Crouched behind the bed with my back to the wall, my brain chaotically races through the possibilities. But the only viable explanation I can dredge up is Daniel. My heart hammers loudly in my chest as the minutes crawl by and the alarm continues to blare. But nothing else.

Finally, the alarm stops, and I hear feet pounding up the stairs.

A voice shouts from the hallway. "Ms. Evans, building security!"

I chew my lip for a moment. If they managed to turn off the alarm, they must be legitimate, I reason. I creep to the door and peek out. The man is indeed wearing the building's security officer uniform, and his gun is drawn and pointed at the floor. I open the door wider.

"I'm here," I call. "Is it safe?"

His head swings toward me and he holsters his gun. "Yes, ma'am," he affirms.

I step out of the bedroom, still clinging to the bat. His eyes drop to it and he instinctively rests a hand on his gun. I quickly drop the bat to my feet. A uniformed police officer appears at the top of the stairs.

"Downstairs is clear," he relays to the security guard.

He notices me in my oversized shirt. "Ma'am, if you'd like to get dressed and come downstairs, we can talk."

I nod meekly and duck back into my room to change as the security guard checks the other bedrooms.

When I descend the stairs a few minutes later, the two men are standing in the entryway talking. I approach carefully, waiting for a break in their conversation, but they stop talking when the security guard notices me.

"Ms. Evans, I'm Security Officer Bridges. I'm sorry to inform you that someone did break in through your front door tonight. We still aren't sure how they escaped, but we're checking the security footage now," he assures me.

"Were they gone when you got here?" I ask, wrapping my grey shawl tightly around me.

"Affirmative," Officer Bridges replies. "You will need to meet with our security chief tomorrow to review the situation."

I nod in understanding. With the adrenaline finally wearing off, fear starts to settle in. And I'm putting all my effort into controlling the shaking that is starting to rip through my body.

"Ma'am, your door will need to be replaced," the police officer notes. "It's probably best if you stay somewhere else tonight, or until you can get it fixed. Is there anyone you can stay with? Or can we escort you to a hotel?"

"She can stay with me," a deep voice says from the door.

I whirl around to see Bryce towering in the doorway, in sweats and a T-shirt, looking like he just fought a bear. He's out of breath, with a crazed look in his eye, and his hair and clothes are disheveled. The second he lays eyes on me, he strides into the room and pulls me into his arms. I gratefully embrace him, burying my face in his broad chest, inhaling his familiar, comforting scent.

Bryce extends a hand to the police officer, and it's clear that they know each other. "Jack," he says to the man. "Good to see you."

Officer Jack shakes Bryce's hand. "You too, Bryce." Officer Jack looks at me. "Looks like you're in good hands."

I nod gratefully. "Thank you for your help, officer," I reply.

"We'll be in touch tomorrow," Security Officer Bridges assures me. "I'm terribly sorry about this, ma'am."

"Thank you," I respond. "It could have ended much worse if it wasn't for you."

He gives me a small smile. "Just doing my job." He looks up at Bryce. "Take care of her."

Bryce squeezes me tighter. "I will. Thank you," Bryce responds.

The officers leave, closing the door. And I can see the

broken frame and lock rendering it useless. I bury my face back in Bryce's chest and choke back a sob. He rubs my back gently.

"You have no idea how relieved I am that you're okay," he murmurs into my hair. I look up into his face. He looks exhausted and scared, and it pushes me closer to falling apart to see him upset.

"How did you even know?" I ask, confused. He strokes my cheek with his thumb and smiles.

"The alarm company notified me when you didn't respond. I'm still listed as your emergency contact," he explains.

"Well, thank god for that," I reply.

As his expression softens and my immediate terror recedes, I become painfully aware that we're still locked in a tight embrace, staring ardently into each other's eyes. And that I'm still tipsy enough that I don't have full control over my thoughts. And they're definitely headed down a path that ends in rejection. I make to push away from Bryce and he frowns, pulling me closer and dropping his face closer to mine, inhaling deeply.

"Have you been drinking?" he asks.

"What time is it?" I respond. He gives me a funny look.

"Almost two a.m."

"Not today, I haven't." I smile innocently up at him. "I take it you haven't talked to your sister recently."

Now he really looks confused. "Not since yesterday afternoon. What does that have to do with anything?"

I smile cryptically in response. Something tells me he wouldn't appreciate our talking about him.

"I'm going to go pack a few things," I say, dodging the question. "I'll be right back."

I make a quick exit before he can press any further. And once I'm upstairs I chug the water next to my bed. Time to finish sobering up fast. I don't want to push this night from awful to the worst night of my life by following up a breaking-and-entering situation with drunkenly pursuing and being rejected by a man who is likely back with his ridiculously gorgeous ex-girlfriend.

I sigh heavily as I stuff clothes into a bag. When Bryce appeared and put me under his protection, I was so relieved. But as the reality of the situation sets in, I realize how awkward this is going to be. Because just as I'm sure he's fallen out of love with me, I think I may be doing exactly the opposite.

SIXTEEN

I put on my game face as I descend the stairs, my small pack slung over one shoulder. I find Bryce crouched, examining the door. He runs a finger over the doorjamb and shakes his head.

"This is pretty amateur stuff," he mumbles. "Looks like they just used a crowbar to open it."

"So much for high-tech security," I grumble.

He stands, wiping his hands on his sweatpants. "Hey, that high-tech security saved your ass," he reminds me. He looks me up and down and gently tugs the pack off my shoulder. "Come on, let's get you back to bed." He tucks me under his arm and together we make our way to his place.

I'm quiet the whole way, half trying to make my tired brain absorb the events of the evening, half trying to stay awake. But when we get to Bryce's place, I fail epically at the latter. The last thing I remember is slumping against Bryce in the hallway before everything goes dark.

∾

I'M WOKEN AROUND SEVEN BY BRYCE'S WEIGHT SETTLING onto the bed. I open one eye slowly, blinking against the daylight.

"Good morning, sunshine," he teases me. "I have to go in a minute."

He's still dressing in all black and looks about as rested as I feel. In other words, hardly at all. I instantly feel horrible for adding to his already full plate.

I sit up groggily and take in my surroundings. It's clearly a guest bedroom and, thankfully, I appear to still be fully dressed in my leggings and shawl, with just my shoes removed and set on the floor beside the bed.

I look back to Bryce, who is regarding me tolerantly as I regain functionality.

"Thanks for letting me stay," I say. "I'll get out of your hair as soon as I can."

He smiles dimly. "Stay as long as you'd like," he assures me. "There's coffee in the kitchen. Just lock up on your way out."

I nod in understanding, biting back all the things I really want to say to him as the reality of what almost happened hit me. And how sharply it's thrown into contrast what's important to me. Who is important. But Bryce rises from the bed before I can even put it all to words.

"Bryce?" I call after him.

He stops in the doorway and looks back at me questioningly. I scramble off the bed and hurry to wrap my arms around him before he leaves. I try to throw all my unspeakable emotions into the gesture, not trusting myself to give a proper voice to them now. He hesitates before squeezing me back, and I let go more quickly than I'd planned, suddenly very self-conscious.

"See ya, Sera."

"See ya, Bryce."

I slump back onto the bed as soon as I hear the front door close. Tears start to flow unreservedly down my face. It's all too much. Again.

When I've collected myself, I call in to take a personal day. I explain the break-in to Brooklyn, downplaying the danger. But I want her to know, both so my absence isn't unexplained and in case it's relevant later. In case it was Daniel, or someone acting on his behalf. I shudder lightly at the thought and gather my things to head home. It's time to find out what happened.

"There," the day security officer, Katlyn Ferris, points at the screen. "That's where our external feed first picks them up."

I watch the hatted, gloved figure deftly keep their face hidden from the camera as they enter the building. Officer Ferris taps a few keys and the lobby feed picks up, following their progress. The intruder shoots across the lobby suddenly, yanking the stairwell door open and disappearing. A few more taps. "And fifteen minutes later." A third camera feed picks up, in the hall on my floor. My door is farthest from the camera, but you can see the figure step close to the door and, with quick movements and minimal noise, slip a crowbar from inside their garments and expertly pop the door open in seconds.

The chief guard, a stern, fit Englishman in his sixties named Bernard Shaw, looks on grimly as the figure dashes back to the stairwell the moment the alarm sounds.

"That will do," he instructs Officer Ferris, who kills the feed. Bernard turns to me primly. "The perpetrator then waited at the bottom of the stairs until the coast was clear and walked right out the front door. Not a single camera captured their face."

I slump into the uncomfortable metal chair in the security office. "So we have nothing?" I ask dully.

Officer Ferris looks nervously at her boss. "Not exactly," she hedges. "There are several things the feeds tell us. This person knew where the cameras were. They also knew the parts of the lobby that were more visible from the front desk. So they'd been observing the building or were given insider knowledge. And, finally, they were unaware that there would be additional security once they entered your unit. Which leads me to believe that it is unlikely that they had inside help. Because any of our security officers would have known that."

"Why did they take the stairs?" I ask.

Mr. Shaw peers at me over his spectacles. "To get to the elevators you must pass the reception desk and security office. The stairs are closer to the door and, while visible from both of those vantage points, they are less obvious and easier to navigate to," he explains. "We will continue to review our past feeds to see if there is any unusual activity. But for now, we will question anyone who might have seen this person and review the security tapes. It is highly unlikely that they will attempt to gain access to your condominium again."

It should make me feel better, but somehow I'm still uneasy. I rub my eyes, the exhaustion catching up with me. "When will the door be fixed?"

"It's being done as we speak. You are free to reenter at any time," Mr. Shaw offers. I nod dully and switch to rubbing the back of my neck.

"Thank you," I murmur, rising from the chair. "Please keep me informed."

"Of course, madam," he responds. "And if there is anything else we can do, please let me know."

I shoulder my pack and head home. As the elevator carries me back to the scene of the crime, the familiar terror of feeling unsafe creeps through me. But this time the danger happened in my own home. That's a little harder to run from.

I announce myself to the workman at the door and he lets me pass. I walk to the window wall and perch on the edge of my favorite chair, not comfortable enough to sink into its depths quite yet. In fact, having my back to the door is so nerve-racking that I switch to sitting on the floor, leaning against the windows. The view is spectacular, but my slight fear of heights kicks in if I dare to look down for too long. Instead, I stare at the horizon, trying to suppress the overwhelming panic and appreciate the beauty of the late-summer day.

But I feel baseless. Like home is no longer home. This condo was a symbol of my achievement, a well-earned indulgence so that I could enjoy and appreciate the fruits of my labor. And despite the tumultuous months past, including the events of the previous evening, I don't want to leave it. But I don't want to be alone, either.

For a moment I let myself imagine being a normal girl. In love with a normal boy. With normal lives. We could live together. Make each other breakfast. Make love on every surface of this spacious abode. Just be. Happy and safe. It seems like too much to ask. But what scares me the most is that, a few months ago I would have wanted all that with Alessandro. But now, even if he'd stayed, I know that there was only a fleeting time with him that things were simple and easy. Most of the time it has just been so *hard*. And this, well, whatever we are now, is the most difficult of all. Because I don't know if we're even still anything to each other. Or where he is. If he's okay. And if he is, why he hasn't contacted me in more than a month.

And I realize I've spent more of our short relationship wondering where we stand than not. When all I need is someone here, now, ready to comfort me in my time of need. And I know the one person who has been there for me through all of this, who I'm just starting to realize is everything I need, everything I want .... I shake my head, willing myself out of my pity party. It's too late. I realized it too late.

My phone rings, breaking the silence around me. Bryce's name flashes on my phone's screen.

"I was just thinking about you," I say after I answer the call. I bite my lip, wishing the words back into my mouth.

"Oh? Good things, I hope," Bryce's deep voice responds. He sounds amused.

"The best. Thank you again for letting me stay last night," I say softly.

"Anytime. What's the sitrep on our perp?" Bryce asks.

I chuckle and resist the urge to tease him about his language, instead relaying what I know. He chews on it thoughtfully.

"It definitely doesn't sound random. And with the timing …" he begins contemplatively.

"I know," I agree. "Daniel. It was my first thought too."

"Well, maybe. But it sounds like this person did quite a bit of recon prior to the fact. And while you weren't on the best terms with Daniel, it doesn't sound like there was anything serious enough to warrant that kind of behavior from him. Besides, if Daniel wanted to attack you, he seems like the kind of guy who would do it himself. And on his own turf."

"Huh," I respond. "I hadn't thought about that. Then who?"

"Didn't you say your half-brother didn't seem happy about your being back in your father's and his life?" he asks.

"Hunter? I seriously doubt …"

"You don't know him at all, Sera," Bryce interjects. "The kid has anger issues." The implication of his statement sinks in instantly.

"Damnit, Bryce, do you investigate everyone even remotely connected to me?" I demand.

His low chuckle sounds over the line. "I can't help it," he replies winningly. "Force of habit."

"Isn't that like an abuse of your position or something?" I pout.

"I promise I only use my powers for good," he teases back. "Speaking of which. Tomorrow. I'm picking you up at eight."

"In the morning?" I ask.

"Yes. Is that a problem?" he replies archly.

"I've been traumatized. I think I need to sleep in," I whine. I meant it to sound serious and pitiful, but it's hard to hide the smile in my voice.

"That is letting you sleep in," he says.

"What the hell time do you get up on a Saturday?" I demand jokingly.

"I'm up at five every day, Sera. I work out. I have breakfast. Take a shower. By eight my morning is practically half over," he explains patiently.

The words *take a shower* ring through my head, and the memory of Bryce in a towel drifts through my mind again.

"Fine," I concede. "I'll see you at eight."

"Good." I can hear the triumphant smile in his voice. "Wear something you can move in."

∞

"WHEN YOU SAID I SHOULD WEAR SOMETHING I CAN MOVE in, this isn't what I thought you had in mind," I tell Bryce nervously as we walk through the gym.

While I would normally enjoy the eye candy, the bevy of tall, insanely muscled men covered in tattoos surrounding us is a little intimidating. Not to mention their open ogling that is definitely making me regret my choice of cute blue-and-green fitted capri yoga pants with a matched tank bra.

I wrap my arms self-consciously around the sliver of soft midsection showing, wishing I'd thought to throw a T-shirt or light hoodie on over the tank. Bryce smirks at me and continues to lead me through the machines to one of a few small rooms in the back of the gym.

The room we enter is bare but for the mirrors covering the longest wall opposite the door and the thick, black mats on the floor. I stop in the middle of the room, anxiously awaiting whatever Bryce has planned. He squares off opposite me, hands on his hips. I size him up in his black basketball shorts and black oversized sleeveless shirt. He's more distractingly gorgeous than any man here, which is saying something.

"What is this place?" I ask. "Why do all these guys look like ridiculously good-looking gang members?"

Bryce laughs, and his smile lights up a small, forgotten part of my heart. It's been a long time since I've seen him smile like that. It's almost his patented sunshine smile. I like it more than I care to admit to myself.

"If by 'gang' you mean 'military,' then yes, they're

gang members," he replies. "I guess the Navy can be a *little* like a gang." He's still grinning inanely at me, and I can't help but laugh. He looks like a little kid.

"Geez, Bryce, I didn't take you for the type to fall in with such a rough crowd," I tease. Bryce raises an eyebrow and gives me a look of disbelief. "What? What did I say?"

"Nothing, I just thought you knew," he replies. "But then, maybe I never specifically told you."

"Told me what?" I ask, confused.

"I was a SEAL. Did you seriously not know that? It's on my bio on the company website, and there are pictures and stuff all over my apartment," he says. Then after a moment, he teasingly continues, "Geez, Evans, for a smart chick you're not very observant."

I blush furiously. I did *not* know that. But it explains a lot.

"Why don't you talk about it more?" I deflect.

He shrugs. "It was a long time ago."

"You're only thirty-four, Bryce — it couldn't have been that long ago."

"It feels like a long time ago," he amends. He levels a look at me that says this part of the conversation is over. "In any case, I brought you here to teach you the basics of self-defense."

Oh. OH. "That sounds like a really good idea," I

admit. "Considering the only self-defense I've learned is from movies."

He nods, clearly unsurprised by the information. "The biggest thing they get wrong is *why* you react," he says. "You're not trying to be a hero here and lay the bad guy out on his ass so you can fire witty remarks at him until the police magically show up. Be aware of your surroundings, try not to get in a place where there isn't someone around. But if you do, and you're attacked, assume help isn't coming — so your objective should always be to get away. You may not be a small woman, but most men are going to have the advantage over you. Even if they're shorter or skinnier or much older, they're likely stronger. So don't get cocky and think you can take someone on. Do what you need to do to run. And whenever you see that opening, take it."

I nod. "So are you going to attack me a bunch now?" I ask hesitantly. I must look scared because Bryce laughs.

"Yes, Sera, that's exactly what I'm going to do." He grins maniacally at me. The bastard is going to enjoy this. "But I'm going to teach you a few things first."

"Thank god," I breathe. "All right, Yoda, let's do this."

He shows me how to hold my arms up in front of me when threatened so I can use them to strike or deflect. Then he shows me how to kick effectively, standing or from the ground. I'm feeling pretty confident until he starts the next part.

"This time you can only learn by doing. I'm going to teach you how to use the momentum of someone pushing or pulling you against them."

"Do I get to flip you over?" I ask excitedly.

He rolls his eyes. "Lord, no," he scoffs. "Don't ever try that. You're likely to seriously hurt yourself. Think simpler — move *with* your attacker to land a punch or kick that will help you break free." I give him a completely confused look. "I know. I just have to show you."

"And how exactly are you going to do that?" I ask meekly. I'm not frail by any stretch, but at around a hundred and sixty pounds I'm guessing Bryce easily has eighty or more pounds on me. Of pure muscle. Not to mention a good seven inches of height.

Bryce loosens his posture and stands in front of me. "Don't worry, I'll tell you what I'm going to do before I do it. And I'll go easy at first until you get the hang of it, okay?"

"Okay," I squeak nervously.

But he dives in anyway despite my obvious hesitation. "Now, if I go to grab you with one hand," Bryce reaches his left arm up slowly and grabs my right shoulder gently, "you lean into the motion on that side." I roll my shoulder back. "And lash out with the heel of your other hand like I showed you before." I swing my left palm up to meet his nose. "Good. Again."

We repeat the motion several times, faster each time.

Then we switch to the other side and do the same. Bryce takes me through a full series of face-to-face grabs with various combinations. And by the end, I'm feeling much less vulnerable than the break-in of a couple nights ago had left me.

"Good, you're really getting it," he says. "You're just going to have to practice. A lot. Until it's instinct."

I give him a wary look. "You're not going to randomly start grabbing me, are you?" I ask.

A shit-eating grin breaks across his face. "Not unless you want me to," he replies huskily, and I blush. He clears his throat and reverts to teacher mode. "Let's try grabs from behind."

He turns me around gently and tucks me against his body, wrapping his arms around my front. He starts demonstrating the various ways someone could pull my body, but his mouth is at my ear, his breath hot on my neck and, pressed up against him this way I'm suddenly finding it very hard to concentrate. The feeling of his hard body against my back reminds me of the almost-kisses. And how long it's been since I've had so much contact with someone.

"So you want to lean to one side, hook your leg around to pull theirs out from under them." He nudges my right leg with his until I wrap my foot behind his knee. "Then strike backward with the opposite arm."

It takes all my effort to pull myself back to the present

moment and nudge my elbow into his stomach. "Like this?" I ask.

"No. With your arms pinned you don't have any distance to put force into swinging your elbow," he explains. He releases his left arm and straightens mine out, flattening my hand so the heel of my palm is pointed backward, and slowly swings my arm to his crotch until it's a hair from touching his shorts. "Like that. Hit them in the groin."

And I don't know who shifts — him or me, but my hand grazes him through the fabric. His sharp intake of breath tells me that I touched exactly what I thought I did. The thought sends a flush of heat through me, and I can't help myself — I turn my head to look back up at him. His eyes meet mine and my breath catches in my throat. I slowly turn myself in his arms until I'm facing him.

"They're definitely going to be holding you too tightly to do that," he murmurs hoarsely, staring down into my eyes.

Looking up into his dancing blue eyes, I'm suddenly not sure I can make a move. I tentatively place a hand on his chest, feeling the hard muscle through his thin shirt. The arm that had been holding me in front of him is now wrapped around my waist. But Bryce's expression closes abruptly, and he folds his hand over mine and gently removes it from his chest while stepping back.

"I think that's enough for today," he declares huskily.

He looks uncomfortable and turns away.

A cold tide of rejection washes any remaining heat from my body. "Bryce, I'm sorry, I didn't mean to …" I start, but he turns back around, raising a hand to stop me.

"Don't," he commands.

I bite my lip to hold back a small, strangled cry that is trying to break free. Tears sting the back of my eyes. Bryce, seeing my distress, crosses the short distance he'd put between us. He grasps my chin, titling my head up to look into my eyes.

"Stop. Whatever it is you're beating yourself up for right now," he insists. He draws a deep breath before he continues, his voice softened considerably. "You've been through a lot lately. And you're vulnerable right now." He pauses, and I can tell he's struggling with how to say what he wants to say next. Finally, his eyes looking searchingly into mine, he continues, "It seems like ever since we met you've been torn in pieces. If you choose me, I want it to be with all of you. I won't settle for anything less."

His words tug at the edge of my reason. In this moment, I want all of him. I want him to hold me until all my fears, uncertainties, and insecurities fall away and all that's left is us. But he's right. Until I can give him all of me, it's just not a fair thing to ask of him. I nod softly, and he drops his hand from my chin. He suppresses a sigh as I follow him quietly out of the room, more confused and defenseless than ever.

SEVENTEEN

I meet Allie as planned on Sunday at our favorite brunch spot. And the sight of her is so familiar and comforting it makes me want to cry. She stands outside the restaurant, nervously smoothing her peach tulle skirt and tugging at the hem of her white eyelet-lace sleeveless top. Her long, strawberry-blond hair has been carefully braided over one shoulder. The only trace of the ordeal she's been through is her green eyes — they have a dull look and are rimmed in red. But as soon as she sees me, they warm as her face breaks into a smile.

"Sera," she breathes, embracing me tightly. "It's so good to see you."

"I missed you," I reply, squeezing her back. I let her go, holding her at arm's length. "You look fantastic."

She blushes and waves a hand at me. "This old thing?" she jokes. We both laugh, and the sound warms me. "Let's do this. I'm starving."

If I didn't know better, I wouldn't think there was anything different about her. Pleased, I hold the door open and follow her in.

We make small talk about things like the weather and traffic. Once we're seated and have ordered ridiculous amounts of breakfast foods, I smile patiently at her, waiting for her cue to talk about anything more serious.

"If you're waiting for me to spill my guts, it's not gonna happen," she says quietly into her mimosa.

I huff a small laugh. "Whatever you want to talk about, Allie," I offer. "I'm just so fucking happy to see you, you don't even know."

She snorts. "Been boring without me?" she teases. The smile slides off my face and she raises an eyebrow. "You just went completely pale."

"A lot has happened," I admit. "But I'm sure you have enough on your plate."

"Please," she replies, rolling her eyes. "I promise I won't break. I could use the distraction from my own problems."

I eye her skeptically. "Are you sure? Because some of it's pretty serious," I say. "Well, most of it, actually."

She presses her lips together and sighs heavily. "I'm

sure. I promise. We can talk about my issues when I'm ready. But for now, I would really like to not be treated like I'm made of glass," she insists.

I'm silent for a few moments, unsure of how to begin. "I can't even remember when to start," I admit.

Allie taps her fingers on the table while she thinks about that. "We'd finished moving to Sutton Developments." She pauses. "And Heather quit." Another pause. "And I think you were supposed to meet your brother?"

I blanch, realizing how long it's been since we've talked. Really talked. "Alessandro was in Italy, and I wasn't talking to Bryce," I recall. Allie nods. "God, that seems like a lifetime ago."

She eyes me quizzically as our food arrives. "It was just about a month, Sera," she replies flippantly. She dives into a stack of pancakes, talking through a mouthful. "What could you possibly have gotten into in that short a time?"

Suddenly, I'm not so hungry. So I talk instead. Slowly and carefully filling Allie in on everything that's happened. Carefully because I want to watch her reactions, to make sure I'm not overwhelming her, and taking small bites of food when I feel like she needs time to process.

As I relay it all, I realize how much it is, and I start to understand the tightness I didn't even notice in my chest until now. I start with the lunch that didn't happen and the brother who seemingly isn't ready to have anything to do with me. I'd almost forgotten that particular sting. Then I tell her how I stopped hearing from Alessandro and started talking to Bryce again, and how different he's been. Only to be followed by the passing of his father, and our growing closeness. I'm especially careful with those parts, though, telling her what happened but reserving how I feel about it all. But there's no fooling Allie.

"If this Madison chick hadn't showed up, do you think you two would've ..." she stabs at the air with her fork and I can't help but laugh.

"No," I reply firmly. "That was not the time to go starting anything. We were still figuring out how to be around each other when his dad passed. I didn't want to make it worse."

"Were?" she asks shrewdly.

Damn. I forgot how sharp she is. I shrug, feigning nonchalance as I shove my last piece of bacon in my mouth.

"That was a week ago. A lot has happened," I reply after swallowing.

She stares at me incredulously. "You keep saying that. Out with it then," she prompts.

I chew on my lip anxiously, not sure how much to tell her about Heather.

"Come on, Sera, it's me. I know I've been struggling, but you're not going to damage me."

"You keep saying that," I joke. "But I'm not so sure."

She sighs heavily in response and sets down her fork. "Look," she starts seriously. "I get that what I went through, what I'm going through, is scary for the people who care about me. It's been *super* hard for David, and I'm trying to be patient with his doting on me constantly like I'm a fragile creature that needs shielding from this cruel world." Despite her claim, even I can hear the obvious impatience in her tone. "But I need to get back to life again. Real life. And I thought I could count on you, of all people, not to treat me like I need to be sheltered. It's my own problems I'm struggling with, not other people's. I *want* to hear that I'm not the only one who is going through things. That my problems aren't the end-all-be-all. Really."

I can't help but smirk. "Be careful what you wish for," I reply.

She levels an impatient look at me, and I laugh.

"Okay." So I tell her. All of it. About what really made Heather quit. About our time at the police station, and my conversation with Charles the next day. And about the middle-of-the-night break-in after a night of drinking that left me terrified and led to the ridiculously confusing self-defense training with Bryce.

Allie's frown deepens throughout, and when I'm done we both fall silent for a while. I take the opportunity to finish the last of my food.

"Who'd you go drinking with?" she finally asks. I'm taken aback by her question, and not just because it wasn't the part of my story I expected her to hone in on.

"Bryce's sister, Emily," I reply. Her brows knit together in a scowl. And I realize she's *jealous*. "I needed someone to talk to. Who *didn't* know me well. I just needed to get things off my chest. Loosen up a little." And while Allie looks a little reassured, she is still pouting a bit.

"So I haven't been replaced?" she asks.

I suppress a laugh, knowing that won't help. But I can't hide my smile, and it loosens her frown a bit. "Of *course* not," I reassure her. "Nobody could ever replace you."

"Good," she concedes. "Now, about you and Bryce."

I press my lips into a thin line and huff a breath out through my nose. "I'm just not sure how to feel right now," I admit. "I think there's too much going on. With the break-in. With not knowing what the hell is happening with Alessandro. Bryce is right. I'm in no place to trust my feelings right now."

Allie squints at me uncertainly. "You don't have to trust them, but don't pretend like you're not having them," she replies. "Don't go backward, Sera."

"I'm not going backward," I promise. "But I feel like I can't go forward, either. How can I possibly decide when everything is still so up in the air?"

"Nobody is asking you to," she points out. "You've never been one to fully commit to something without *knowing* it's the right thing. But that time will come, and then you'll know exactly what to do."

"You think?" I ask skeptically.

"Yes," she replies confidently. "Deciding to really be with someone with everything you've got is not exactly a fact-based decision. Which, let's face it, is more in your wheelhouse. But you've got good instincts, Sera. Pay attention. See things for what they are. Then listen to your heart. I don't think it's going to lead you astray."

"I hope not," I reply, unsure.

"Well, you can talk to me," she says. Then a grimace flashes across her face. "Or Emily."

I feign an unamused glare at her. "I think you'd like her," I respond. "No need to be catty."

She smiles innocently. "Who's being catty?" she asks.

I can't help but laugh. "It's good to have you back, Allie."

"It's good to be back, Sera."

And as we smile at each other across the table, a small ray of hope shines on my leaden heart.

I CAN'T HELP BUT STILL BE ON EDGE THE FOLLOWING DAYS — and nights — as being in my own home is no longer the refuge it once was, and I know it's going to be a long while before I feel safe again. I'm trying my hardest not to think about Alessandro, or Bryce, or Daniel. It's all just too much. So I trudge through, sinking into the monotony of work.

It's not until Wednesday morning when I enter my office that the routine is disturbed. As soon as I walk in, I know something is different. It takes me a few minutes of carefully scanning my desk, the cabinets, and the furniture to put my finger on it. And once I do, I realize it's because it's extremely subtle. Something I wouldn't have even noticed if I wasn't so anally retentive.

It's only a few small things — files that were perfectly aligned on the cabinet now askew, pencils and pens shuffled in their holder where they were separated, objects on my desk in slightly different positions. Someone has been rifling through my things. I carefully back out of my office and check in with Maggie.

"Hey, Mags," I greet her as she sets up for the morning.

She looks up, startled. "Everything all right, Sera?" she asks.

I smile, pleased that she's finally comfortable calling me by my first name. "I think so," I reply. "Did anyone go in my office after I left yesterday?"

She looks at me quizzically. "Not that I know of," she responds slowly. "Is anything missing?"

"I'm not sure, actually, I just had a funny feeling," I reply, brushing it off. "Never mind. Thanks, Maggie."

"Of course," she murmurs as I go back to my office.

I close the door behind me and settle carefully in to conduct a more thorough search to see if anything is, in fact, missing. But a few minutes later I come up empty handed. Nothing gone, everything just slightly off. I frown, unable to shake off the violated feeling.

I realize I'm probably just being overly sensitive. With the break-in last week, my radar is just on extra-high. It's almost certainly nothing. Maybe Charles looking for a client file or something similarly innocuous. I shake myself out of my reverie and hunker back down into my routine.

At home that night I find it hard to stay out of my own head, so I decide to make a few phone calls. First, I check in with Bryce, then Emily, then Allie. I leave my mother for last, knowing it will be a long call since we haven't spoken in some time. She is understandably angry that I didn't share everything sooner and concerned for my safety. I do my best to reassure her, but it sounds hollow even in my ears as, if I'm being honest, I'm still terrified myself.

By the time I'm done, I'm drained. But I still can't turn

my brain off. I sit in my favorite chair, staring out into the summer night. Could my mystery prowler really be Hunter? While I tend to side with Bryce, that it just doesn't seem like Daniel's style, I find it hard to believe the brother I've never met would have such an extreme reaction toward me. But then, I never would have guessed Gabrielle Grayson would hatch an elaborate plan to destroy me and, ultimately, try to kill me. There's just no accounting for crazy sometimes.

And while I'm thankful for Bryce's involvement, it occurs to me that he has to deal with this sort of shit all. The. Time. And while I blindly didn't realize he had a military background, I should've realized it had taken extensive training to give him the skillset to do what he does. But the roll-with-it attitude is all Bryce. He's just the right combination of laid-back and assertive. And, as usually happens when I think about him for too long, I eventually am revisited by the mental image of him in that towel. I wonder briefly if my feelings for him aren't simply borne of sexual frustration. But then, that totally ignores the feelings I've always had for him and suppressed for other reasons. Or one sexy and charming Italian reason named Alessandro Giordano.

I sigh deeply and decide it's time to break out the wine. But before I can open a bottle, I'm suddenly reminded of the last time I indulged and was caught still tipsy in a dangerous situation. My stomach lurches and I decide against it. Instead, I head to bed where I rest fitfully, plagued by nightmares once more.

EIGHTEEN

On Thursday morning, Heather calls me. She wants to update me on the case but is reluctant to discuss it on the phone, so we arrange to meet after work at her parent's house in Mountlake Terrace.

I arrive at six as planned and find Heather waiting just inside the door — she manages to open it before I even knock. She ushers me in and nearly knocks me over with a tight hug.

"Nice to see you too, Heather," I tease her. She pulls back, swinging her long braids over her shoulder and smiling self-consciously.

"Thanks for coming," she replies. "My mom made dinner. I hope you're hungry." She leads me toward the dining room where an array of amazing aromas drift toward me.

"I'm suddenly ravenous," I reply appreciatively.

"Good, because my parents can't wait to meet you," she admits. She smiles mischievously. "And nothing makes my mom happier than feeding people. Just be warned — we're all huggers."

I laugh and shrug, following her into the dining room where a tall, athletic man in his fifties is setting the table. Heather introduces him as her father, Ronald. As warned, he uses my proffered hand to pull me into a tight hug.

"Thank you so much, for everything you've done for my daughter," he says fervently as he releases me.

I blush hotly, unsure of what he knows. "Heather is an amazing young woman. I wish I could do more for her," I hedge with a small smile.

"Nonsense," he replies as a curvy, ebony-skinned woman enters from the kitchen. If it weren't for the grey streaks in her hair I'd swear she was the same age as Heather. "Catherine, this is Serafina Evans." Catherine sets the roasting pan she was carrying on the table and hurries around to deliver my third hug in as many minutes. I can't help but laugh.

"Welcome, welcome," Catherine says excitedly.

"I certainly feel welcomed," I say, laughing still. Once I'm released and her parents are busy bringing food in, I catch Heather's eye and quietly ask to speak to her. She slips around the table and we turn away from her mother and father. "How much do they know?" I ask softly.

"It's okay," she assures me. "They know pretty much everything. The big stuff, anyway."

I nod, relieved. "And how are you doing?" I ask.

She pushes out a deep breath and shrugs. "I'm nervous, but ..."

We are interrupted by Ronald declaring it's time to eat. We all slide into our chairs and the talk veers into more neutral areas. They want to know all about how I came to do what I do, and it comes out that Heather has apparently built me up to them as some sort of paragon of real estate success. It's very flattering but also fairly embarrassing. I play up Heather's strengths as much as I can to divert the conversation from myself. Thankfully, it mostly works, but by the end of the meal I can tell Heather is ready to take a break from the spotlight.

Ronald and Catherine assure us that everything is taken care of and encourage us to adjourn to the living room. We settle into a well-worn tan microfiber sofa, full and comfortable after the delicious meal.

"Your mom is a fantastic cook," I tell her, reiterating the compliment I'd just given Catherine.

"She is," Heather says absently.

"So are you going to tell me what's on your mind or what?" I tease her.

She smiles vaguely. "They've just issued an arrest

warrant. They're bringing charges against Daniel," she says succinctly.

I gasp, my hands flying to my mouth. "Really?! That's fantastic," I breathe. "Why don't you look happier?"

She shrugs lightly. "I guess I just feel like I've been looking over my shoulder ever since it happened. But even more so since last week," she admits. "And until they actually have him in custody, I'll just feel like every shadow is him, waiting to get me." She shakes her head.

"Hey," I say, catching her eye. "I completely understand. Believe me. Have you talked to anyone about this? A counselor maybe?" Heather nods that she has, and I release a breath.

"Yes, Officer Ramirez set me up with someone first thing," Heather replies. "And I don't want to keep being the victim of what he did, but it's going to take some time. And going to trial isn't going to be easy." She twists her fingers nervously in her braids.

"Do they need you to testify?" I ask, hoping there's some way to not make her face this all over again for the coming weeks.

"Need? I don't know. But I'm going to," she replies. "Moreover, I want to be there. I want to see justice done. I need to see it. But that doesn't mean it's going to be simple. They're preparing me, though, so I know what kind of questions I'll be asked. So I won't feel blindsided, at least."

I rest a reassuring hand on her knee. "I'll be there with you, if you need me," I respond.

Her answering smile is so bittersweet that my heart breaks for her. "Thank you," she says, brushing away a tear.

She changes the subject, and we talk about her new job for a while before I head home for the night. Of course, not before I receive a final round of hugs from every Irving. I'm a little jealous of the love in their house as I climb into my car, my heart warmed from having experienced it.

It's not until I'm merging onto the freeway that it occurs to me the same car has been behind me since shortly after I left their house. I try to shake off the feeling. Surely the freeway is a common enough destination that it's a coincidence. Though some of Heather's paranoia may have heightened my own, I can't help but remain concerned as it continues to stay a comfortable distance behind me for miles.

I switch lanes as a test, and it follows shortly after. The nervous feeling in my gut grows, and a few minutes later I switch lanes again, this time traversing two lanes. And it follows. My throat constricts, and I'm just about to use my car's Bluetooth to place a call when the car exits the freeway one exit before my own. I release the air in my lungs, my shoulders slumping in relief. Though I'm left feeling something like a suspicious nutjob as I finish the drive home.

∽

IT'S NOT UNTIL FRIDAY MORNING, WHEN BRYCE CALLS TO tell me that Daniel has been taken into custody, that I realize I forgot to call him and tell him about my dinner with Heather. After I explain that I've just been distracted, I can tell he's not mad, but the concern in his voice is unmistakable. And I silently wonder how many times this man is going to have to watch me come undone before he decides it's just not worth the drama. I reassure him that I'm fine and we make plans for the next day.

The tone in the office is somber as word spreads of Daniel's arrest. I decide to check on Charles that afternoon after some very tense and unusually short meetings. I knock on his door and wait for his response to enter.

"Yes?" he calls. I pop the door open. When he sees it's me, he gestures for me to come in. I close the door behind me and perch in one of the chairs opposite his desk.

"Hi," I say feebly. Charles huffs and gives me the smallest of smiles. "I'm so sorry, Charles. I can't imagine how hard this must be on you."

"It's no picnic," he agrees. "But I'm hard-pressed to feel put out. I'm still struggling to come to terms with my son's behavior."

"Has he admitted to anything?" I ask, curious.

"Not that I know of," Charles replies, peering at me shrewdly. "He never was one to take responsibility quickly. And certainly not when it could come with jail time and the ruin of everything he holds dear."

"But you think he's guilty," I reply. It's not really a question. I can tell by his words and his tone that he thinks Daniel did it.

"The opinion of an old man is neither here nor there," he responds vaguely. "At the very least, I must now accept that Daniel's suspension is more than temporary. Suraj has been managing Daniel's department, but I'd like to split it between the both of you starting next week. If that's okay with you."

"Of course," I reply. "Anything I can do, just let me know."

"You'll be heading both project management teams now," he responds. "That will more or less even out the numbers between you." He heaves a deep sigh. "I've also engaged services to help manage the legal and external aspects of this development."

I scrunch my brows together. "External aspects?" I ask, confused. And then it hits me. "You mean, like PR? You're afraid of the bad press?" I'm a little aghast that *that's* one of his concerns right now.

"In a sense," he admits. "I simply want to make sure nobody here says or does anything to interfere with Daniel's trial."

Oh. Not the angle I was expecting. "You're not worried we'll lose clients?" I persist.

"Of course I am," he responds. "I'd be a fool not to. And if there's anything to be done to that end, we will. Within the bounds of my discretion."

I eye him warily for a moment but realize I'm going to need to trust his judgment. The path ahead is going to be rocky enough without more internal drama.

"I trust you," I assure him. "As I said, if there's anything I can do, let me know."

Charles rubs his chin in a way that reminds me of Alessandro, and a pain totally unrelated to the situation shoots through my chest.

"Thank you, Sera, I appreciate that more than you know," he admits wearily.

I leave him to his thoughts and lose myself in work once more.

When I next think to look at the clock it's after seven and everyone has clearly gone home. I start my own journey home, exhausted from the day, the week, these past few months. It's hard to say what exactly.

But almost as soon as I'm on a main road, I'm once again plagued by the suspicion that I'm being followed. The car behind me is the exact make and model of the one I swore was following me the night before. I decide to make a complete loop of right turns, all on main roads, to test the theory. The dark sedan follows me from a few cars back this time, until I'm done with the loop, and I can tell they must realize what I've done, that I'm onto them, because they don't hide behind other cars anymore, moving up to stay right on my tail.

Panic starts to flutter in my chest, but I suppress it, trying to think of who to call. I rule out Bryce, not wanting to drag him into my web of crazy again. And as tough as Allie seems, I can't lay this at her doorstep right now. The only other person I can think to call is Emily.

As her phone rings, I pray hard that she answers. And quickly. And she does.

"Hey, Sera, how's it going?" She sounds so cheerful I almost feel bad.

"Emily, I hate to do this to you, but I think I'm being followed. Can I meet you somewhere? Right now?" I ask, struggling to contain the terror in my voice.

"Holy shit, Sera, why didn't you call Bryce?" Emily demands.

"Please, Emily, can we talk about that later?" I beg.

"Fuck. Yes, of course. I'm just at home. Fire Station 25 is a block from my house. I'll meet you there," she directs. I plug the destination into my navigation system.

"I'll be there in less than ten minutes," I reply. "Thanks, Emily."

"Be safe, Sera, see you soon," she responds.

I hang up and accelerate through the next turn, hoping to lose my tail. But they stick on me like glue. I glance in my rearview mirror, trying to get a look at the driver, but it's too difficult to make anything out without stopping to draw them in closer. I scrap any hope of getting the license plate number safely and focus on getting to the fire station.

It's not long before I arrive to see Emily and a firefighter in a plain, navy uniform standing on the main steps. She waves me down and points at the driveway spot next to the walkway they're on. I pull in tentatively and swivel my head around in time to see the dark sedan continuing to accelerate down the street. I breathe a sigh of relief and hop out, hugging Emily tightly.

"It was the black car behind me." The words topple out of my mouth and are barely understandable. The firefighter nods.

"I got the plates," he replies, and I want to cry with relief. "There's a police station just a couple blocks from here. I'll go with you to make a report."

"Can I hug you?" I ask, holding back tears.

He laughs and nods. "Sure thing, ma'am," he replies. And I can't help but embrace him gratefully. "I'm Brad, by the way. Brad Hanson."

"Well, Brad, today you're my knight in shining armor," I reply, releasing him. "Shall we?" I climb back into the car and Brad folds his long frame into the passenger seat, while Emily pops into the backseat.

The police station is, in fact, literally just a couple of blocks away, and there is no sign of the black sedan on our short journey. There is ample parking on the street in front of it, and we park quickly and enter the building together.

Firefighter Brad enlists the officer at the desk and together they take down the details quickly. The officer pulls up the information on the vehicle. We are all disappointed to find the plates are old, no longer registered, and the last vehicle they were registered to does not match the description of the one that was following me. The officer offers to take the report anyway. Emily insists that we do, and Firefighter Brad takes his leave.

"Too bad he had to go," Emily whispers to me as the desk officer continues to type into her computer. "He was cute!"

I glance back at his retreating form, noting that I suppose she was right. "I hadn't really noticed," I admit. "Do you really think we need to finish the report?"

Emily eyes me levelly. "You've already excluded my brother from this. He'll kill me if I don't make you," she replies.

And I know she's right. Thankfully, it doesn't take long, and within a half hour an officer escorts us to my car and we make the short journey to Emily's place without incident, parking in the underground, gated garage for her building.

Emily leads me up to her apartment, which is small, cozy, and covered in crazy posters, fabrics, and musical instruments.

I point at a mandolin. "Do you really play all these?" I ask, in awe.

Emily grins and plops in a crocheted-blanket-covered armchair. "Yep!" She pulls the instrument into her lap and plucks a short tune with a smile. "Now, are you going to tell me why you didn't want to call my brother?"

I sink into the small, patchwork couch next to her and bury my face in my hands. "You're going to think it's stupid," I grouse. I hear her put the instrument down and feel her tug at one of my arms.

"Come on," she prompts. "I'll let you stay overnight! It'll be like a slumber party. But I can't harbor a fugitive from Bryce Hoyt. I know better. Spill."

"You're going to call him, aren't you?" I reply miserably, catching her implication.

She shrugs. "He has a way of finding these things out on his own," she reminds me. "I'm not going to tell him."

I eye her skeptically. "You want *me* to call him," I respond.

She smiles beatifically. "I would if I were you," she replies in a singsong voice.

It's enough to crack my mood, and I laugh appreciatively. "Fine, I'll call him. It's not like I wanted to *hide* it from him. I just feel like I interrupt a lot of his days with my drama. I'm like a magnet lately."

"I don't think he minds," she replies drily, picking up the mandolin again and strumming it softly.

"I'm not sure why you think that," I reply. "But even if he doesn't, I do. I hate relying on other people. And I feel like I rely on him *a lot*."

"But he can rely on you too," she points out. "That's what having a relationship is all about."

I can't help the dirty look I shoot her. "Except we don't. Have a relationship, that is. Not like that," I correct her.

Emily shrugs. "If you say so," she replies, again in her singsong voice.

I sigh resignedly. "I'd have to tell him anyway. I'm supposed to see him in the morning for another training session of some sort. He won't tell me what, so he was going to pick me up."

"Good. The less time I have to hide this from him the better. You can use the balcony if you'd like," she replies. She points at a small door next to the kitchen.

"Thanks." I grab my phone and head out onto the slip of a balcony and place the call. I stare at the setting sun as I wait for him to answer. It takes a while, and I can't stop my mouth from settling into a concerned frown.

"Sera," he finally answers, out of breath. "What's up?"

"I didn't interrupt anything, did I?" I ask nervously.

There's a beat of silence on the other end.

"It's okay, I have a sec," he replies.

"I won't keep you, then. I just wanted to let you know

you can pick me up at your sister's place tomorrow morning," I say quietly.

"You're at Emily's?" he asks, confused.

"Yes," I reply simply.

Another beat of silence.

"You can tell me more tomorrow. I have to go," he says abruptly.

"Okay, sorry to have bothered you. See you tomorrow," I mumble.

He ends the call without responding, and I can't help but wonder — *what the hell?* And then an explanation pops into my head. A blond one.

I go back inside and the expression on my face betrays me.

"He was mad, wasn't he?" Emily squeaks.

I shake my head, disturbed. "He was busy," I say softly, my eyes wide. "And out of breath. He wouldn't answer the phone while he was ..." I trail off, shaking my head and looking back out at the descending twilight.

Emily pales a little and her nostrils flare. "He could just be working out," she suggests feebly. I roll my eyes. "Not *that* kind of workout. I meant ..."

"Save it, Emily, it's his business. And we both know he works out in the morning." I pause, suppressing a disgusted shudder. "You know what? I actually really don't want to know who or what he was doing."

Emily grimaces and slinks into the kitchen, emerging moments later as I sink into the couch.

"Booze?" She holds an icy bottle of vodka and two shot glasses aloft with a conciliatory smile.

I laugh drily. "I don't think vodka is the answer to my problems. But it's worth a shot," I joke.

Emily groans as she settles into the couch next to me. "That will be funnier once I've had a few of these," she replies, pouring the shots.

"Do you always drink this much?" I tease her after her first couple of rounds.

"Pretty much," she replies, expertly slinging back another shot. "Just remember, Sera — nobody ever told an epic story that started with, 'Dude, this one time I ate so much salad.'"

I know I shouldn't encourage her, but I laugh anyway. "So what's new with you? Seeing anyone?" I press her, setting down my shot glass.

Emily pulls a face and shakes her head while pouring another shot. "I'm on my fourth shot of vodka and it's not even nine p.m. on a Friday night. What do you think?" She downs the shot and sets her glass next to mine.

"Okay, then," I concede. "Ever fallen stupid in love with the wrong person?"

Emily gives me some serious side-eye. "Of course. Who hasn't? But that wasn't a loaded question at all." She pauses. "So are we talking about the Italian guy right now? Or someone else?"

I contemplate the ceiling for a moment, the vodka pleasantly warming and numbing me.

"Yes," I respond. I look over at Emily, and we both burst out laughing. After the laughter subsides we sit in companionable silence for a bit.

"Sera," Emily says softly.

My head snaps up and I realize I must have started drifting off. The living room lights are off now and the light over the stove casts a dim glow that allows me to still see most of what's around me.

"Lay down right here, okay?"

I lean into the couch as she slides a blanket over me. And I'm out before I can even thank her.

NINETEEN

Despite my early bedtime, I manage to sleep until almost seven a.m. Emily isn't up yet, so I scrounge the supplies to make coffee and hope the smell doesn't wake her. I take my cup onto the balcony and sit in the small metal chair there, holding the hot cup close in the cool of the early morning.

I don't realize how long I've been out here until Bryce appears through the small door, his large frame even more pronounced in the tiny space. I barely glance at him as I continue to survey the buildings around me, watching them come to life with activity.

"You sleep in that?" he finally asks.

I look down at my cranberry shirtdress. It's rumpled but perfectly serviceable. "Yes. But I'm sure I can borrow clothes from Emily if I'm violating dress code," I reply drily, still avoiding his gaze. I realize I'm more bothered by what I suspect he was up to last night than I thought I was.

"Wear what you want," he replies dismissively, folding his arms over his broad chest. I try not to stare at his rippling biceps as he eyes me speculatively. "You care to tell me why you were at the East Precinct last night?"

I shoot him an angry glare. "I'll show you mine if you show me yours," I reply snarkily. And after a moment's pause, "You know what? I take it back. No, I don't care to tell you. And I don't really care to have all of my movements monitored."

His expression remains stoic, his gaze fixed on me. "I was going to teach you to shoot today," he says offhandedly. "But I think that's off the table."

"Oh? Why's that?" I can barely contain my annoyance.

"I don't think I want to put a gun in your hand when you're this angry with me," he replies evenly. "Why *are* you so angry, Sera?"

I clench my jaw, realizing he's right. I'm unreasonably angry, and he's free to spend the night with whomever he wants. Maybe I'm just mad at myself for thinking he was still waiting for me. For hoping, even though I knew better, that I still had a shot with him.

"Why do you even need me to tell you what happened?" I grumble, diverting the conversation. "Can't you just read the police report?"

A muscle twitches in his jaw and he shifts his weight to his other foot. "I did, actually. But I'd still like to hear it from you," he replies.

He looks so concerned that my anger melts until only sadness remains. And I realize that that's what the anger was protecting me from. I set my coffee mug down on the small table next to me.

"I'm just tired of all this drama," I reply, digging the heels of my hands into my eyes. "I just want it all to go away. The more I talk about it, the longer it lives." I move to running my hands through my hair, frustrated.

Bryce crosses the short distance between us and squats down next to me so he's looking up into my face.

"We'll get through this," he promises. "But to help you, I need to know what's going on."

My eyes rove over his short, thick chestnut hair. I note that it's grown out a little, and it makes me want to run my fingers through it. His sky-blue eyes sparkle with intensity as he stares at me. I have to bite my lip hard to hold back the tears threatening to form.

"It's all in the report," I sigh. "Someone was following me when I left work yesterday. I called Em and she met me at the fire station. They escorted us to the police station to make the report." I pause. "Though I can't remember if I told them that the same car had followed me the night before. But it took off when I was still deciding whether I was being paranoid."

"You did," he replies softly. "You really didn't get a look at the driver?" I shake my head. He sighs and sinks onto the concrete, his back against the balcony railing. "I have other news."

I look at him expectantly. "Well? Are you going to tell me, or should I go get more coffee?" I ask, irritated.

Bryce's eyes flick up to mine. He has a wary look about him that makes my heart sink in my chest.

"You're killing me here."

"Daniel posted bail this morning," he replies hesitantly. He shifts against the rails.

I frown. "How is that possible? Are violent criminals really given that option?" I ask.

"The judge must have thought he was low enough risk not to re-offend or run. Though his bail was quite high," Bryce amends.

"Okay," I say slowly. "So that's not good. But I guess honestly I'm not that surprised, either." Bryce looks away guiltily. "There's more, isn't there?"

His eyes return to mine. "There's more," he agrees. He clears his throat and leans forward, draping his long arms over his knees. "My sources located your boyfriend. They spotted him walking into a bank in Rome with another man two days ago. He was unharmed and didn't seem under duress."

I'm struck dumb by the information. It takes my brain

what feels like an eternity to even make full sense of the words.

"He's alive? He's okay?" I finally manage. Bryce nods. "Do they know where he is? Where he's staying?"

Bryce's expression clouds over. "Damnit, Sera, you're not going after him," he snaps.

I open my mouth to protest, but I know he's right, so I close it. And as the information truly sinks in, my composure begins to crumble. I can see in Bryce's eyes that he expects it. I summon every bit of willpower left in my tired, ravaged heart and force down my reaction until I can fully experience it privately. I return to staring numbly at the horizon. Bryce is still looking at me apprehensively.

I meet his gaze and shrug. "If you don't want to tell me, don't," I say evenly.

"I couldn't even if I wanted to," he admits. "They weren't able to track him back to wherever he's holed up. But …"

"What?" I ask sharply.

Bryce looks at me imploringly. "The bastard doesn't deserve you if he can't even be bothered to man up and break things off instead of leaving you in this purgatory." His every word is filled with venom.

I close my eyes and shake my head. I refuse to discuss this with Bryce when I haven't even had a chance to process it. "Why does it matter to you what he does? Or what I do about it?" I ask, not really expecting or looking for an answer. I sigh heavily.

"Because you matter to me," he replies. I bite back a retort, but he sees it. "Spit it out."

"If I matter so much, then answer one question," I respond. He looks at me anxiously, waiting. "What were you doing last night that you could barely talk to me?"

His expression closes so fast that I don't even need him to confirm it. Not really.

"I answered the phone, didn't I?" he responds tightly. "But I'm not at your beck and call. I can't be everything, everywhere you want always. I'm your friend, Sera, not your personal security guard."

"I know," I agree. "But that wasn't my question." I rise from the chair and step over him to get to the door. I stop with the door open and turn back to him. "If we're friends, there's no reason for you not to tell me. And if we're friends, then whoever I choose to love is not really your decision." *Even if it's you.*

I slip back into the apartment, still numb, to find Emily hovering in the kitchen. Clearly, she's heard every word.

"You okay?" she asks softly.

I huff out a breath and set my coffee cup in the sink. "No. Thanks for the place to crash, Em," I reply.

And with that, I take my leave of both Hoyt siblings. But I can feel their eyes on my back as the door closes behind me.

❦

Back in my favorite chair with a bottle of wine at my feet and a glass in hand, I finally feel the pressure of other's expectations lifted enough to start handling what I learned this morning.

Alessandro. Alive. Unharmed. Casually strolling into a bank with a friend. Yet not a word or whisper for six weeks to reassure me or at least let me know where things stand. I can't help but think his silence speaks louder than anything he would have to say on the matter. Because if he truly cared for me, even if he couldn't be with me anymore, wouldn't he find a way to tell me that? Surely, he must know how worried I've been.

My mind races with a thousand explanations that excuse his lack of contact. I shake them out of my head, frustrated. There's no point in guessing. All I have to go on is what I know. So I decide to switch tactics. If someone I cared about was in this position, what would I think?

I sink into the frame of mind and, trying to put myself outside of the situation emotionally, spin through the events. Say Emily started dating a man who'd pursued her for months, only to find out a month later — after falling in love with him — that he was married. Then another month later, something horrible happens to her after which she finds out he's gotten divorced, but he still can't be with her because he's got to run off to figure out why his crazy ex-wife is making serious threats against him that could affect her own safety. And then he's gone for a month when she stops hearing from him. And another six weeks later, realizing she's falling for the one man who's actually been there for her through all of this, she's sitting around wondering what to do about it when she learns her paramour has been just fine and dandy this whole time.

Even I realize how ridiculous it sounds. But the missing piece, and what there is no accounting for, is love. The force I've resisted all these years due to its destructive nature, its ability to make even the smartest among us do some truly unwise things.

I think back to Bryce's demand — that he won't settle for anything less than all of me. And the truth of that condition is undeniable by either logic or love. How can you be with only part of someone? Painfully, is the answer, I realize. Because that's what it's always been with Alessandro, and what he protested against from my side at the beginning of our relationship. But even before I gave all of myself to him, I only ever had part of him. Even when I let myself fall in love with him, I didn't know he still technically belonged to someone else. Even after it tore us apart I still loved him, but we couldn't be together. And we haven't been able to be together since, for this reason and then that.

But the hardest part is not knowing. Is Alessandro still

working on clearing the obstacles in the way of our being together without mortal peril hanging over our heads? Or has he simply changed his mind and hasn't been able to bring himself to tell me? Neither explains his complete lack of contact. And I know he'd be furious with me if our roles were reversed. But would he give up on me without knowing?

I stand, pacing nervously in front of the glass wall, the heat of the waning summer radiating off its smooth face. I feel like a caged, wounded animal. It's no wonder I lashed out at Bryce this morning. I contemplate going for a walk to clear my head, but I know that's a bad idea when Daniel has made bail and I've had someone following me the last two nights. Not to mention the break-in. And I still can't shake the feeling that it's all connected.

I'm torn from my reverie by a soft knock on the door. Warily, I approach soundlessly and peer through the peephole. I breathe a sigh of relief when I see Emily's familiar chestnut waves. I open the door to find her chewing her lip, looking completely contrite and cheerless.

"Why am I not surprised?" I greet her. "Are all you Hoyts just big, fat meddlers?" I give her a small smile to let her know I'm not serious and step aside, gesturing for her to enter.

She steps past me into the condo and I close the door behind her. Before she says anything, she gives me a brief, tender hug. "I can't help it," she finally replies. "If you saw your face when you left, you'd be here too." She pauses. "That made a lot more sense in my head."

I can't help laughing. "I get what you meant," I assure her. "Come, sit down. There might be some wine left." I grab another wine glass and a second bottle from the kitchen as she settles into the overstuffed white couch next to my chair.

When we're both seated with full glasses, she looks contemplatively into hers as she swirls the dark liquid in circles. "I just didn't want you to be alone," she finally says.

I throw her a grateful smile, blinking away tears. "Thanks, Em," I reply softly.

She beams at me. "I noticed you've started calling me that," she says.

"Is it okay?" I ask tentatively. I've heard Bryce call her that so many times that it's clearly rubbed off. But it was so subconscious that I didn't even register it and consider that it might be too personal.

"More than okay," she assures me, leaning over to squeeze my free hand. "Now. Talk."

I can't help but grimace. "Really? I feel like such a drain," I admit. "I swear I'm not always this much drama."

Emily shakes her head and smirks. "We all go through phases where it seems like everything is going wrong," she replies. "And even aside from that, we're all going through something pretty much all the time anyway. It's okay to need someone to listen. Or be a sanity check. Or whatever it is you need."

I take a deep breath and let it out in a sigh. "You're right," I agree. "I guess I'm still learning to let people in." Emily sips her wine tolerantly as she waits for me to continue. "I know I've told you about Alessandro before, so I'm guessing you pretty much understood what you heard this morning?"

"Pretty much," she confirms. "So you haven't heard from this guy in weeks and now you find out he's been on a Roman holiday. Must sting a bit."

"Six weeks," I clarify. "And yes, it stings. A lot."

"It's the people we love the most who have the greatest capacity to cause us pain," she responds.

"Preach," I reply with a sigh. "It feels like falling in love is part choice, part fate. But how do you decide when to *stop* loving someone?"

Emily fingers the stem of her wine glass as she considers her response. "I don't think you ever stop," she finally offers. "I think all you can do is decide when it's not worth beating your head against a wall anymore."

"Easier said than done," I grumble.

Emily laughs. "Touché." She pauses. "Do you want my opinion?"

"Can't hurt," I reply drily.

She catches and holds my gaze. "This dude is selfish. You don't want to be with someone selfish. You're a giver, Sera. You want to be with a giver," she says plainly.

I'm not surprised by her take on the matter. But it still feels contrary to what I know about Alessandro. "I don't think he's selfish. He has his reasons. I just don't know what they are right now," I reply with a sigh.

"Yes, because he's not sharing, because there's nothing in it for him. Look," she says, staring at me squarely, "I get that you love this guy. But he's lied to you, hidden things from you, and still isn't being forthcoming. Whatever his story is, it doesn't matter. He's quite obviously doing things in a way that works for *him*. I'm not saying he doesn't love you. I'm saying he can't love you the way you deserve to be loved."

"Now you just sound like your brother," I reply sullenly.

Emily throws a hand up. "Thank god one of us does," she replies. "Bryce may let people walk all over him sometimes — okay not people, women — but he's been through a lot and has seen even more. And he has a gift for cutting through the façade people put on and seeing them for who they are."

"You mean researching them and finding every sordid detail of their past," I grumble.

Emily raises an eyebrow. "Who has he done that to?" she asks.

I roll my eyes. "Um, everyone remotely connected to

me? It's obnoxious. I don't know how you stand it," I grumble.

She looks at me, confused. "He's never done that to me," she replies slowly. She's silent for a moment. "But he *can* be very protective."

I snort. "That's an understatement," I scoff, burying my face in my free hand.

"What are you waiting for?" Emily asks softly.

"What do you mean?" I ask, dropping my hand back into my lap.

"What has to happen for you to move on from this guy? How long are you going to wait for him?" she presses.

"I don't know," I reply honestly.

Emily taps the side of her glass in thought. "I don't blame you. I can't say I'd find the decision easy if it were me. But there's an opportunity cost," she eventually says. "To waiting."

Her words jog something in my memory. "I'd rather regret doing something than doing nothing," I murmur.

Emily snaps her head up. "Then do something," she urges me.

I look back at her sadly. "I think I've done everything I can," I reply despondently. "I can't reach Alessandro. There's nowhere for me to call. He either didn't get or is choosing to not reply to my email. And not even Bryce could find where he's staying in Rome.

And despite your brother's low opinion of me, I'm not stupid enough to go there and wander around looking for him."

"I wasn't suggesting that," Emily responds. "I agree completely — you've done everything you can do. Except move on."

Her words sink deeply into my consciousness. And I realize she's beyond right. The only thing I can do now is choose to keep waiting for him to decide to contact me, or I can decide to go forward with my life. And waiting isn't doing anything at all.

"You're absolutely right," I breathe. "I'm done waiting." The immense sorrow I feel at the decision is only matched by the feeling of freedom that follows. Tears flow out of my eyes at the release, and I set my wine glass down before it can tumble out of my shaking hand.

Emily sets aside her own and opens her arms to me. I crawl onto the couch next to her, gratefully accepting the offered embrace. She holds me for a good while until the tears finally stop.

"So are you going to go after my brother now or what?" Emily murmurs into my hair once I've settled.

I pull away, facing her on the couch. "I'm not sure I can even be friends with him anymore," I admit. "I thought for a while there he might still ..." I sniff deeply, reigning back my emotions in the aftermath of the tears. "But if last night is any indication, I think he really has finally moved on. I don't want to keep making things harder for him."

Emily scowls and eyes me sternly. "That's not doing something, Evans," she reprimands me. "You don't know anything for sure. Would you rather guess or know? Because this is one case where you *can* know. You just have to be brave enough to ask."

I huff a small laugh and shove her shoulder playfully. "You're really smart, you know that?" I tease her.

She smiles widely. "Yes, I am," she agrees imperiously.

I laugh. "And so humble," I tease.

"One of my many virtues," she jokes back. "But seriously, no matter what happens, let's still be friends. Pinky swear on it?" She holds up her little finger.

I chuckle and hook mine with hers. "Pinky swear," I agree.

TWENTY

It takes me hours after Emily leaves to work up the courage to go see Bryce. Knocking on his door is the hardest part. Because until I do that, I can always turn back. Before I can chicken out, I give three hard raps on the door. And my stomach immediately goes from a ball of butterflies to a clenched knot. I count to distract myself. When I'm to fifteen I realize expecting him to be home on a Saturday night might have been ridiculous. At thirty I stop, and I'm debating whether to knock again or give up when the door swings open.

Bryce's eyes travel over my face for several heartbeats. But we're both silent. I take in his casual attire — navy basketball shorts and a plain, white T-shirt and am thankful that at least I don't appear to have interrupted anything.

"Can we talk?" I ask, breaking first.

Bryce shrugs and steps back. I enter, hovering near the door, unsure whether he really wants me here. He seats himself on the couch and gestures for me to sit. When I'm perched reluctantly on the other end, I find myself needing to work up my courage once again. He sighs impatiently.

"What is it you wanted to talk about?" he prompts. He's not going to make this easy.

"You said something this morning," I start, my voice cracking with the strain of trying to keep my tone even. "You called him my boyfriend." I look up to meet his steely gaze. "He's not. He hasn't been for months. And no matter what you think, I have no intention of going after him."

Bryce's expression softens ever so slightly. "You still love him, though," he replies.

I nod, biting back a wave of tears. "I do. But I'm done waiting. I'm done chasing the wrong guy. Because you were right. What he's doing," I pause for breath, "it doesn't matter why. It's not okay. And I'm tired. Of waiting for answers. Of wasting my energy worrying about someone who ..." I shake my head.

"Who what?" Bryce leans forward, clearly eager to hear the end of the sentence.

"Who is selfish," I say simply. "But I'm not here to bad-mouth Alessandro. I'm just over it. And I ..." My rambling train of thought is interrupted by a soft knock on the door. Bryce looks at me, clearly confused. "Go ahead and get it."

He rises from the couch, and I take the opportunity to wipe away the tears that had formed at the corners of my eyes and to collect myself as he answers the door.

"Hey, soldier, you lonesome tonight?"

My head whips around at the high, feminine voice. And just around Bryce's side I see her. All blond hair, short dress, and tall heels. The Funeral Barbie disguise dropped, she's clearly gone full seductress. And every fear I had about what Bryce was doing and who he was doing it with comes to life in front of my eyes.

"Now's not a good time," Bryce responds tightly, but she pushes past him anyway.

I rise frantically from the couch, a lump in my throat. Madison catches sight of me and freezes.

"Oh, I didn't know you had company," she purrs in my direction.

Bryce continues to hold the door open behind her. "Madison. Not. Now," he says commandingly.

She glances back at him coquettishly. "Ask nicely, Bryce, darling," she prompts him.

"Please," he replies through gritted teeth.

She casts a simpering smile at me, flaunting her control of him over me. "Okay," she agrees, slinking back to his side and planting a kiss on his cheek. "I'll just come back later."

"I think it would be best if you didn't," he says tightly.

She cocks an eyebrow at him. "Some other time then," she suggests as she exits. She blows him one last kiss over her shoulder as he closes the door.

The silence hangs heavy in the air for several heartbeats.

"Since the funeral?" I ask.

He turns back to me slowly. "It's not what you think," he says.

I keep a tight rein on my expression. "I just want to hear it from you, Bryce," I reply pleadingly. "Same as you wanted to hear about the police report from me."

"Yes, since the funeral," he confirms.

I nod, choking back the emotion threatening to overtake me. "The rest is a two-way street too. We're just friends. I have no business telling you who to love," I say. My voice sounds far surer than I feel. Inside, I'm falling apart.

"Sera, I don't …" he starts.

I hold a hand up to stop him. "You don't owe me an explanation. I think I'm done here. You should call Madison and tell her to come back. Maybe you can still salvage your evening," I manage to get out. I push past him and head for the door.

"I may not owe you an explanation, but I'd like to give you one," he growls.

I take my hand off the doorknob and spin to face him.

"I'm not stupid, Bryce, there's nothing to explain. You're back with your ex. I get it. Message received loud and clear. I just …" I bite back the nasty comment I'd been about to make. "I need to stop. Now. Before I say something I can't take back." I turn and leave, not giving him a chance to draw me into another fight.

Furious, I burst out of the building into the cool night air. I make for where I thought I'd parked around the corner, but don't find my car. Remembering I'd parked somewhere different this time, I whirl around, angry at Bryce for distracting me so badly that I can't even properly recall where I put my vehicle, when someone grabs me hard from behind. It takes me only a fraction of a second to realize whoever it is isn't tall enough to be Bryce. And they sure as hell don't smell good enough to be Madison.

I throw my head back and my feet fly out from under me as my assailant lifts me up.

"Let me go *now*!" I screech, writhing in his vice grip.

"You're a bossy little bitch," a low voice growls in my ear. I feel myself being hauled backward toward a dark clump of bushes. "Shut your fucking mouth, or I'll show you who's the *real* boss."

My blood turns to ice, but I don't give myself time to think about why the words bother me beyond the obvious threat.

With an intensity I didn't think myself capable of, I

focus on remembering Bryce's lesson. I throw myself to the right, hooking my foot around the thick leg behind mine. Pulling as hard as I can with my foot, I simultaneously leverage as much distance as possible and slam the heel of my left hand back hard. Both efforts bear fruit and my attacker cries out in pain, falling to the ground. His arms spring open, and I barely manage not to spill onto the concrete in front of me as I break free. I don't waste time looking back, breaking into a sprint to get back to the building's entrance. As I round the corner, I see Bryce standing on the walkway ahead of me and I bolt toward him. His head whips in my direction and his eyes go wide as saucers as I slam into him.

"Someone," my breath comes in sharp pants, making talking difficult, "grabbed me."

"*Fuck*. Get inside. Now," he barks. He drags me wordlessly back into the building and up to his apartment. He doesn't let go of me as he finds his phone and calls the police. When he hangs up, he pulls away, leveling his face with mine. "Stay here. Don't open the door for anyone but me." He leaps back into action, disappearing into the back of the apartment and returning with a pistol in his hands and an ID case strapped to his waistband.

I want to beg him not to leave, but I can't even form the words. And once he's slipped out the door, locking it behind him, I'm glad I couldn't. Because it gives me time to break down in private. And to remember where I'd heard those words before. My frantic brain pulls the memory out. Of Daniel. Warning me not to tell anyone about his threats against me. It's hard to remember, but his exact words were something like, *If you say anything about this, I'll have to find another way to show you who's the real boss around here.* Terrifyingly similar. A deep shudder rolls through my body. I try not to think more about it, but as the minutes tick by it gets harder.

Finally, I hear sirens. And a few minutes later a knock.

"It's me," Bryce's voice calls through the door.

I scramble to open it and find him there with a uniformed officer at his side, a portly man a bit older than Bryce with straw-colored hair and a mustache. "Sera, this is Officer Abbott."

"Ma'am," Officer Abbott offers with a tip of his hat. "I'm sorry to hear about what happened tonight."

Bryce leads us to the living room, leaving the door partially open and setting his holstered gun on the kitchen counter. I glance at the door nervously and Bryce catches my look.

"His partner is still checking outside," he explains. "He'll be in shortly." I nod and fold myself into the corner of the couch facing the door, ready to get this over with. Again.

Officer Abbott gives me a sympathetic look. "I know this is probably the last thing you want to do right now.

But it's important that I take a statement while events are still fresh in your mind."

"It's okay," I reply. "I'm unfortunately getting kind of used to it."

Bryce grimaces from the armchair next to me but stays silent. I sigh and give them the facts in as fine a detail as I can. I must do a good job of it, because there are no questions from the peanut gallery, and Officer Abbott is heading out the door before his partner even has a chance to join us. His radio crackles briefly and he exchanges words with someone.

"Nothing outside. I trust you'll be in to the station tomorrow, Bryce?" Officer Abbott asks.

I look at Bryce, who nods in reply.

"Thanks, Al," Bryce replies.

With a last tip of his hat, Officer Al is gone. Bryce turns to me, looking wearier than I've seen him since his father's funeral.

"I can take you home if you want, but I'd prefer if you stayed here," he says.

"I'll stay," I reply meekly. "There's something I didn't tell Officer Al."

Bryce raises an eyebrow and presses his lips together. "And why not?" he asks through gritted teeth.

"Because I'm not sure. It didn't sound like Daniel. I mean, I think they were trying not to use their real voice, but …" I feel like a stuttering mess, so I stop and take a breath. "What he said, about showing me who the real boss is? Daniel said those *exact* words to me in his office the day he threatened me."

"Ah." That's all Bryce says. But he looks as troubled as I feel. He looks back down into my eyes. "I'll talk to the detective in charge of his case tomorrow. Try to get some sleep. You're safe here." And without so much as a reassuring glance, he retreats to his room.

TWENTY-ONE

Bryce

As soon as I'm alone, I take a swing at the punching bag in the corner of my bedroom. Bare-fisted, I pummel it until I'm breathing hard and have burned off a good amount of rage. Rage at Madison for her unannounced appearance. At the bastard stalking Sera. At myself. I could go on, but I finally give in to my exhaustion and flop onto the bed.

The dull ache in my knuckles and arms keeps me awake. But not as much as remembering the look of terror on Sera's face. Eventually, I slip into a restless sleep.

∿

I WAKE AT MY USUAL TIME, THOUGH IT'S THE ONE DAY I don't bother with alarms. Not that I usually need one anyway. I trudge toward the kitchen set on making coffee when I spot Sera asleep on the couch.

"For Pete's sake," I grumble. I turn around and open the guest bedroom door before scooping her up gently. She stirs against my chest as I move her, but I manage to get her onto the bed without waking her fully. Closing the door behind me, I head back to the kitchen.

More than an hour later I've managed to get through two cups of coffee and most of the newspaper when Sera emerges.

"I was fine on the couch," she grouses, pouring herself a cup of coffee.

I raise an eyebrow but remain silent.

She plops into a dining chair across from me. "I didn't know anyone still read the paper."

"Well, I have since I was ten. Not about to stop now," I say shortly.

"You read the newspaper when you were ten?" she asks doubtfully.

I glance up at her. "Okay, fine, I used to just read the comics," I concede. I can see her trying not to smile and for a moment I'm hopeful that we can get through all of this.

"Can I go home now?" she asks testily.

I fold the last section that I was reading onto the table.

"If you want," I allow. "And I know you had a rough night, but first I'd like it if we could talk about what happened before that."

She sets her mug down and pushes it away. "I'd rather not, if it's all the same," she grumbles.

I grimace and loose a sigh. "I don't want there to be bad blood between us," I explain.

She levels an angry glare at me. "Then maybe you should've been honest with me in the first place," she retorts.

I clench my jaw at the accusation in her words and tone and choose my response carefully. "Exactly how was I dishonest?" I ask.

"'If you choose me, I want it to be with all of you. I won't settle for anything less,'" she mimics. She's throwing my words back at me with spite. "But you weren't exactly in a position to offer that yourself, were you?" Her fury morphs quickly into something far more devastating as tears fill her eyes.

"Madison means nothing to me," I reply evenly.

She scoffs. "Bullshit," she fumes. "You're just like him. You say you want me under your terms, like I'm not living up to your exacting criteria, then I find out it's a complete double standard. You want all of me without having to give up your little side pieces. I'm so fucking sick of it."

"It's not like that," I protest.

"Which part? You wanting me? Or her being your side piece?" she demands. But she quickly rises from the table, not waiting for an answer. "I'm leaving. It's daytime. I remember where my car is now. Thanks for everything." She turns on her heel to go.

"So that's it? You just leave every time the conversation gets a little difficult?" I call after her.

"Yep," she responds flippantly without turning around. "And you don't need to bother trying to follow me this time. I'm sure you have to report to your girlfriend to give her a good fuck before church, soldier." The door clicks shut behind her.

Well, shit. That didn't go as planned.

I clean up and throw on a pair of khakis and a blue polo. And then I head to the police department. Because, despite what Sera thinks, the tradition of going to church every Sunday died with my father. He's the only reason I went anyway. Hell, he's the only reason I did a lot of things.

ABBOTT LEFT A NOTE THAT HE HADN'T FOUND ANYTHING yet to add on the assault file, so I head to talk to Detective Jacobs, lead on Daniel Sutton's case. And though it's Sunday, I know he'll be here. Even without the high-profile case the guy's a workaholic. Always has been.

And sure enough, I see his full head of messy brown hair bowed over his desk, examining something with a magnifying glass. I rap my knuckles on his door to get his attention.

"Hey, Tim," I call out. He pops up from scrutinizing the paper in front of him and gives me a wide grin.

"Hoyt!" he exclaims, jumping up to clap his hand in mine and throw his other arm around me. He gives me a one-shoulder hug and releases, shoving me jokingly. "They keep letting your ass in here? Gotta tell them to up the security in this place."

"You're just pissed I didn't let them seduce me into this gig," I joke back. "I mean, I know SEALs gotta stick together, but this is all you, man."

He laughs and settles into his chair. "Yep. You know how much I love this shit," he replies, offering me a seat with a gesture. I slide into a chair. "But I'm guessing you're not here to catch up."

"Not today, Timmy," I lament. "I'm here because Serafina Evans was attacked last night."

Tim's eyebrows shoot up. "The chick that works with Sutton?" he asks. I can tell I have his full attention now. "They catch the guy?"

I shake my head. "She didn't even get a look at him. But he said something to her. Threatened her, actually. With the exact wording Daniel Sutton threatened her almost a month ago. And she was followed home from your vic's house on Thursday night." Tim's eyebrows climb so high this time, they're threatening to merge with his hairline.

"Is that so?" he murmurs. But other than surprise, his expression gives nothing away.

"It is. Any way it could've been your guy?" I watch his face carefully, but he wipes any expression from his face and levels a blank stare back at me.

"You know I can't tell you anything," he replies evenly. I hold his gaze. "But I'll look into it. Who took the report?"

"Al. At almost ten last night."

I purposely don't mention her being followed on Friday night, since Sutton was in jail at the time. An accomplice wouldn't be out of the question, and he's still my number one suspect. But I know Tim. If he had that information he wouldn't pursue Sutton with the same gusto. Especially since nothing much came of the stalking or the assault. A bloodhound, this one, but not terribly excited when there's no blood, so to speak.

"I appreciate it, Tim." I let silence hang in the air a bit, seeing if he'll offer anything else. But he doesn't.

"Anything for you, Hoyt," he replies when he's done sizing me up. I huff a laugh, doubtful. But I'll take what I can get. And I know I'm not going to get anything else out of Tim Jacobs today. I toy momentarily with the idea of going directly to the DA. But I both don't have the kind of connections with that office that I do with the Seattle PD, and I don't dare go around Tim. I've got to think about the long game and not piss off some of my best allies.

"I'll let you get back to it," I respond. "Nice seeing you, Timmy."

"You too, Hoyt."

I leave, still relatively unsatisfied and fairly certain Tim will take his dear sweet time looking into it. Time in which I'm not willing to gamble with Sera's safety. I silently thank my father for insisting I not join the force after being discharged. Because if I were a police officer I wouldn't be able to do what I'm about to do. It's time to ask the bastard himself. Once I'm back in the car, it doesn't take long to find Daniel Sutton's address.

I PULL UP AND AM IMMEDIATELY DISGUSTED BY THE obnoxiously modern, overly lavish residence in the exclusive Medina neighborhood. Looking around the front of the house, I don't see a garage or any vehicles. The driveway must be on another side of the house. Deciding to look later, I pull a pistol from the glove compartment and hang it from my belt, adding my ID holder next to it. As I approach the front door, I note the security cameras and realize I'm going to have to play this one more conservatively than I'd like.

I take a deep breath and ring the bell. An older Hispanic woman answers almost immediately. "Yes?" Her expression is stern, her voice full of suspicion as she glances at the gun on my hip. "You police?" Despite her small stature, I can immediately tell she's not someone to mess with.

"No, ma'am. My name is Bryce Hoyt. I'm a private security consultant. I'm here to talk to Mr. Sutton," I respond.

"You have an appointment?" she asks sharply.

I can't help but smile. Sutton doesn't deserve such a faithful helper.

"I'm afraid I don't. But it's in Mr. Sutton's best interest to speak with me," I reply calmly. She eyes me a bit longer before nodding her head.

"You wait here." She closes the door.

I'm guessing by her guarded nature and failure to admit me to the house that I'm not the first stranger to come looking for answers from Daniel Sutton.

When the door reopens a few minutes later, the most average looking man I've ever laid eyes on stands before me. I'm not sure what I expected. Someone as vicious or ugly outside as he is inside, perhaps, even though I know that's not how it goes. But even his expression and his body language are unremarkable. Though he looks as exhausted as I feel.

"Can I help you?" he asks sharply in a likewise ordinary voice.

I hand him the business card I'd pulled from my ID holder, hoping it will help put him at ease.

"Mr. Sutton, I'm Bryce Hoyt. I run a private security company. I'd like to speak with you about some information I have related to your case," I explain carefully. I stay loose, fixing a casual expression on my face. I just need to get in the door. If he lets me in, I may have a shot at getting something useful out of him. But there's no overcoming the disadvantage of standing on a threshold.

He throws me a skeptical glance. "I've never heard of you. What could you possibly know?"

I cautiously select the truths to present. "I know Heather Irving. I met her when I did security work for Evans Realty Services. And I was at the police department the day she filed a report against you."

Daniel glances nervously toward the street, clearly afraid of who might have heard. He steps back, swinging the door open. I internally breathe a sigh of relief.

"Come in, Mr. Hoyt," he offers. "It seems we may have things to discuss after all."

He leads me through the vast foyer and into a formal living room stuffed with overwrought furniture and antiques. The place looks like it was decorated by a seventy-year-old woman.

"Nice place you've got here," I murmur. One lie won't hurt.

He offers me a seat on a stuffy, hard-backed tufted leather divan and settles into a matched armchair across from it.

"Thank you," he replies stiffly, then turns toward the back of the room. "Estella!" The Hispanic woman who answered the front door appears through an archway. "I'd like coffee, please." He turns to me expectantly.

"Nothing for me, thank you," I say. He nods curtly, and the older woman disappears.

"So who exactly are you working for, Mr. Hoyt?" Daniel asks, turning his weak blue eyes on me questioningly.

I get the sense immediately that he's not as smart as he thinks he is. "I'm afraid that's confidential," I reply apologetically.

"You said you did some work for Serafina Evans," he points out shrewdly. "She wouldn't happen to be who you're working for now, would she?"

Maybe he's not as stupid as he looks. But I seize the opportunity to turn it to my advantage.

"Lord, no. I haven't worked for Ms. Evans since her company was absorbed by yours," I reply, feigning disgust. The revulsion is meant to draw him in, but technically the rest is true. I don't work for Sera.

Daniel smirks at me. "You're lucky you don't *have* to

work with her," he responds. "If it was my choice, I wouldn't, either."

"Oh? What did she do to *you*?" I ask with practiced indifference and the subtle insinuation that I'm a fellow "victim" of hers.

"Nothing much," he says. But his wrathful tone betrays him. "Just poison my own father against me. Attempt to steal my hard-earned place in the company I helped him build into what it is today. And I'm fairly certain that she also had something to do with Ms. Irving's fabrications."

"Fuck," I respond, snorting. "It sounds like you have more of a beef against her than I do."

"You don't know the half of it," he seethes. He starts to say something else and then stops.

"It's okay," I reply, sensing his struggle. "I know you probably can't say anything with everything that's going on." Daniel sighs, relieved.

"Exactly," he agrees. "But let's just say, since this whole thing started I've steered clear of anyone and everyone, even my own family, but I hope I'm around when someone takes her down. I'm just sad it won't be me."

"Right. If I were you, I'd want to see her in a world of hurt," I agree zealously.

Estella enters with a tray and sets it on the table next to Daniel before exiting once more. Daniel picks up the coffee and sips it thoughtfully.

"You know, as long as she's professionally destroyed, it's all the same to me," Daniel finally replies.

I keenly note his purposeful use of the word *professionally*. Not exactly the singular focus I'd expect of a deranged stalker. Which makes me think that, while he's deranged, it's unlikely he'd go after Sera in the ways she's been pursued these past weeks. He just wants her to keep her paws off his perceived birthright.

"But enough about Ms. Evans. You said you have information?"

I clear my throat. Having already learned most of what I needed to know, I need to wrap this up in a way that seems plausible and possibly even confirms my conclusion further.

"Given that the investigation is still ongoing," I hedge carefully, "I can't divulge everything. But I'm trying to prove, on someone else's behalf, where you were this past Thursday evening. Or where you *weren't* to be exact."

"If this investigation has to do with my case, this is the first I've heard of it. To what end are you trying to prove my whereabouts?" Daniel asks distrustfully.

"I didn't say it was your case," I reply, smiling politely. "But it is related. If I can establish where you were, I may be able to head off any future issues for you."

And this is really the moment of truth. Have I established enough of a rapport for him to trust me? If not, I'll settle for him being gullible enough to answer anyway. I try not to hold my breath as I wait for his answer.

"As I said, I haven't been to see anyone. In fact, I haven't left the house since …" he pauses to think about it, "Since I stopped working last Wednesday."

I nod, focusing on not letting out a sigh of relief. "I presume your housekeeper and security cameras will corroborate that?" I ask.

"Of course," he replies unflinchingly.

"Good," I respond, stopping short of warning him to be prepared to provide that evidence when the police come asking. I'm already toeing the line of obstruction of justice. "I appreciate your cooperation, Mr. Sutton."

Daniel looks at me incredulously. "That's all?" he asks suspiciously.

"That's all," I assure him. "I'm sorry I'm not able to tell you more. But you've been extremely helpful." I rise and offer my hand, which he also rises to take. His handshake is uncomfortably firm, and I smile, unsurprised. This guy obviously has a *lot* to compensate for. He smiles back, thinking the gesture friendly, and I suppress a laugh. "Best of luck to you." *You're gonna need it.*

"Thank you, Mr. Hoyt," he replies, seeing me to the door. As I descend the steps of his front walkway, he calls after me. "I trust you'd rather I didn't mention this visit to anyone from the police department?"

I turn around and spread my arms open, offering a

final smile. "By all means, tell whomever you wish," I encourage him.

He nods curtly and closes the door. This guy really is a pompous asshole if he thinks that kind of test is going to work. But I'm fairly confident his even asking, and then accepting my response, means he's highly unlikely to say anything anyway, since he obviously thinks there's a shot I'm trying to help him.

I finally let out that sigh of relief. And on my way out, I drive around the corner and eye the cars in the driveway leading to the back of the house. Flashy red sports car. Tan SUV. Green coupe, probably the housekeeper's as it's the only practical vehicle. Nothing matching Sera's stalker's vehicle. I'd gone in expecting to find him linked in some way. But I'm leaving fairly convinced he's not. It's a relief on one hand, but a troubling mystery on the other.

My stomach rumbles, and I decide to stop for lunch before heading to my next destination. I'm going to need all the strength I can get to deal with Madison.

BY THE TIME I KNOCK ON HER DOOR, I'M SWEATING AND cranky from struggling to find a parking spot in the hilly Green Lake neighborhood on a hot and sunny late summer afternoon. So much for being at the top of my game.

She finally answers, fanning herself lazily with a

folded piece of paper and looking ridiculously racy in pink barely-more-than-underwear shorts and a tiny white sports bra.

"Bryce, darling," she greets me. "I'm glad to see you." She pulls me into the apartment, standing on her toes with her hands around my neck, trying to land a kiss. I firmly disentangle her arms and step back.

"I'm not here for that," I reply.

She settles onto a spot on the couch with a fan pointing at it. I sit on the opposite end, facing her with my knee crooked up to discourage her from getting too close.

"What *are* you here for then?" she asks, pulling her blond locks off her sweaty neck. She's continuing to lay the sexy act on thick, unaware that I've resolved not to fall for it anymore.

"You had no right to show up like that last night," I reply.

She eyes me speculatively. "I just thought you might be up for a little fun," she pouts. "Haven't we been having a good time, darling?"

"Please don't call me that," I snap. "And I wouldn't exactly call it a good time. Momentary weakness, perhaps."

"You and I have different definitions of momentary," she replies, smirking. "Three times is a pattern, dearie."

"It's over is what it is," I correct her.

She arches an eyebrow and purses her lips. "Your little

girlfriend wasn't happy to see me, I take it?" she asks shrewdly. "To be honest, I was surprised to see her there after you came running to me last Saturday with a case of blue balls."

"Don't be so crass, Madison, it's unbecoming," I snap.

She grins at my choice of words. "Yes, there's been lots of coming. But I guess no more," she sighs. "Oh, well, it was fun while it lasted."

"Can you be serious for a minute?" I growl, frustrated. "Look. I'm sorry. I'm not trying to blame you. I just haven't been myself. But I can't do this anymore. I won't. So please, just don't call me, don't come to see me, and I'll do the same. Everything will go back to how it was."

Madison's expression softens and the pity in her eyes is almost worse than the attempted seduction. "It's not something you can take back," she replies. "But if that's what you want, then okay."

I look at her skeptically.

"Really. Cross my heart." She runs a finger in an X over her left breast.

I snap my eyes back to hers, so I don't stare.

"Thank you," I breathe, relieved. I rise from the couch. "Take care, Madison. I'm sorry for everything."

She opens the door for me and gives me a sad look. "And here I thought your coming to me that one time meant you were giving in. Can't lie, I'm a little disappointed. But I'll get over it," she says, leaning on the door.

I suppress an eye roll. I'm sure she'll be over it by being under someone else in no time flat. She certainly didn't waste any time doing exactly that as soon as our relationship ended the first time.

"I have no doubt," I reply wryly. "Bye, Maddie."

I don't even wait until I'm back at the car to call Sera. It rings once and goes to voicemail.

"Son of a bitch," I mutter, trying to suppress my annoyance. I place the call again. And again, after one ring it goes to voicemail. Now I'm *really* annoyed. I call her one final time, ready to leave a voicemail if that's how she wants to play it. But this time, she actually answers.

"Boy, you just can't take a hint, can you?" She sounds as angry as I am annoyed.

I don't even bother with apologies or small talk, as I know my window to keep her listening is short.

"I saw Daniel." My words are met with silence, and I know I have her attention.

"*Excuse me?*" Now she sounds furious. "What did you do, Bryce?"

"Don't worry, I used all my best super-secret security guy tricks. He's none the wiser. But I'm also fairly certain he had nothing to do with following or attacking you," I reply.

"And exactly how do you know that?" she asks, her voice echoing on the other end of the line.

"Where are you?" I ask suspiciously.

"I'm in the garage in my building," she replies impatiently.

"Coming or going?" I demand.

"Relax. I just went through a drive-through coffee stand. I ran out," she responds snippily. I hear the noises of an elevator.

"You think someone won't follow you again just because it's daytime?" I press.

She heaves a dramatic sigh. "Fine, next time I'll call you and make you get my coffee. If you're not my personal security guard, you can be my errand boy," she responds, her voice dripping with sarcasm. Man, she's really pissed.

"I'm just worried. If Daniel isn't the one after you …" I pause. There's a soft ping on her end and I hear her moving. "I'm not sure how to figure out who is." Sera suddenly sucks in a sharp breath. There are a few beats of silence, and I'm wondering why that was so shocking when she finally responds.

"I think I might have an idea," she replies, her voice quavering.

My hackles rise. "Are you okay?" I ask, fighting a sudden tightness in my chest.

"I'm fine. We'll talk about it later. I have to go," she replies vaguely. And the line goes dead.

TWENTY-TWO

I concentrate on not dropping my phone or my coffee as I approach the door, my heart pounding in my chest, eyes locked on Alessandro. I slide my phone blindly into my back pocket as I stop a few paces away.

Alessandro stares back. Now that I'm close enough, my eyes can't drink him in quickly enough. His thick, dark brown hair is disheveled, his chocolate brown eyes filled with love and longing. His dark jeans and black T-shirt are loose — he looks like he's lost weight from his already lean frame. In fact, he looks gaunt. Haunted. And he's just as at a loss for words as I am.

"Are you really here?" I finally manage.

"I'm here," he affirms, his voice tired and more lilting than I recall. He steps forward and wraps his arms around me. I sink into his warm embrace, fighting back tears as I inhale deeply of his familiar wine and spice scent. When he pulls away, he stays close, brushing the hair from my face, running his fingers down my jaw. I look up into his eyes, still unable to believe what I'm seeing. "Did you miss me?" His thumb drops to my lip and traces a line that sends fire shooting through my core. I almost forget to be angry. Almost.

I slowly wrap my free hand around his and draw his thumb away from my mouth, vigilantly working to control the myriad of emotions roiling inside me.

"Let's go inside," I reply. I unlock the door and he follows me in.

Once I've put my coffee down, we settle onto the couch. Well, perch on the edge of our seats is more like it. The tension in the room is palpable, and I know he's confused as to why I stopped him from touching me.

"I'm glad to see you're okay," he finally says, breaking the awkward silence. "But I'm a little surprised you don't seem completely happy to see me."

I stare at him, shocked and bemused, unsure which part of that to unpack first. "Why wouldn't I be okay?" I ask.

He frowns and leans back into the couch, crossing his legs and clearly agitated. "That's a long story," he hedges.

"It would be shorter if you'd bothered talking to me these past weeks." I don't even try to keep the annoyance and rage out of my tone.

A look of understanding crosses his face and he leans forward, earnestly folding his hands around mine. "For that, I am truly sorry," he says solemnly. "You must understand it was necessary."

"Well, I don't. Care to explain it to me?" I scoff. Even I feel like I should be more relieved to see him. But I'm not. Now that the initial wave of relief has passed, I really am just mad.

"Serafina, please don't be so angry with me," he pleads.

I want to throw my hands up in frustration. He and Bryce really are more alike than I'd realized. Both completely unaware of the impact of their actions and words.

"I *am* angry. Wouldn't you be?" I ask, turning it back on him.

He runs a finger under his chin thoughtfully and the memory of all the things that gesture used to make me feel makes me want to cry.

"Yes," he concedes. "I'd be infuriated." He looks so forlorn, so defeated, that my anger collapses in on itself. "*Mi dispiace, mio tesoro.*"

The apology is my final undoing, and hot tears spill down my cheeks, a wretched sob tearing itself from my throat. He's holding me in an instant, his warm, rough hands tracing my jaw, his legs pressed against mine. I wrap my hands around his forearms, but only to hang on as the sobs rip out of me. His forehead meets mine, and I can feel him desperately trying to calm me with his touch.

Finally, his lips crash into mine, hot and wet. My overwhelmed body responds, my lips parting to receive his tongue. Our mouths work together fervently, as if their dance can erase the pain and confusion of our separation and subsequent reunion. Long-suppressed need awakens in me, and I nearly swoon with desire for him. It's so overwhelming, it takes a conscious effort to rein it in.

As my control returns, I break away, panting. My gut twists, and I have to search myself to name the feeling that is rising to the top of the ocean of emotions churning inside me. It's disloyalty. As if I'm betraying Bryce.

My anger turns inward at the thought. At how foolish I've been to feel so deeply for two such different men with the same disastrous results. Because now, even though I've consciously chosen Bryce, he hasn't chosen me. He's chosen someone else.

But touching Alessandro still feels wrong. Like an insult to myself, to the decision I'd made. Because his reappearance makes it no less valid. No less likely for there to be an explanation that changes things.

I collect myself completely, the flow of tears stopping, before I dare to speak again. I look up into Alessandro's patient eyes, the same sorrow I feel etched on his face.

"Why are you here?" I ask quietly, calmly.

"Because you are in danger," he replies. "And it's my fault."

I stare into his devastated face for what feels like minutes before it clicks. "The break-in, being followed, the *attack*," I whisper. "It was all because of you?"

Reluctantly, Alessandro nods.

"Explain. Now." My words hiss between my teeth.

Alessandro looks up at the ceiling, blinking back his own tears. When he looks at me again, I try to smooth the anger from my features, knowing it won't help now.

"It was exactly what I feared," he begins. "After we last spoke all those weeks ago, I gave in. I couldn't find the answers on my own. So I contacted a friend who I knew could help. And what we found was much, much worse than I even dreamed. That is why you didn't hear from me. Because I didn't want it to lead them to you. But yesterday we learned they'd found you anyway. Through an email you sent. It didn't take long from there to learn that they were going after you, to drag you to Rome to use against me. I came immediately. I can't even tell you the panic I've been in. How happy I am that you're okay. But now you must come with me. So I can keep you safe from them. If they know I'm here ..."

I throw up a hand, having heard enough. "Please," I breathe. "Stop. It's all too much."

He nods understandingly. "I realize how it must have

seemed to you," he agrees. "Everything you must have felt, how serious this all is …"

"No," I interrupt quietly. He stops, staring at me, confusion written all over his face. "It's too much of the same. The same vague nonanswers. The same excuses for keeping me in the dark. The same threats looming in the background keeping us from just being together and living our lives free of the worry of what *might* happen."

"I assure you, these are very dangerous people and the threat against my life, and now yours, is very real," he replies somberly. I search his eyes and find no exaggeration. He's truly terrified.

"I'm sorry you're going through this," I say slowly. "But I don't see how uprooting my life to hide with you in Italy is going to be any better."

"We'd be together," he says earnestly. "I have the contacts there. It wouldn't be a prison, Serafina. You would be protected. You wouldn't have to fear for your safety any longer."

I laugh humorlessly. "At what cost?" I ask. "Giving up everything and everyone else I care about? And what about your safety? If what you say is true, you'll be in danger regardless."

"For now," he admits. "But not forever."

"Can't you protect me here? Can't you just stay here with me, where we met? Where we fell in love? Where our lives are?" I beg. "I just want to go back to that. Is there any way?" I have to ask. But I already know the answer even before his face falls.

"I wish there were, *amore mio*," he murmurs. "But no. My life is no longer here. There are things I must go back and do. And I can't leave you here, where I can't protect you."

"Alessandro, I'm not yours to protect," I reply. I may as well have slapped him in the face. He starts to rise, but I pull him back down. "Please. I need to say this." He sits back down, a solitary tear falling down his cheek. "I love you. I do. But it's not enough. You left. And then I stopped hearing from you. I was out of my mind until I realized that it was pointless. Whatever your reasons, you've kept me out of it. And in doing that you separated yourself from me, and made decisions on your own that affected me, without so much as checking in."

"I had to, I couldn't …"

"Even before you left, Alessandro. You were doing this. You asked me to be with you completely or not at all once while keeping from me that you weren't mine completely. Then even after you were free to be with me and all *this* started, you still kept it from me. I had to hunt you down and seduce it out of you, for fuck's sake." I shake my head, staring down into my hands. "I've hung on because I love you. But it's only gotten harder. You've only pushed me farther away. And now you're asking me to give up everything after shutting me out completely for *six weeks*. While I sat here, not knowing if you were dead or alive. Not knowing if you still loved me, or if you'd changed your mind. And not knowing the true nature of the danger I was facing." I stop to take a deep breath.

Alessandro is still, silent, and pale. I stare at him sorrowfully. None of this is what I wanted for us.

"You're right," he admits. "I'm selfish. To ask this of you after everything."

"Thank you," I reply simply.

He shakes his head and runs his hands over his face. "I understand if it's too much to ask," he says. "But please think about it?"

I huff an incredulous laugh and shake my head. "I can't go with you," I reply firmly. "It's too late."

His lower lip starts trembling and he grabs my hands. "Don't say that," he insists. "I know this is hard. It's hard for me too. To ask this of you. To ask more of you than you've already given. But everything I've done …"

"Please, please, please, do not say you've done it for me," I object vehemently, withdrawing my hands from his. The ashamed look on his face confirms that's exactly what he was going to say. "If that were really true, you would've asked what *I* wanted. What *I* thought *we* should do. You've done all of this for *you,* Alessandro."

And with those words, the last glimmer of hope for us inside me dies. Because their truth rings through the room. And even he doesn't have the balls to deny it.

My heart softens, watching him grapple with the knowledge that it's over. I fold my hand back over his and squeeze. He looks at me, a perfect picture of misery.

"I wish I could go back and do things differently," he says sorrowfully.

I smile sadly back at him. "But then you wouldn't be the man I fell in love with," I reply.

"I don't know how I can leave not knowing whether or not you'll be safe," he admits. "I'll do what I can from my end. But even if they know we're through, it won't take away how much you mean to me. That's why they're after you."

"Staying won't help that," I point out.

I contemplate telling him how I escaped my attacker. About the security features of the building. And that I still have Bryce. Until a sharp pain in my chest reminds me that I don't. And remembering that renders me unable to speak. I try to control my breathing as panic threatens the edges of my composure.

"I could ask Marco to look out for you," he offers.

I laugh. "Marco has enough to worry about right now, I'm sure," I reply. "Besides, I'll be fine. I promise. You were the one who once extolled the virtues of hiring personal security guards. Lord knows I have the money to hire the best protection."

Alessandro considers that for a moment. "You're not going to hire the giant, are you?" he asks reticently.

I want to laugh, but pain shoots through my chest again. "No," I reply softly. "That's not an option." I look up into Alessandro's soft, sad eyes once more. "I'll make some calls as soon as I can. I'll be protected around the clock. You needn't worry."

"Nonetheless, I will," he says softly.

He smiles my favorite sideways smile and I can't help it, I pull him to me and wrap my arms around him fiercely. He embraces me readily, stroking my hair and holding me tightly until I let go. I rise, taking his hand in mine one final time, and walk him to the door.

"Be careful," I plead.

He nods and gives my hand one last squeeze. Then he leans in, touching his lips gently to mine.

"Goodbye, Serafina Evans."

"*Arrivederci*, Alessandro Giordano."

TWENTY-THREE

True to my word, I spend the rest of the day researching private security online. It keeps me focused enough so the last shattered piece of my heart that belonged to Alessandro doesn't completely incapacitate me. It wouldn't be so bad if that part wasn't right next to the crushed piece that belongs to Bryce. But I'm proud of myself for finally sticking to my guns and not settling for being treated like shit. Even if, in the end, I'm alone. Funny how that's exactly what I used to prefer. Now, who knows? Allie would probably call that growth. I call it exhausting. My whole world has been upended more times than I can count lately.

I shake away the depressing train of thought and refocus on the screen in front of me. Resigned to my task for the following day, I email work to let everyone know

I'll be taking the day off. I save the list of companies and shut down my computer, ready to drink myself numb to ride out the rest of the evening.

~

I'M REGRETTING MY ALCOHOL-RELATED DECISION THE NEXT morning when I wake with a pounding headache. But somehow it occurs to me, while I wait for the ibuprofen to kick in, to ask Maggie which of the private security companies on my list had the best recommendations, and if there are any others she'd discovered when she did her search several months ago. Besides Hoyt Corporate Services, of course.

It turns out to be a huge time saver as only two of the companies I'd sourced were well recommended *and* do personal armed security. And only one has availability to start immediately. I schedule an in-home meeting for the afternoon to get set up.

And then I spend the rest of the morning cleaning out the downstairs bedroom to ready it for its new occupants.

~

AT SEVERAL MINUTES PAST THE HOUR OF THE MEETING, I sit in the dining room, cradling a cup of tea and tapping my foot impatiently. Finally, the doorbell rings.

I open the door to a put-together blond woman with a sleek bun and a no-nonsense plum-colored bespoke suit and a tall, stern man with salt-and-pepper hair who appears to be in his forties.

"Ms. Evans?" the blond asks, extending a hand.

"Yes, you must be Ms. Pruitt," I respond, shaking her hand. "Please, come in."

"Please, call me Lisa," she responds as she enters, scanning the room appraisingly. "And this is Mr. Wallace." She gestures to the stern man. He dips his head briefly and firmly shakes my hand.

I lead them both to the living room and they take a seat on the couch as I settle into my armchair.

"Thank you for seeing me on such short notice," I say. "As I explained on the phone, having been attacked the night before last, I'm ready for some peace of mind."

She leans forward eagerly. "I can imagine. Any of the incidents you described would be cause for concern. In any case, I'm confident we can help you," she agrees.

"I'm glad to hear it. I've reviewed the contracts you emailed, and everything seems fine. Why don't you tell me a little more about the practical aspects of the arrangement?" I prompt.

"Certainly," she responds. "Your contract includes one guard, to be present at all times. Actually, it will be three guards, each working an eight-hour shift. As each guard will be present for a different portion of your day, each may have recommendations on security precautions, schedule modifications, or other adjustments to ensure your continued safety. It is, of course, up to you which recommendations to follow. We will always do our best to protect you in a way that suits *your* needs, as long as there is no immediate danger."

"Sounds reasonable," I agree.

She nods curtly and continues. "We have received your deposit, so I simply need to verify your identification and witness your signing of the contracts. As a reminder, you can cancel your contract at any time, for any reason, with seventy-two hours' notice. If for any reason there is a particular security guard you feel isn't a good fit, please let us know and we will remove them from your rotation, no questions asked. Do you have any additional questions?" Her speech done, she looks at me expectantly.

"The contract was fairly thorough," I allow. "I understand that I will be responsible for all costs including food, travel, and incidentals, but am I understanding correctly that the guards will not actually be living here?"

"That's correct," she agrees. "They'll simply need to use the room requested as a base, especially for the night shift. But they will only utilize it as necessary for the eight hours they are each assigned to your security detail."

"What are the shift times?" I ask.

"There is some flexibility, and we recommend

adjusting them to your schedule," she explains. "What time do you usually start and finish work?"

"I start between seven and eight a.m. and usually finish between six and seven p.m."

"Then I think shifts starting each at six a.m., two p.m., and ten p.m. would be best. Does that work for you?" she asks. She's all business as she primly folds her hands in her lap, awaiting my response.

"Well, I'll let you know if it doesn't," I reply with a small smile.

Her perfect mask doesn't crack. "Certainly," she agrees.

I want to chuckle. This woman is like a robot. But I suppress it and focus on the paperwork she's laying out on the coffee table.

"Please initial here to acknowledge that your guard, and therefore you, are GPS-tracked at all times," she points, and I obligingly scribble my initials. "And here to accept use of the provided driver service as your primary method of transportation." Another scribble. "And sign and date here to accept the full contract terms." A bigger scribble. "And that's it. Oh, and as stipulated in the contract, each guard has signed nondisclosure agreements as part of their general employment requirements not to share any personal information regarding their clients for both the duration of your utilizing our services and after termination."

"Naturally," I reply drily, glancing at Mr. Wallace.

He's barely moved a muscle this whole time. Maybe they're all robots. I almost giggle.

Lisa rises, extending a hand once more. "It's been a pleasure meeting you," she says mechanically. "I'll leave you and Mr. Wallace to get acquainted."

I see her to the door, and immediately notice my new, Mr. Wallace-shaped shadow tailing me. I glance over my shoulder at him. This is going to take some getting used to.

Once we are alone, I size Mr. Wallace up a bit more thoroughly. His impeccable black suit and tie and white shirt look starchy and uncomfortable. Or maybe that's just his stiff demeanor.

"Mr. Wallace," I say. "Do you have a first name?"

His stern façade cracks just a bit as the corner of his mouth lifts. "Yes, ma'am," he replies. His first words. His voice is commanding and just as severe as his demeanor. "Ross, ma'am."

I let out a small cough to cover a laugh. "I see," I reply. "May I call you Ross? Or would you prefer Mr. Wallace?"

"Ross is fine, ma'am," he responds.

"Call me, Sera, please. No need for 'ma'am,'" I encourage him. He nods. "Thank you. Now, is there anything we need to cover before I give you a tour?"

"We can cover most things as we go. But most important," he says, holding up a cellphone. "This is the cellphone assigned to only you that your guard or driver will carry at all times. You should program this number into your phone. It is how you will let whoever is on duty know when you are ready to be picked up from a location. It is your connection to us."

I nod and pull out my cellphone and he helps me program the number in.

"Okay," I say when it's done. "Let me show you around."

As we stroll the rooms he asks questions about my habits, my work, my visitors, that sort of thing. It's clear he'll be filling out some sort of report, and I can't help but mess with him a little here and there. Through that, I'm pleased to find he clearly does have a sense of humor, it's just carefully controlled as part of the whole serious bodyguard schtick. Most important, though, I find I'm more comfortable with him than I thought I'd be. Which is huge. Because the last thing I need right now is more difficult shit to deal with.

AT THE TEN P.M. SHIFT CHANGE, HOWEVER, A NEW KIND OF challenge presents itself in the form of Bodyguard Number Two. From the moment Ross lets him in, I know I'm in trouble. Because he's one of the most attractive people I've ever seen. At just over six feet, with blond hair, green eyes, full lips, and a swimmer's body under his well-tailored black suit, I'm immediately mesmerized. He extends a broad hand and flashes a dazzling smile full of bright white teeth.

"Tristan Thomas," he introduces himself. His honeyed voice matches his Midwest good looks perfectly. I'd put him in his late twenties. I clear my throat.

"I'm Sera," my voice comes out a squeak. I inwardly roll my eyes at myself. I'm sure he gets this reaction a lot, but I somewhat despise myself for letting him have this effect on me.

His smile widens, and my hand lingers on his for what feels like a fraction of a second too long. "I'll just be a few minutes. Ross and I should sync up before he leaves," Tristan excuses himself.

I retire to the kitchen to finish the dinner dishes and watch them talk as Ross gives Tristan the tour. And in less than ten minutes, Ross is wishing me a good night and heading out the door. Tristan stands at the window wall, gazing out at the city sparkling in the velvety blue night.

"Nice view," he remarks.

I set down the dishtowel and approach, stopping a few paces behind him. "It is," I agree.

He turns to note that I've come closer.

"I should be getting to bed soon."

Tristan nods. "I'll be in the guest room, then," he replies. "Does the security system have multiple modes?"

I take him to the panel in the living room and flip through the settings. He chooses a door and window monitoring setting, leaving him free to roam without setting off any alarms.

"Help yourself to anything in the kitchen or whatever you need," I say. "Is there anything else I can get for you before I go to bed?" I keep my eyes locked on his, refusing to let them travel down his gloriously attractive body. I do not need to leave him thinking that I'm on that list of things he can have before bed, despite how hard my heart is pounding in my chest being close to him. *God, what is wrong with me?*

Tristan smiles knowingly. "No," he replies. "I'm just going to go call my boyfriend before he goes to bed."

I'm sure the shock passes over my face, but all I can think is, *Oh, thank god.* "Sounds good," I respond, trying not to sound as relieved as I feel. "Goodnight."

As I fall asleep, I briefly wonder if Tristan really is gay, or if he realized that an icy shock is the fastest way to douse an inferno.

BEING DRIVEN TO WORK WITH YET ANOTHER BODYGUARD beside me is a trip, to say the least. Thankfully, this one I like the best so far. Aiden Green is a slim, dark-haired man in his fifties. He's incredibly laid-back and very friendly, and with his Irish accent, subtle deference, and impeccable manners, he makes me feel like royalty. Or someone very important, anyway. It's hard to describe. But for the first time I'm not self-conscious at all for needing to be under the watchful eye of an armed guard. Though the thought of getting comfortable with it is strangely disconcerting too.

Work is a welcome reprieve from the drama of the past few days, and I happily surrender to the familiar ebb and flow of meetings, deadlines, and decision making. I allow myself to sink deeply into a new routine, my only companions out of work being Ross, Tristan, and Aiden. But I know it can't last forever. Especially if the mounting log of missed calls and text messages is any indication.

My mother, father, Allie, and Emily have all contacted me. And I've ignored them all in turn, unable or unwilling to remove myself from the careful bubble where I don't think about the one person I haven't heard from — Bryce. He's the one person I want to talk to the most. The one person whose silence pains me more than I allow myself to think about. But every time I start to wonder if I'm truly so easy to forget, I force my emotions back down.

Dodging my own thoughts and the attempts at communication of my friends and family gets easier when Tristan is switched to swing shift on Wednesday. I still find him ridiculously attractive, but with the pressure of any possible sexual tension removed, I find he's actually the best companion of my three protectors. It makes sense since he's the closest to my age. But it turns out he's also a sweet, intelligent guy. And he's very interested in what I do, so we have plenty to discuss to keep my mind off other things.

But on Thursday evening, ignoring everything I can't deal with finally catches up with me when someone furiously pounds on the door. Tristan jumps up from the couch beside me, hand on his gun.

"Serafina Evans, I know you're in there," Emily's voice calls through the door. I heave a sigh and climb out of my armchair, signaling Tristan to stand down. "You pinky swore! You'd better open the door this instant, or I swear to god I'm going to force my brother to come down here and …"

I swing the door open and level an annoyed glare at Emily. "And what?" I demand with a smirk.

Emily pushes past me into the condo. "Moot. Why have you been ignoring me?" she demands. She stops dead as she spots Tristan. "Oh."

"Tristan, this is my friend, Emily. Emily, Tristan."

Emily looks Tristan up and down. He's removed his jacket, but he still looks like hot, sexy business in his crisp, fitted white shirt, skinny black tie, and slim-fit black slacks.

"And Tristan is?" Emily's face is filled with questions and something bordering on anger.

"A bodyguard," I reply simply. "Tristan, can you please give us some privacy?"

Tristan nods curtly, clearly alarmed at the sudden, demanding intruder.

"You know where I am if you need me," he assures me. He ducks into the guest room off the entryway, and I turn back to Emily, who has settled herself on the couch.

"Did I just step into a movie? Because that dude is unnaturally hot," Emily says.

I huff a laugh. "Yes, he is. And so, so gay," I reply.

"Damnit," Emily jokes. "Oh well. Probably out of my league regardless. A bodyguard, huh?"

I sigh heavily as I sink into my armchair. "A bodyguard," I confirm. "I'm not sure if you'd heard …"

"About the attack?" She nods. "I'm so sorry, Sera. I wanted to give you some space, with everything, but when you didn't message or call me back, I kinda freaked out."

"And then came barging over here?" I say sweetly.

"Ehhh, sort of. I tried to get my brother to come, but he refused. Something about you promising to call him back and then not. So he figures if you want to talk to him you will."

Oh, shit. With everything that happened, my mind glitched out on promising to talk to him later about whoever was following me.

"Fuuuuuck," I respond. "I'd completely forgotten about that. What else did he tell you?"

"That you got the wrong idea," she replies.

I snort. "That's rich. I think I got exactly the right idea," I grumble.

"Meaning what?" she asks sharply.

"Meaning he's a double-standard-setting, unavailable, demanding jackass, just like Alessandro," I snap.

"Wow, tell me how you really feel," she responds.

"Seriously, Emily. He's fucking Madison. And he had the balls to make me think *I* was what was holding us back from being together," I retort.

"*Was* fucking Madison," she replies.

I wave a hand. "Whatever. It's doesn't matter anymore. He made his bed, and he clearly didn't really want me in it," I say, starting to shake with suppressed emotion.

"Why would you say that?" Emily asks sadly. She is sincerely confused, and I wonder how much he told her.

I sigh heavily, unsure of where to even begin. I start by telling her my version of what happened after she last visited me here. I explain that I tried to tell Bryce about my decision, and what I felt for him, but only got to the former before Madison showed up. And then after I was attacked, the next morning was so difficult. Because his actions and his words were so mismatched, it was unbearable. And how I lost hope that day. Only to fortuitously be tested about the decision that started it all when Alessandro reappeared.

When I tell her about our conversation and how I stood

my ground, a proud look settles over her. And when I tell her that all the danger I've been facing is tied to him, she looks as grim as I feel. But she lets me finish, lets me explain how, even in the face of all that, I still stayed strong. And I feel better for having relived those painful moments.

"It made me realize something," I explain, finishing my story. "They both wanted something from me that they weren't prepared to give themselves. So you were right about Alessandro. I saw his selfishness in every word he said to me. But you were wrong about Bryce. Maybe he hasn't moved on, but what he did was just as selfish."

"Maybe," Emily concedes thoughtfully. "But I've been there for him through everything you guys have gone through. You're not perfect either, Sera. And I say that now, knowing you, and knowing that you aren't a selfish person. But that's the thing. Everyone can be selfish some-times. Especially when they're hurting."

Her words break the bubble I've wrapped myself in, and my carefully stoic demeanor collapses. Because she's right. I know how much I've hurt Bryce throughout all of this. And how much he's been going through. How much we've both been going through. It abruptly all rushes back, and it's too much. I can't catch my breath, and panic over-takes me as the tears I've suppressed all week finally come all at once. Emily looks at me, a heartbreakingly sad expression on her face, and it makes it so much worse.

"I can't …" my sobs stop me from finishing. I shake my head as the tears pour out. I breathe in deeply, fighting to control myself until I've regained the ability to speak. "I have nothing left. Even if I could make it right. I wouldn't begin to know how anymore. And I swear to you, Emily, I know how good Bryce is. I can forgive his selfishness, because you're right. I've done the same to him. Probably worse. But if he really wanted me, why was I the one chasing him?"

"Does it matter who chases who?" she asks, fighting her own tears. "I just want to see you both happy."

I shake my head. "Twice now I've decided to be done with Alessandro. I told Bryce I was. And I guess I didn't believe it myself until I had to say it to Alessandro himself. But I am. I wasn't lying, and I've proven that. But all Bryce said was that Madison doesn't mean anything to him. Not that he was done. Not that he wanted me. He hasn't said that …" I can't think since when. I shake my head again. "I can't even remember the last time. Too long. I've made a fool of myself."

"Sera, please, just try," she pleads.

I snap my head up, angrily wiping away fresh tears. "Has he told you that he loves me? That he's not seeing Madison anymore because he wants to be with me?" I demand. Her blank stare is all the answer I need. "Exactly. So you, Emily, please, just stop. If you want us both to be happy, let us move on. There's nothing else I can do now."

"You're not wrong," Emily's voice quavers with emotion. "He hasn't said any of that to me. But he doesn't need to. I know him. He's in love with you, Sera."

I laugh a tired, tearful laugh. And I don't want to be cruel to Emily, but she's crossed the line into meddling. And I'm so, so tired of it all.

"If that were true, wouldn't he be here telling me that instead of you? It's not exactly an epic journey. He lives about ten minutes away. I'm the one who's been repeatedly stalked and assaulted. And now I'm basically a prisoner to my circumstances until this all blows over. I've got enough on my plate, for fuck's sake. I've told him where I stand. If he has something to say about it, maybe he should try not sending his sister to do it for him." I expect Emily to be offended at the very least.

But she's not. She just looks sad. "You're right," she murmurs.

I catch her eye, trying to apologize silently, trying to communicate the affection I have for her. That I know she just wants to help. I'm not sure if I manage it, but we both sit in contemplative silence for a bit.

"I should go." Emily rises from the couch and I follow, with no intention of stopping her.

She stops at the door and turns to embrace me. I squeeze her tightly, putting my frustration aside. When she releases me, I hold it together long enough for her to leave.

I'm on the floor, slumped against the door for who

knows how long when I feel Tristan's strong body slide down next to me, his solid, warm arm wrapping around me from the side. I lean into him and let go, my hot, salty tears staining his crisp, cool white shirt. And since I'm pretty sure this is outside his job description, I'm especially grateful that he makes no move to stop the wanton destruction of his uniform as I let all my grief out. Finally.

TWENTY-FOUR

Friday is miserable. Tired from a night of little sleep and plenty of tears, I struggle to make it through the day even with large doses of caffeine. But it's not so much the exhaustion as it is that I've embraced the reality of everything that's happened. And it's a lot, but I know I'll be okay. I've survived worse, after all.

Tristan meets me after work in front of the building, escorting me into the back of a black sedan. And I just want to go home and bury myself under blankets and booze for the weekend. As we start our drive, I stare out the window at the gathering rain clouds. Summer has finally started to melt into the first vestiges of fall. While it's still warm, a humid darkness threatens the sky, coordinating well with the darkness of my mood.

When we get home I silently grab a bottle of whiskey from the kitchen and settle into my chair with a fuzzy brown blanket wrapped around me, intent on watching the rain and getting stinking drunk. But before I can bring the bottle to my lips, Tristan kneels in front of me, his green eyes clouded with worry.

"Sera," he says softly. "I hate to do this to you, but I need you to not drink yet. My boss is coming by."

I stare at him quizzically. "Your boss?" I ask dully. "Why?"

"He wants to check on things here. If he sees you drinking like this, he might think I'm not taking very good care of you," he explains.

I snort. "I didn't know keeping your charges from drowning their sorrows was part of your job," I reply.

Tristan frowns, and I'm immediately sorry.

"Tristan. Forgive me. Of course, I won't drink until he's gone."

Tristan nods solemnly. "Thank you," he replies, clearly relieved.

I sigh and heave myself from the chair to return the bottle to the cupboard. "Will I need to speak to him?" I ask dully.

"Yes. I'm sorry for the short notice, but I only heard this afternoon," he replies.

I sigh resignedly. "It's okay. I'll go get cleaned up then. How long do I have?" I ask.

"He'll be here soon," Tristan replies apologetically.

I suppress my irritation and nod, heading up the stairs. My dress is crumpled, and I could use a long, hot shower, but I'll have to settle for a quick rinse and an even quicker change of clothes.

Ten minutes later I'm headed back downstairs in black yoga pants and grey T-shirt when I hear a voice downstairs. Tristan is filling someone in on the week's events, which is to say, basically explaining my going back and forth to work. I pause for a moment to see if he'll mention Emily's visit and my subsequent breakdown, but when I halt on the stair it creaks and Tristan stops speaking. My cover blown, I continue down the stairs. As I round the corner into the main living space, I'm stopped short. Standing next to Tristan in the dining area is the last person I expected to see.

Bryce's clear blue eyes meet mine, and my heart drops into my stomach. It's so pronounced that I physically grab my midsection in surprise, tears springing to my eyes. He looks the same as he always does. Heartbreakingly handsome in khakis and a white polo, his chestnut hair freshly cut, though he's perhaps a tad leaner than the last time I saw him only five days ago.

Tristan glances nervously between us as I approach. I didn't even realize my legs were carrying me forward until I stop next to Tristan, my eyes breaking from Bryce's to stare accusingly at my should-be protector.

"I thought you said your boss was coming by," I say accusingly. "What the hell is this?"

Tristan looks deeply uncomfortable, but it's Bryce who answers.

"I *am* his boss," he asserts. "The company you contracted is the private security company we acquired in order to offer those services to our clients."

I glance between the two, Tristan continuing to remain awkwardly silent. And I realize what a difficult position this must put him in.

"You can go, Tristan," I assure him.

Tristan looks at Bryce, who nods in agreement. And I've never seen anyone move so fast. When the guest room door closes behind him moments later, I look back up at Bryce.

"Why are you here?" I ask, my heart heavy with pain and longing. Even now, amid the anguish and sorrow of the past week, I just want to reach out to him, to feel his arms around me. It's a special kind of torture having to be this close to him.

"I talked to Emily last night," he replies, as if that explains everything. I shrug and crumple into a dining room chair. "God, Sera, you look like hell." He pulls out the chair next to me and sits down facing me.

"Gee, thanks," I reply sarcastically, picking at my fingernails. "You look like you're doing just fine."

"I'm not. I've been worried sick about you this week," he replies.

I look at him skeptically. "Did you know? When Alessandro came back? Did you get one of your notification thingies?" I demand.

A smile tugs at the corners of his mouth. "No," he admits. "I stopped monitoring the situation after he was located."

"Oh," I say softly. "How much did Emily tell you?"

"I made her tell me everything. She wasn't happy about it. Said she was betraying your confidence," he replies.

"Then why did she do it?" I asked, annoyed.

"Because she's worried about you too. About us," he responds softly.

"There is no 'us,'" I remind him.

His lips press into a thin line and his nostrils flare. "I think it's time to set a few things straight," he responds slowly. "But I want you to promise me that you'll finish this conversation and not run in the middle of it. I want you to have all the information before you decide to hate me."

I stare at him, somewhere between sad, angry, and confused. I don't bother correcting him by explaining that I could never hate him. "Fine," I whisper. "I promise."

Bryce nods, leaning back in his chair and running a hand

over his hair. "When we had that fight the week after you came back from San Francisco, I was at the start of one of the most difficult periods of my life," he admits. "You know I was in love with you." The past tense and his averted gaze are like a knife to my heart, but I only nod and stay silent. "And we knew something was wrong with my father. Nobody talked about it, but we all knew. And it was making work, well, you remember." I nod again, and he takes a deep breath.

It's a minute before he continues again. "I decided after our fight that I wasn't going to go after you. If you wanted to talk to me, that was on you. And if you did, I was determined to keep you at a distance until I didn't have those kinds of feelings anymore. And then my father died, and I was a fucking mess. Much worse than before."

I can see his agitation as he runs his hands over his hair repeatedly, hard and fast. It makes me want to hold his hands in mine to steady him. Because even knowing what comes next, I can't stop what I feel for him. Even if he can.

"Everything was jumbled. And you were such a pillar of strength for me that week. The day of the funeral, lines were blurred. It was harder for me to wish away my feelings. When you left that day, I was weak again. And I admit it, I let Madison seduce me, even though I knew better."

I raise an eyebrow. I'd like to tell him it's cheap to

blame her, but I also acutely remember the pain and confusion grief can cause.

"And after that?" I point out.

He grimaces. "The next time was after the day in the gym," he admits. "I was frustrated. I didn't intend for it to happen again. And I meant what I said to you that day. But I didn't think for a minute that I was what you really wanted. I just didn't want you to think you could try it out without being serious about it. I didn't want to start things up again just to have them stop like they had before."

I realize it's time to tell him what I couldn't get to when Madison showed up the night I came to confess everything to him. Because even though it may do no good, he's being honest with me. And he deserves the same in return.

"You were," I reply, but he looks confused. "What I wanted," I clarify. "That's what I was trying to tell you before the attack. But even before Madison showed up, I was pretty sure you'd been with her the night before."

He looks surprised at that bit of information. "Then why didn't you tell me that after she was gone?" he asks incredulously.

I shrug, twisting my fingers together in my lap. "Suspecting it was one thing. But seeing her there, the way she talked to you, I knew I didn't have a shot once I was sure you two were together," I say, my voice barely above a whisper.

He shakes his head miserably. "That last night with her was another huge mistake. And not one I sought out. I should have put a stop to it then, but I hoped I could just avoid it happening again. I never meant for you to be hurt by it. And I meant it when I said she means nothing to me. Madison did some awful things that caused me to end our relationship in the first place. I would have never, in my right mind, gone anywhere near her like that ever again."

His explanation makes sense but brings me no peace. I close my eyes and inhale deeply through my nose. His evergreen summer scent flows through me, causing another sharp pain in my chest. When I open my eyes, Bryce is staring at me. The compassion in his expression is almost too much, and I shift uncomfortably in my chair.

"I believe you," I respond, sensing he was waiting for me to say something. I'm not sure what else to say. But it seems to satisfy him anyway.

"I ended it on Sunday. It's not what I wanted in the first place. If I could go back, I wouldn't make that mistake again. And I never meant for it to hurt or confuse you," he explains.

I pull a leg up to my chest and wrap my arms around it. "Well. Now I know. Thank you for setting the record straight," I reply tiredly.

"I'm not done," he persists.

Tears sting the back of my eyes. I'm not sure how

much more he can expect me to take. But I promised. "Go on," I allow.

He laughs and shakes his head. "You don't get it, do you?"

I look up at him, annoyed. "I don't get what's funny about this," I agree.

He smiles and shakes his head, leaning forward intently. "It's funny because I'm an idiot. From the moment I met you, Serafina Evans, I've been crazy, ridiculously, madly in love with you. I'm an idiot for thinking I could snap out of that. An idiot for letting Madison worm her way between us. But mostly, I'm an idiot for not accepting you on whatever terms you wanted me. Because, all of you or not, any of you is better than none."

My heart stops as I gape up at him.

He drops to his knees in front of me, pulling my leg down and taking my hands in his. He looks earnestly into my eyes, his handsome face awash with worry. "Can you forgive me?"

I continue to stare at him, bewildered, a thousand emotions running through me at once. "I guess Emily didn't tell you *everything*, then," I murmur.

His expression falters, giving way to confusion.

"I've hurt you too, Bryce. I've been selfish. I've jerked you around. I never meant to, same as you, but sometimes the path our hearts take isn't straight or easy. But I know in my heart that you are good. So good. Maybe too good for me. So yes, I forgive you. Do you forgive me?"

Bryce laughs, full and hearty, and it's hard not to smile in response. "Considering I just told you you've had my undying love from day one, yes, I think I can forgive you," he replies, his eyes sparkling. "But I'm not. Too good for you, that is." His expression is suddenly serious again. "And I'm not going to pressure you. I just want you to be happy. And if you're really happier without me ..."

I pull a hand free and press it over his mouth. "You really *are* an idiot," I say, laughing. "You don't get it, do you?" I can feel the grin break across his face under my hand as he realizes what I'm about to say. "I'm crazy, ridiculously, madly in love with you too, Bryce Hoyt." I drop my hand from his face. And there it is. My sunshine smile. My heart leaps in my chest, a different and wholly welcome pang of emotion.

Through a mist of happy tears, I watch his hands rise to my face. Then I feel them, warm and rough, holding me gently as he brings his mouth to mine. Our lips meet softly, wet with the tears streaming down my face. Warmth spreads through me as his mouth presses into mine more insistently. His tongue parts my lips, meeting my own fervently as I slide my hands over his shoulders and down the firm muscles of his back. He moves a hand to my lower back, and pulling me with him, he settles on the floor between our chairs, forcing me to sit astride him as he plants kisses down my jaw and neck. It's bliss, being in his arms finally.

And when his lips find mine again I'm dizzy and flushed, and a small noise escapes me as his hands rove over me. But I'm also suddenly very aware that we're groping each other in the middle of the dining room floor. I push him away gently, so we can slow down, and I take the opportunity to look deeply into his eyes.

"This isn't anything like the first time I kissed you," I remark.

He laughs easily, pulling me up from the floor. Now standing, he holds me against his body, leaning in to whisper huskily in my ear. "No, it's not," he agrees, running his nose along my earlobe and sending jolts of electricity shooting through me. "But you were a bit distracted then." He continues to softly kiss my neck.

With my cheek resting against his taut chest, I'm finding it difficult to do anything but breathe through the pleasure of his touch. "I'd say I'm pretty well distracted now," I huff.

He pulls away, laughing once more and flashing his sunshine smile.

I touch it with the tips of my fingers, a reflecting smile on my face. "I missed this."

His eyes sparkle as he runs his fingertips down my jaw.

"It's getting late," he murmurs, suddenly distracted. "Shift change is in an hour."

Reminded of Tristan in the other room, I disentangle myself from Bryce and sigh. He looks disappointed for a fraction of a second, so I lay my hand reassuringly on his arm.

"Stay," I say.

A sexy smirk settles on his face and his eyes dance with desire, sending warmth shooting through my core. Bryce turns toward the guest room.

"Tristan," he calls.

I slide back into my dining room chair, attempting to breathe normally and push back the rosy flush I feel on my cheeks. Tristan pops out of his room and rejoins us.

"Shifts are suspended until further notice."

Tristan eyes my red face and disheveled clothes and is unable to suppress a smile. "Yes, sir," he agrees happily. He gives me a friendly smile and wave. "Bye, Sera." I can almost hear the unspoken, "Have fun."

I laugh. "Bye, Tristan," I respond.

Bryce and I are both still as Tristan takes his leave. When the door has quietly closed behind him, Bryce's large, warm hand tugs at mine, pulling me back into a standing position.

A sudden bout of shyness overtakes me as I realize we are alone together, for the first time in a long time, with the expectation of more. But this time is so very different.

Because I want him more than I've ever wanted anyone or anything. He's been my protector, my best friend, and my rock. And I know I can trust him with all of me. That he sees me, warts and all, and still chooses me. I've never been so vulnerable. Or so happy.

He stares down at me patiently, his hands lightly skimming my arms.

"What are you thinking?" I ask him.

He smiles furtively. "That I'm the luckiest bastard alive," he replies. His eyes darken, his hands wrapping firmly around my waist. "And that it's about damn time I took you to bed."

A pleasurable shudder shoots through me, and I wrap my arms around his neck, pulling his face to mine. I expect the intensity of his kiss, but I don't expect the slow, sensual exploration as our bodies meld together. When I'm nearly breathless with desire, he pulls back for a moment, stroking my face gently. He slides his finger down to my chin, then pulls my lips back to his. This time his mouth is unrelenting, taking mine in greedily, his tongue still slowly stoking the fire in me.

And suddenly he's lifted me up, wrapping my legs around his torso. He supports my weight with his hands under me as his lips continue to work with mine. He carries me upstairs, and I feel my back hit the bedroom door.

He uses the flat surface to pause, pressing me against it

and grinding his hips into me. A low groan rumbles through his chest, and I break my mouth from his, sighing with pleasure. But he doesn't stop, and his mouth continues greedily kissing and sucking down my neck. Finally, his hand reaches for the doorknob and we spill into the bedroom.

He lays me gently on the bed, hovering over me, staring into my eyes as if he could derive all his pleasure from the simple act of seeing my love for him there. Abruptly, he rears back and hooks his thumbs in his collar, pulling his shirt forward over his head and removing it. A small noise escapes me as I'm face to face with the mental image that's been haunting me for weeks. But now I can use my hands to explore the perfect planes of his chest and stomach. My fingers are icy on his warm skin, but he leans into my touch nonetheless. I bite my lip, concentrating, as I drop my hands to his belt.

Bryce pulls back, smiling and shaking his head. "Tit for …" he trails off. "Well, you know." He winks, and I have to laugh.

I wriggle into a sitting position and let him remove my shirt. As he tosses it over the side of the bed, I deftly reach behind my back and unhook my bra, tossing it after the discarded shirt. When he sees me topless, his lips part and his tongue slides across his bottom lip. But his control is flawless as he leisurely leans down and blows a hot breath across the tip of my breast.

It tickles slightly, and I bite my lip to suppress a giggle. He smiles up at me before running his nose over the sensitive flesh. It responds, the peak lengthening, the skin around it tightening. He groans appreciatively and sinks his warm mouth over it, gently working it with his tongue. He sucks away as he pulls up, and I groan involuntarily at the sensation. He languidly trails more warm kisses down my stomach, stopping at the top fold of my pants. His fingers travel along the thick seam, teasing my sensitive flesh as he drops occasional kisses along the way. My hips are twitching in anticipation.

"So impatient," he laughs. He crawls up the length of my torso to plant a firm kiss on my lips.

For a moment, I savor his weight on me, the feeling of his tight muscles against my soft chest, and the warmth of his lips. Then, with a stroke of his nose on mine, he drops away again, and before I'm even aware of what he's doing, his capable hands have pulled my bottoms off completely, leaving me naked. With another decisive lunge, his strong hands separate and lift my legs, exposing me to his waiting mouth. He gives me a final, sexy smirk as his head disappears between my thighs.

The first slow, gentle touch of his tongue sends a jolt through me. I work to still myself, eager for more. He masterfully increases his pace and pressure so that I'm not overwhelmed, but the intense ache that begins to build almost immediately is borderline unbearable. So when he adds a finger to the mix I can't control the arch of my hips. But he hangs on, his skillful tongue and hand following my movements as I work myself involuntarily with his motions. When he inserts another finger, though, I nearly fly off the bed. The now-rapid pressure inside and out is driving me insane as the ache builds to an intense explosion. I cry out, the ascent to my climax more slow and intense than I've ever experienced. And just when I think it's about to end, he flexes his fingers inside me and redoubles the weighty caress of his wicked tongue. Pleasure so deep and powerful carries me over the edge, and my body shakes with the immensity of my orgasm. As I crash back to earth, he slowly withdraws, leaving one last gentle, hot kiss on my inner thigh before sliding up next to me.

I turn toward him as his mouth finds mine, and the taste of me on his lips is another level of eroticism I was unprepared for.

It takes me a moment to stop panting, to regain control of my jelly-like limbs, and to find my voice again.

"That was insane," I admit.

He laughs and kisses my neck. I weave my fingers through the short, thick, chestnut hair on top of his head as his tongue plays along the tender skin of my clavicle.

"Good insane?" he asks.

"Mind-blowing, life-altering insane," I assure him. "Let's-call-off-the-shifts-for-the-rest-of-the-weekend insane."

"Wow, and I thought *I* enjoyed that," he teases.

I look at him in disbelief. "You really are a giver, aren't you?" I ask incredulously.

He kisses me deeply, pulling back and sliding his teeth across my lip along the way.

"I suppose. I certainly enjoyed giving you that orgasm. You have no idea how sexy you are when you're coming in my mouth," he responds.

And I didn't think it possible again so soon, but I feel myself grow wet at his words. "Bryce Hoyt," I say in mock shock. "I had no idea you were so dirty." I push him onto his back. "I like it."

And intent on returning the favor, I remove his pants, only to discover the largest, most beautiful cock I've ever seen. He smiles down at me proudly as I take it in, running my hands over it to convince myself it's real. It's a little daunting for what I had planned, but I accept the challenge happily.

As Bryce did, I take my time pleasuring him, using my lips, tongue, hands, and anything else that occurs to me to slowly build his pleasure. He's so huge that taking the entire length of him into my mouth isn't possible, but it's a fun challenge nonetheless. And the next pleasant surprise is the amazing noises he makes, affirming his pleasure the whole way with low moans, pleased gasps, and guttural groans. It's almost enough to make me come all over again. And I can tell I've brought him close when his breathing takes a sharp turn toward sustained, wailing gasps.

"Ohhhh, baby," he pleads. "If you don't stop, I'm going to come in your mouth."

I don't answer, simply catching his eye as I bear down on him, sliding him all the way back in my throat as I twist my grip around the wide base of him. His lets out another groan and throws his head back as he finds his release. His every cry, the taste of him, watching his long, muscled frame contract with pleasure under my touch almost over-whelms me with ecstasy. And I realize fully Emily's point about being with a giver. Because the bliss found by two people who would do anything to please each other is staggering.

And when I return to his arms, there's no need to say anything. He simply folds himself around me as we both drift into a deep, satisfying sleep.

TWENTY-FIVE

For once Bryce sleeps past five. I actually wake up before him, the first vestiges of daylight peeking around the shades. His heavy frame is draped all around me, making escape impossible. Not that I mind terribly. Even though the places our bodies touch are warm and slightly tacky with the sweat that's dried between us, it's intensely gratifying to be so close to him. To be his at last.

After a few minutes of laying naked underneath his gorgeous body, I'm unable to keep from touching him. I trace the bulging muscles in his arms lightly with my fingers, marveling at their definition. With my hand resting in the crook of his elbow, my thumb hovers close to one of his nipples. And I can't resist rubbing it in a firm circle over the dark flesh, watching it pucker and snap to attention. It finally stirs him, a low groan rumbling through his chest as his hips reflexively press into me.

He starts to harden before his eyes even open, and I can't help slinging a leg over him, pulling in to him so I can feel him stiffen against me. His baby blues peek out from under his eyelids and a smile curls his lips.

"Best. Wake-up. Ever," he mumbles, finding my lips with his. He abruptly rolls on top of me, sliding himself fully between my thighs.

I gasp in surprise, but his mouth tugs at mine, cutting me off with his kiss. When he pulls away to give attention to my neck, I wrap my legs around him.

"You haven't seen anything yet," I reply, tilting my pelvis up to capture him. And it's a good thing that he wasn't fully hard yet, because even at half mast, he fills me completely. My gasp isn't hampered this time as he's buried his face in my neck, his own groan of pleasure escaping his lips. "Don't stop." My plea stirs him, and I can feel him harden fully as I expand around him.

Ever so gently, he rocks into me, sending shockwaves of intense pleasure crashing through me.

He rears up over me, resting on his forearms, so he can watch my face as he picks up his pace. I can tell he's making sure he's not hurting me, and the tenderness makes me want to cry. I urge him on with my moans, and soon we're hurtling toward ecstasy together.

He pulls back onto his haunches, and it pulls him out

enough so the pressure isn't as intense. But it also allows him to use his thumb to start circling the sensitive nub above where he's thrusting. The unexpected move upends my control.

"Ohmyfuckinggod," I gasp. Bryce looks at me questioningly and eases off. I shake my head violently. "Don't. Stop."

He smiles and leans in to kiss me. His lips are soft and sensual as he continues to gently slide in and out. He runs his nose along my cheek and drops his mouth to my ear. "Love you, baby," he whispers.

I whimper from the pleasure of it all, unable to respond. He seems to understand as he rears back once more, renewing his patient thrusts and dexterous stroking, adeptly increasing his speed until we're both moaning loudly.

"Holy ..." I gasp. "I'm going to ..."

Bryce nods, pressing into me with his thumb and speeding the tilting of his hips into a bed-shaking frenzy. The added sight of his muscles tensed and the sweat sheening on his chest from his concentrated efforts drive me straight into orgasm. And if past orgasms shattered me into a million pieces, this one sends me into ten million. And over again as he continues to thrust into his own climax.

Amid my trembling descent, I'm barely able to watch the expression of extreme gratification pass across his features before he collapses over me, still buried deeply inside.

His heavy breathing tickles my ear, and I numbly run my fingers over his slick back, savoring the feel of his damp skin.

"Well, that didn't suck," I joke. Bryce pushes himself up over me, a bemused expression on his face as he starts laughing. I can't help but laugh too, until the sensation causes his receding manhood to shift, tickling me in a whole different way. "Eek, don't make me laugh!" I wriggle under him as he tumbles out, laughing harder.

He rolls onto the bed next to me, still chuckling. "Give me a few minutes," he breathes. "Maybe I can do better next time." His head lolls toward me and I can see that he's smiling.

"Baby, I don't think it gets any better than that," I reply, gently kissing his bottom lip.

He strokes my arm thoughtfully. "That sounds like a challenge," he responds. He looks down at himself, but he's still, understandably, no longer at attention. "Hmmm, might need a bit longer actually."

I shake my head and laugh at him. "Were you a porn star in another life or something?" I ask teasingly. He grins. "You may be ready to go soon, but I'm going to need a break. I can barely move." I demonstrate by trying to lift a shaking arm from the bed and flopping it back down dramatically.

"Good," he replies, scooping me into his arms. "Then you're at my mercy."

He runs his nose over my neck, ears, and jaw, stopping to plant kisses along the way. Each point of contact leaves a hot flush under my skin, adding to my general feeling of being a pleasurable pile of jelly. Eventually the deep relaxation seeps out of my limbs, and I feel like I may actually be able to walk again. But lying here in Bryce's arms is its own kind of heaven. A reprieve from all the pain, sorrow, tension, and strife that we've both been through. But something is still niggling at me, even through the bliss.

"I don't want to spoil the mood …" I start.

Bryce pulls his head back and cocks an eyebrow. "But?"

"But while I'm glad most of this is over, there's still the issue of whoever is after Alessandro. They're still out there, trying to get at him through me." I pause, unsure of how to voice my concern. "The bodyguards have been a huge weight off my shoulders, in one sense. But this whole week I think it's contributed to me isolating myself. I can't imagine living a normal life being followed by armed guards, waiting for someone to try something. Even with them here I feel like I'm constantly waiting for the other shoe to drop."

"You'll get used to them being here," he assures me, sliding a leg between mine and using it to hook me and pull me closer. "And trust me. These goons who are after you have been biding their time, trying to catch you alone. Once they figure out that there will always be a guy with a gun between you and them, they'll give up."

I try to ignore the feel of his leg between mine, our hips lightly touching. "I get that having guards here is a trade-off. But I feel like I have to play hostess all the time," I object. He starts to contradict me, but I shush him. "I know they don't expect me to. But it's how I am. I can't help it. And it's nerve-racking."

Bryce looks at me, and I can tell he doesn't understand, but he's heard me. He strokes my thigh reassuringly. "Okay," he replies. "No more guards in the house."

I look at him quizzically. "Where are they going to stay?" I ask skeptically.

He shrugs. "They're not. Someone can pick you up each morning and be on call while you work. Then at the end of the day, they go home," he explains. "With one catch."

Ah. Yes. It sounded too easy.

"Which is?" I ask suspiciously.

Bryce's mouth twitches. "I stay," he says simply, grinning.

"I thought you weren't my personal security guard?" I ask, eyeing him skeptically.

"I'm not," he agrees. "But you're safer with me anyway. Right here. In your bed." He kisses my neck persuasively.

"Mmmm, using your newfound powers over my body is fighting dirty," I respond. I can feel him smile into the crook of my shoulder as his kisses go lower.

"I told you, that's how I do it now," he replies, amused. His tongue finds my nipple and I'm momentarily breathless.

"But won't that be a huge pain? Trucking back and forth all the time?" I ask.

Bryce releases my nipple and laughs. "Wow. Seriously, Sera. For someone so smart, you can be very dense." He shakes his head at me, and his expression becomes serious. "I'm saying we should live together."

My eyes go wide, but his amused expression returns despite, or perhaps because of, my obvious shock. "Isn't that kind of fast?" I squeak.

His hand travels to my backside, gently stroking it in a way that's both distracting and relaxing as he thinks about what he wants to say next.

"Not really," he eventually replies. "I mean, it doesn't have to be permanent. Not that I'd object if it was. But if it's too soon for you, I understand." He takes in my doubtful expression. "Listen, gorgeous. We've known each other for months. And I knew from the beginning what I wanted. And even if this part of our relationship is only starting, I'm still solidly on the side of the line where I'll take as much of you as I can get."

"Don't you think you'd get sick of me?" I ask.

"No," he promptly replies. "We've been through a lot, Sera. More than most couples who have been together for years. And we've fought. And made up. And so much more. I have no doubt that we can do this. I'm here because I realized all my doubts were about me. I have no doubts about you."

"I don't have any doubts about you, either." The words are out of my mouth before I even remember forming them.

He looks as surprised as I am. "Really?" he asks incredulously.

I chew on my lip. Really. I really don't. Bryce has always been there for me. Even when he was unsure how to behave around me. He was always the one wanting to persevere, to have the difficult conversations when I was running away. Which I only did because I was hurt, because I thought he was over me.

But the idea of living with him, of waking up every morning like this. Of spending weekends lazily making love, eating together while he reads the newspaper, and actually being able to go out as a couple. I realize there's a part of me that's always known that if I met Bryce first, we would have been here already. And I'd be safe, and always loved and cherished at his side. And of that I have no doubt.

"You said you knew from the beginning what you wanted," I hedge.

He nods reluctantly.

"What do you want?"

He inhales deeply, his eyes dark and serious.

"You. All of you. Forever," he admits. He regards me anxiously after the intense declaration.

And I should be scared. But I'm not. Because in the deepest, purest place in my heart, it's exactly what I want too. I feel the smile spreading across my face.

"That sounded an *awful* lot like a proposal," I tease him.

He strokes my face seriously. "Well, I guess that depends on what your answer would be if it were," he replies carefully.

I raise an eyebrow and laugh. And then I kiss him passionately, unable to put words to the love overflowing my heart. When I break away, he looks happier than I've ever seen him. As happy as I am.

"All of me," I agree. "In exchange for all of you. Forever."

And I know the answer before he gives it. Before we agree to join our lives. Before he makes passionate love to me again, over and over. Forever.

Thank you so much for reading! Please take a minute to leave a review on any retailer, goodreads, and/or

BookBub. Even if it's just a couple of sentences, your opinion is important to potential readers and to me. Thank you!

∾

Want to know what happens to Sera and Bryce? Get *Never Forget* (Book 3) now at https://melanieasmithauthor.com/books-never-forget.html

∾

Sign up for Melanie A. Smith's newsletter to get a FREE book plus all the latest news and more https://melanieasmithauthor.com/newsletter.html

ACKNOWLEDGMENTS

In my first book's acknowledgements, I mentioned that I've always wanted to write a novel. And now I've written two. And again, I must give much of the credit to my ever-supportive husband for not just making the writing time possible, but for lending his own thoughts and suggestions with far more tact than I'm capable of. Our two heads are better than my one, and his saintlike patience while I come to realize that over and over deserves immeasurable praise.

A second round of huge, unending thanks goes to my best friend and copy editor, Jenny Gardner, for making this venture doubly rewarding. I don't miss Los Angeles (sorry L.A.), but I do miss my favorite person there. And through this process the distance feels less, and I'm so ridiculously thankful that you seem just as into this as I am.

As I go through the process of releasing these first couple of books, I've learned so much, but none of it without the immense body of knowledge compiled and made readily available by those who have come before me. And I'm so thankful for the writing and publishing communities that are generally eager to share knowledge and see others succeed. Seeing all these authors putting their work out into the world and sharing their lessons learned reminds me why I push through the vast tedium of publishing. Because sharing the joy of the written word is insanely important for society. It's not just how we communicate — it's how we imagine and grow together.

And that community includes the readers. So thank you, to all of you, for being on this ride with me. It's a blast, and I can't wait to see what happens next.

ABOUT THE AUTHOR

Melanie A. Smith is a former engineer turned stay-at-home mom and award-winning, international best-selling author of steamy contemporary romance. She crafts strong book boyfriends with hearts of gold and smart, self-sufficient heroines. When she's not lost in the world of books, you'll find her spending time with family, cooking, and driving with the windows down and the stereo cranked up loud.

facebook.com/MelanieASmithAuthor
twitter.com/MelASmithAuthor
instagram.com/melanieasmithauthor

Vegas Baby (Hot Vegas Nights)

Pompous Paramedic (A Hero Club Novel)

Short Stories

Cruising for Love

Hot for Santa